C000174304

HIDDEN
WIFE

BOOKS BY WENDY CLARKE

What She Saw
We Were Sisters
The Bride

HIS HIDDEN WIFE

WENDY CLARKE

bookouture

Published by Bookouture in 2021

An imprint of Storyfire Ltd.
Carmelite House
50 Victoria Embankment
London EC4Y 0DZ

www.bookouture.com

ISBN: 978-1-80019-267-6
eBook ISBN: 978-1-80019-266-9

For Bonnie

PROLOGUE

The child is lying a few hundred yards from the cliff path, beneath the braced legs of the electricity pylon, her hair spread out, Medusa-like on the long damp grass. The grey school skirt she put on that morning is soiled with mud, and there's a gaping rip in her grey woollen tights. Over by the scraggly hawthorn bush, one black patent shoe lies upside down, while the other clings stubbornly to her small foot.

The sea mist, that has yet to clear, swallows everything in its path, leeching the colour from the land. It's strangely comforting, this lack of clarity. This blurring of reality. It heightens the other senses: the taste of salt on her lips, the roll and break of the waves far below her.

Either side of the girl, as if protecting her, the metal ribcage of the pylon rears skywards, like a giant puppet, its arms held up by the power lines that join it to the next one... and the next. On and on across the rolling Dorset hills.

She doesn't move – just watches the last of the mist lick at the skeletal frame of the tower. But it isn't long before the sun penetrates through, bringing the world back into sharp relief.

As its rays catch the wires above her head, turning them into silver spiders' webs, the girl smiles. The sun feels nice and warm on her face, and she can smell the seaweedy tang of the air. Hear the waves breaking rhythmically onto the stones, the sea calling to her. She doesn't know why she's lying here, her mist-damp fringe clinging to her forehead, but she doesn't care.

She's at peace.

There's nothing to be afraid of. Or is there?

Someone is calling her name.

Maya. Maya!

It's her father, worry raising the pitch of his voice. She wants to answer, but she doesn't. She can't because then he'll know what *she* knows and will be sad. For what she feels deep inside her chest – in the heart that's pumping against the damp fabric of her white school blouse, despite the calmness she feels – is the certainty that only comes when a loving bond is severed. The bond between mother and child.

Her mother is dead.

CHAPTER ONE

Teresa

The door closes with a satisfying click, and after a few seconds, Teresa hears Louise on reception call out goodbye. A deeper voice replies, then there's the sound of the outside door slamming, and through the partly closed blinds Teresa sees her last client stride down the path to where his car is waiting in the street.

When she hears the engine start, she closes her eyes and massages the area of soft skin between them with her thumb and index finger, relishing the silence. Even though today has been a relatively quiet day, this last client has been particularly difficult. She's been treating him for anxiety-related OCD brought on by his wife's cancer diagnosis, and his progress has been slow. Even getting him to enter her consulting room had been a challenge, and she's shattered, her only thought to get home and run herself a long hot bath. But that will have to wait. She has obligations, and her own needs are a long way down the list.

Shifting herself on the chair to get more comfortable, she focuses on her breathing, concentrating on the sensation of her breath. In through the nose. Out through the mouth.

In.

Out.

Every now and again, the sash windows of the therapy room give a small rattle. It's getting windy outside, and it's forecast to rain later. A part of her wishes she hadn't told her mum she'd visit this evening. After the day she's just had, the thought of driving the fifty minutes to her house and the same again on the way back, isn't something she relishes, especially when the time in between is filled with worry and frustration. But she knows she has to.

Her mind has left her breathing now, wandering to places she doesn't want it to go, but she doesn't let it worry her. She knows that it's natural for your attention to stray when you're trying to clear your mind. The important thing is not to obsess over where your thoughts have taken you.

Gently, she pulls her wandering mind back from her mother and focuses again on her breathing. Visualising the air moving through her nose, filling her lungs, the rise and fall of her chest. Thoughts of her mother slip away. She's in the here and now. Aware only of her breathing. In out. In out.

The sharp rap on the door makes Teresa jump, and she opens her eyes, turning her head to the door just as it's opening. For a second, she thinks it might be her client returning to check, for the third time, that their consultation will stay confidential, but it's not, it's Stephen.

He frowns as their eyes lock, noticing her surprise. 'Sorry, were you busy?'

Just hearing Stephen's calm voice makes her relax. 'No, I was just trying to wind down a bit before I go home.'

Stephen comes in and takes the seat across from Teresa. He rests his feet on the low coffee table between them, and Teresa feels the warmth of his smile. How is it that, however hard her day has been, he always manages to make her feel that she's not alone?

'I find a large glass of wine works for me,' he says with a chuckle.

But Teresa can see the tiredness written in the bags under his eyes. He looks just like she feels.

'Busy day too, huh?'

'Not particularly,' he replies. 'One cancelled this afternoon, which, to be honest, was a relief. I haven't been sleeping well. Don't know what it is. Perhaps I'm feeling anxious.'

She looks at him, taking in his soft check shirt and cords, the beard that is a tad too long and the unruly greying hair. Despite the difference in their ages, they've been good friends as well as colleagues for many years, and Teresa knows him so well. Her own serious, exacting temperament has been a foil to his more laid-back one. They've worked well together, treating people at his Wellbeing Clinic for the last three years.

'You're looking tired, Stephen. Things all right at home? Is Maya okay?'

She watches as he slides out the pen that's clipped to the pocket of his shirt, clicking the nib in and out distractedly.

'Yes, she's fine,' he says.

'That's good. Working at the care home must take it out of her.'

'It's good for her. She likes the routine.' He looks as though he's going to say something else but doesn't, and Teresa wonders if he's being honest with her. She's only met Stephen's daughter a few times, but she'd made an instant impression on her with her fair curly hair and gentle demeanour. She'd liked her, and she wonders whether it might be because she's so much like Stephen.

'Any boyfriends on the scene?'

Stephen frowns, and Teresa wonders if she's been too nosy. After all, it's none of her business.

'No,' he replies eventually. 'Nothing like that.'

Teresa studies him, waiting to see if he'll open up more, but he doesn't. In all the years she's known him, he's preferred to keep his private life to himself. Maybe that's why she's never been invited to their clifftop house. Once, out of curiosity, and wanting a change of scene, she'd parked the car in the village where Stephen and Maya live and walked along the beach from the Heritage Centre to where the cliff folds in on itself before sweeping back towards the sea as if in greeting.

That day, as she'd climbed the barnacled rocks below the bluff, she'd been hoping to reach the small bay on the other side. But she hadn't checked the tides. The waves were already hitting the rocks below her in a spray of foam and, in the little cove beyond, the stones and coarse shingle glistened with every lick and retreat of the sea's white tongue.

Teresa hadn't gone any further, it would have been foolish to do so. Instead, she'd turned back, stopping for a cup of tea at the little café next to the Heritage Centre. But not before she'd seen the house standing high on the coastal path, its gabled windows and large conservatory looking out onto the sea.

Then her eyes had strayed to the rocks at the cliff's base and what interest she'd had in the house had quickly waned. For the one thing Stephen has never discussed since she started working at the clinic is the wife who had been swept away by the sea at the bottom of that very same cliff twelve years earlier. There'd been an inquest and accidental death had been the conclusion, but rumour had it that it had been suicide. Whatever it was, the result had been the same. A young child left without her mother.

She shakes her head. Crewl Point was where it had happened. *Cruel* more like.

'Penny for them?'

'Oh, it's nothing that interesting,' she lies.

Stephen raises his eyebrows at her, and immediately Teresa feels guilty. She looks away. The last thing she wants is for him to know that she read all about him in the paper all those years ago, that she's spent hours wondering what happened: how a happily married couple could fall apart like that. How a mother could abandon her child. Trying to make sense of it all. Trying to work out why Stephen hadn't reached out to her after it had happened. Why he never talks about it. Sometimes, he'll take a day off work, blaming it on a migraine, but she wonders if it's because looking after that big house and bringing up Maya single-handed for the last twelve years has taken its toll.

Several times, since she started working at the clinic, she's found herself on the verge of asking him about it, but each time she's stopped. If Stephen had wanted to talk he would, and she has to remind herself that time is the greatest healer. He'll reach out in his own good time and, when he's ready, she'll be there for him, like he is for her.

And who is she to judge anyway? Her clients might see a well-adjusted professional when they come to her with their problems, but they're not to know that behind the proficient demeanour she's just as human as they are. One who's worried sick about a mother who lives alone, fifty minutes away, and who's becoming more forgetful by the day. One who finds it increasingly hard to face the thought of going home to her husband.

Stephen's not the only one who's good at keeping up appearances.

Today, though, he looks nervous, distracted, as though his thoughts are not on anything in this room and certainly not on her.

'Want a quick coffee before we leave?' she asks him. The thought of him leaving makes her heart sink.

He looks at his watch. 'No, I'd better make a move.'

'Yes, of course.' She tries to think of something that might make him stay a little longer, wonders if saying something about Gary would be enough, but already he's standing, slipping the pen back into his pocket. Preparing to leave before he's said anything to her of any note. She's used to it, but there's something different about him today. She cocks her head to one side trying to work out what it is. Despite the distractedness, there's a lightness to his actions. An extra warmth to his voice.

'Going somewhere nice after work?' It's a guess, but there must be something that's brought on this new mood of his.

He shakes his head, and the smile that had been hovering on his lips slips a little. 'No, just home. I promised Maya we'd eat together tonight as her shifts don't always make it possible.'

'That's nice.' She knows Stephen and his daughter are close, and it must be a comfort to them both. On a couple of occasions when Maya was still at school, he'd brought her along to the clinic and Maya had sat in reception with Louise, helping her with the appointments. The first time it had been an Inset day, but the other occasion had been for work experience. At regular intervals, Stephen had come downstairs to check on his daughter, which Teresa had found sweet. And when she'd come out to consult Louise on something and had found Maya chatting to one of the clients, her calm and easy manner had made it less of a surprise when she'd confided in her that she was considering a career in medicine.

That had never happened though, and now she wonders why. 'Who's cooking?'

He laughs, his good mood returning. 'Oh, Maya, of course.' He raises his hands and waggles his fingers. 'You know as well as I do that these hands are good for writing up notes and that's about it.'

Teresa tuts. 'You're such a dinosaur, Stephen. It's the twenty-first century you know. How did you manage after—' She stops, reddening.

'After what?'

He's looking at her, but she can't meet his eyes. Instead, to cover her embarrassment, she takes a stem of alstroemeria that's started to wilt from the vase on the coffee table, and drops it into the wastepaper bin.

'Nothing. It doesn't matter. Look, it's time I went home myself or Gary will think I've forgotten I'm married. I just need to check on tomorrow's client list.' She gets up and busies herself at the computer, trying to regain her composure. How could she be so insensitive?

She feels Stephen's eyes still on her, but when he speaks again, his voice is cordial. 'I'll see you tomorrow then.'

This time, she forces herself to look at him. 'Yes. I hope you get a better night's sleep.'

He stands with his hands in the pockets of his baggy cords. 'That will depend.'

She raises her eyebrows. 'On what?'

He sighs, a shadow passing across his face. 'On what happens tonight.'

CHAPTER TWO

Maya

The trudge up the hill from the village seems longer than usual, every step exacerbating Maya's tiredness. She looks down at her feet in their black tights and work trainers and wonders how they'll ever take her the rest of the way.

As the houses on the track dwindle to nothing, replaced now by flat fields of cropped grass one side and the open sea on the other, she sees her house at last. Solid. Red-bricked. Its thin chimneys rising from a grey-tiled roof, the top of the glass conservatory just showing above the hedge that borders their windswept garden.

Crewl House. Her home for almost nineteen years. It's far-reaching view of the sea her constant companion as she's been growing up. The folded ribbon of chalky-white cliffs with its coastal path that stretches away from the house, the only scenery she's known. The only place she's wanted to be.

Home. It's not a place but a feeling – conjuring up safety. Security. The world is a dangerous place, but she's always felt that if she stays here, nothing bad can happen to her. More importantly… nothing will happen to her dad.

She's nearly there, and Maya can now see the large bay windows and the long, gravelled drive. As she passes the gatepost, smiling at her dad's car parked in its usual place, the stones crunch under her feet. She walks to the kitchen window as she always does, peering through the glass to see if her dad's there. He isn't. He's probably upstairs, listening to his music – old bands from his heyday she's never heard of and with good reason in her view. Instead of letting herself in through the front, Maya unlatches the side gate and walks around the side of the house. The back door is unlocked, and she steps into the small lobby with its tumble dryer and jumble of walking boots and wellingtons.

'Dad?'

Maya closes the back door behind her and goes into the hall. She puts her bag down and feels the tension she's been holding in her shoulders release as she walks into the kitchen and contemplates what she'll cook them both for supper.

Shrugging off her coat and dropping it onto the kitchen chair, she thinks about the afternoon she's just had – it's been one of those days, as her dad would say. The two new admissions would have been taxing enough, but Alex had called in sick – she was always off with something or other – and was supposed to be training the new care assistant. She'd had to do it instead and, with everything else she had to do, she'd felt distracted, their questions going in one ear and out the other.

Then, just as she was about to leave, Olive King had blocked her way.

'My husband will be here soon,' she'd said. 'To take me to Broadbrook House… for the dance.' This was despite him having been dead for nearly five years. And by the time Maya had led the elderly woman from the front door back to the communal living area and settled her in her chair, it was already half an hour past the end of her shift.

The final refrain of 'Love Shack' reverberates through the ceiling, and Maya smiles as she hears her dad sing along to it. At least it's going to be a good evening, she thinks. She'll be able to forget about her sore feet and the endless beds she's made. Deal with the headache she hasn't been able to shift, brought on by the effort it's taken to stay cheerful. Not every care assistant at the home smiles as they struggle to unravel a story or when it loses its flow midway, but *she* does. She wants each and every one of the residents of Three Elms to feel cared for. Valued and safe in the home that isn't really their home. It's the least she can do. It's the way she feels at home, with her father. Even without her mother.

At the thought of her mother, a pang of longing hits her so hard that she leans forward and grips the edge of the kitchen table. Sometimes, it happens like that... the missing. Coming out of the blue, like a knife in her heart that gets twisted. Even after all this time.

Remembering what her father taught her all those years ago, Maya closes her eyes. She focuses on the inside of her eyelids and one by one the sounds in the room – the ticking of the clock, her dad's music from the room above – recede, to be replaced by different ones. A picture forms, and she starts to relax. She imagines the sun on her face. The whisper of wind. The cry of a gull. As she pictures the sea foaming and hissing up the shingle, drawing back to leave a shiny arc of sand at the waterline, the ache starts to lessen and the tears that prickled and threatened the back of her eyes only moments ago, fail to materialise.

Opening her eyes again, Maya picks up the hessian shopping bag she'd dumped on the floor when she came in and puts it on the worktop. She'd popped into the Co-op on her way home and bought some things for their supper: an aubergine, a courgette and some brightly coloured peppers. She'll make vegetable lasagne and, over a glass of red, she and her dad will compare their days. Of course, due to client confidentiality, he won't be able to tell her much, but he always manages to find a few anecdotes to amuse her with, like the time he got his appointments muddled up and was surprised when the young woman he'd been expecting for relationship counselling had turned out to be a sixty-year-old man with a drink problem. Her own offerings will be a recount of a conversation she's had with one of her favourite residents or a poignant memory dredged up from the cobwebs of a ninety-year-old mind. Perhaps what happened with Olive.

Maya smiles, shakes her head at the memory, which has already become less of a burden, and slides a chopping board from its place between the microwave and the fridge. Placing a pepper onto it, she smooths its shiny surface with her fingers.

'Dad?' she calls again.

She can hear him in his study above the kitchen, the wheels of his office chair running over the wooden floorboards as he moves from computer to printer then back again. He always likes to keep busy. Looking into current research. Keeping up to date.

She's the same. It wouldn't have been so bad today if her manager, Sandra, pulled her weight, but over the last few months she's been leaving more and more to her. Shutting herself in her office off the reception area or disappearing out for meetings that haven't been scheduled in the appointments book. Sometimes, Maya wonders who it is that runs the care home.

Drawing a knife from the wooden block, Maya works the tip of it around the top of the pepper, pulling on the stalk to remove the core. It comes away and a shower of white seeds covers the chopping board. She's just slicing it in half when the music stops. The floorboards above her head creak, and she hears her dad's footfall on the stairs. Out of habit, she watches the door for the first sight of his face.

But she needn't have worried. His glasses are perched on top of his head and, despite looking tired, he's smiling, his brown eyes crinkling at the corners.

Maya lets out the breath she's holding. 'You look happy, Dad.'

'That's because I am.' Going over to her, he places a hand either side of her face and kisses the top of her head. 'It's been a tiring but good day. What about you? How was work?'

He pulls out a chair from beneath the kitchen table, the legs scraping on the tiled floor, then sits, tugging at the knees of his jeans as he does so. Maya watches him, the simple action filling her with a strange sadness. She knows why it is; it's because the elderly gentlemen at the care home do the same thing, and she doesn't want to think of her dad getting old. Not that sixty-four *is* old. Not really.

Narrowing her eyes, Maya studies him. It's his beard that's the problem. Not a close-cropped stubble or five o'clock shadow; if it was, it wouldn't be so bad, but just plain scruffy. Too long to be cool but not long enough to be eccentric. No woman would look twice at him looking like that, but she doesn't care. She loves him, and that's all that matters.

Maya flicks the switch on the kettle. 'Tea?'

'No, you're all right.' He smooths his beard as though aware she's been assessing it. 'As you didn't answer my question, I take it you didn't.'

Maya pulls herself out of her thoughts.

'Didn't what?'

'Have a good day.'

'What? Oh, no. It was fine. Just the usual really. As I was leaving, Olive decided Den was taking her to a dance. It makes a change I suppose, it's usually the cinema.'

'Is that the Den who passed away?' Leaning back in his chair, her dad places one hand on top of the other on his stomach, and Maya's pleased to see that the blue check shirt he's wearing is the one she bought him the previous Christmas.

'That's the one.'

Maya pulls her eyes away from her father's rounded belly. The shirt had fitted him perfectly when she'd got it for him. Now, if he isn't careful, he'll end up with a sizeable paunch by the time next Christmas comes around. She'll have to keep an eye on him; make sure he doesn't let himself go. Even if she isn't able to control what he eats when he's at the clinic, she can limit the number of biscuits he takes from the tin when he's home.

The kitchen table is full of clutter: old photographs Maya has been sorting out of her and her father. Ones she hasn't got around to putting in albums. House and garden magazines she buys with a view to turning their rather ramshackle clifftop house into a show home but whose covers have not been opened. An assortment of pens and pencils.

Her dad picks up a red pen and clicks it absentmindedly. He looked wistful. 'In an odd way, I'm rather envious of Olive.'

Maya looks up sharply, the tip of the knife embedded in the red flesh of the pepper. 'What do you mean?'

'Nothing really. Just that it keeps him with her. It must be a comfort.'

His brown eyes are on her, and Maya feels as though he's trying to communicate some sort of message, though she can't think what.

'Any new clients?' she says, changing the subject.

'Just one this morning. The rest were regulars. Anxiety, relationship problems… the usual. Nothing earth-moving, but we made headway.' He sighs. 'And it keeps the wolf from the door.'

Linking his fingers behind his head, he leans back further until the front legs of the chair lift from the floor.

Maya frowns and puts down her knife. She nods at the chair. 'You're going to break your back one of these days. What have I told you about tipping your chair?'

Righting it, her dad laughs. 'Lighten up, sweetheart. I pity the poor guy you end up living with. He'll be too scared to move without your say so.'

A blush creeps into Maya's cheeks, and she looks down, chopping the pepper with vigour.

'I've no intention of getting married. Not for years anyway,' she replies. She's never quite seen herself anywhere else – anywhere besides at home with her father, staying together, protecting him. Neither has she felt the need to have a relationship… not that anyone's ever shown much interest in her that way. Even her friendships have been limited; the quality time she spends with her dad has always been more important to her than visits to the cinema or pointless shopping trips.

She chops harder, the knife clunking as it makes contact with the chopping board. The conversation isn't one they've had before, and it's almost as if he's sounding her out. Checking to see if there's anyone interested. 'I'm not even seeing anyone,' she whispers, almost as an afterthought to herself.

'You'll leave eventually, my love. But I hope that won't be for a long time yet.'

He runs his hand through his overlong hair. She feels his eyes still on her, and it's unsettling.

'What is it, Dad?'

As if remembering himself, he sits up straight and smiles. 'Nothing. I just meant that one day you'll meet someone who makes you happy and, when you do, I'm going to make sure the poor guy knows to keep his chair legs firmly on the floor.'

Pushing back his chair, he gets up and goes over to the fridge. He stands with the door open for a few seconds, then bends and pulls out a couple of bottles of Budweiser. He offers one to Maya. 'I fancy a change from wine tonight. Okay with that?'

'You drink too much, Dad,' she says, with mock sternness.

He kicks the fridge door shut with his foot. 'And you worry too much. For your information, it's the first drink I've had today. Not that I need you keeping tabs. As you well know, Dan's office is opposite mine, and as an addiction counsellor, he'd make it his job to count the empty bottles on my desk.'

Maya forces a laugh. She doesn't know why she said that. Her dad doesn't drink that much any more, but alcohol is a depressant.

Apart from Dan, it's just her dad and Nina, the speech and language therapist, on the first floor of the Wellbeing Clinic, which her dad set up over twenty years ago. Teresa, the final member of the team, has the office on the ground floor to the left of the waiting room with its white leather-look settees, plantation shutters at the window and the tall bamboo in hessian-covered pots. Maya's met them all, but although she hasn't been there as long as the others, it's Teresa she likes the best. She's a behavioural therapist like her dad, and there's something about her manner that's always put her at ease.

Lifting the chopping board, Maya scrapes the peppers and the courgettes she's just finished chopping into a roasting tin, then starts on the plump aubergine. Her dad wanders over. He leans his back against the worktop, his bottle of beer clasped to his chest. There's a strange expression on his face.

Maya puts down her knife. 'What is it, Dad? You know I don't like you hovering when I'm trying to cook.'

He places his beer on the counter and looks at her. 'There's something I want to tell you. I was going to wait until we were having supper but… well, I'm finding it hard to.'

Despite the pan that's heating up on the stove, the temperature in the room seems to have dropped a couple of degrees. A knot forms in Maya's stomach. She's never liked surprises.

'What is it, Dad?' The knot tightens. 'You're not ill, are you?'

'No… No, of course not.' He takes a swig of beer. It coats the ends of his moustache in white froth. 'Far from it, darling.'

'What then?' Whatever it is, she wishes he'd hurry up and tell her, then things can get back to normal. 'If I don't get the veg roasting, we're never going to eat.'

Her father's large fingers are wrapped around the neck of his beer. Tufts of greying hair sprout from the skin above the wedding ring he's never taken off. Absentmindedly, he moves the bottle in a figure of eight across the worktop. 'You know, Maya, I've always done my best to be a mum to you as well as a dad…'

Maya holds her breath, the knot in her stomach hardening. 'Yes.'

'And you know how much I loved your mum. How she meant the world to me and how I thought we'd be together forever.'

Maya nods. She does know this; her dad has made sure she never forgets. She should encourage him to continue but she can't, as she's scared of what he's going to say next. She's crippled with the certainty that something is about to change.

Don't say it, Dad. Don't say it.

But he does. Even if he notices how pale she's gone, how apprehension has stilled her body, he says it anyway.

'I've met someone, Maya.'

He's looking at her expectantly, and Maya knows he's waiting for her to say something in reply. To tell him how pleased she is. How happy that, after twelve years, he's found someone.

But however much she wants to, she can't. Tears well in her eyes.

'How could you, Dad?'

Brushing past him, she runs from the room, not turning back in case she sees the disappointment that she knows will be written on his face. But she doesn't care, for by letting someone into their home, their lives, he's made it impossible for her to protect their secrets from coming out.

It's what she's always been scared of.

What she's always been dreading.

CHAPTER THREE

Teresa

Teresa manoeuvres her Mini into the tight space between a white van and a car that looks like it's seen better days. Turning off the engine, she sits for a moment surveying the road. It hasn't changed much since she lived here as a child and, as always, it fills her with sadness. Not because she wasn't happy here, her childhood was no better or worse than a lot of other people's, but because of what the place represents now. Worry. Uncertainty. A lack of control.

With a sinking heart, she gets out of the car and slams the door shut. She's had to park a little way down the road and as she walks past the terraced houses, towards her mother's, taking in their neatly tended front gardens, her feet start to slow as they always do. It's not because she doesn't want to see her, of course she does, it's because of what she's afraid of finding when her mum opens the door.

Will it be the mother she knows, her hair brushed and her cardigan buttoned up correctly? Or will it be the one she's come to see more frequently in recent months, her eyes scanning her face as if looking for clues? Stiffening slightly when Teresa hugs her with the arms of a stranger. For weeks now, she's been telling herself her mum's not been haunted by the same dementia that took her own mother, but with each visit she knows she's been fooling herself.

Stopping at the garden gate, Teresa takes a deep breath and presses down on the latch, noticing how it squeaks as it opens. She adds the oiling of it to her ever growing mental list of jobs as that's not all that needs doing: the tiny square of grass on either side of the path hasn't been cut in a while and the faded blooms of the tea rose are browning and in dire need of a deadhead. When she was a child, she'd help her mum with the weeding. They'd crouch side by side on the garden path and throw handfuls of grass and chickweed into a wooden trug. Her mum knew all the plant names and would try to teach her, saying them slowly and making her repeat them. Teresa smiles at the memory, but the pleasure it gives her is short-lived. She knows the back garden is even worse, borders turned green with weeds. Bindweed strangling the small shrubs she planted at the beginning of the summer.

The plan had been to stay longer on one of her visits. Spend time sorting out the house and garden – fixing things and making things nice for her mum. But it's a resolution that's been hard to keep. She tells herself it's because she's tired after work, that after driving here, all she wants to do is have a cup of tea and a chat, but that's not the real reason. What stops her staying longer is the worry of what's going on at home. Whether her son, Dale, will still be sitting behind the locked door of his bedroom, the curtains drawn and the only light the computer screen, or whether Gary will be in one of his moods. A band of pain pulls tight across her forehead. She can't let them be her priority at the moment. It's not fair on her mum. She's the one who needs her the most.

As she walks down the garden path, she tries not to look at the neglected little front garden her mum used to be so proud of when her dad was alive. In all likelihood, she won't even have noticed the state it's in. She's at the front door now and she takes a moment to collect herself. Regaining control of her breathing and bringing her thoughts back to a place of peace. When she feels calmer, she reaches a hand to the doorbell, presses it and waits.

Minutes pass, and Teresa's just about to get out the backdoor key she keeps for emergencies, when she hears the rasp of the door chain being slid out of its metal casing. The door opens and her mum's head appears around it. Out of habit, Teresa scans her face for clues that she's recognised her.

Today she's in luck for her mum smiles and takes her hand. 'Darling. Come in.'

Teresa lets out the breath she's been holding. 'Hi, Mum. It's good that you're using the chain, but you really should keep it on when you answer the door. It's what it's there for. You don't know who might be standing on your doorstep.'

'What do you mean, love?'

Teresa searches for the right words, not wanting to worry her. 'You know what I mean, Mum. We don't want a repetition of what happened the other day.'

Her mum looks at her blankly. 'Happened?'

'Yes, the men who said they were Jehovah's Witnesses. The ones you invited in for tea and cake.'

'They *were* Jehovah's Witnesses, Teresa.'

Teresa closes her eyes a second, then opens them again, trying not to let her frustration show. 'I know, but that's not the point, Mum. You only knew that for sure after I checked. They could have been anyone.'

This had been the moment when she'd realised she'd need to give her mother more of her time, even if it meant forgoing some of her after-work chats with Stephen. When the slight concern she'd had at her forgetfulness had turned into a more insistent anxiety. She wishes Stephen was here to talk to now.

Her mother looks at her as though she's the one who's being unreasonable. 'They were nice young men.'

Teresa shakes her head, wishing she'd never started the conversation. 'Look, it doesn't matter. Let's go in and have a cup of tea.'

Her mother opens the door wider and she steps inside, noticing as she does the piles of magazines and papers stacked on the hall floor. Bending, she picks one off the top of the nearest pile. It's a bank statement.

'Mum, what have you been doing?'

'What does it look like? I'm having a clear-out. You keep saying I should.'

Teresa takes a handful of the papers and flicks through them. There are mortgage statements, pension reports, a letter from her mum's doctor that she hasn't seen before.

Straightening, she massages her forehead. 'Oh, Mum. That wasn't what I meant. I was talking about the newspapers and magazines, your clothes… not important stuff.' She's overcome with a sudden weariness. It's going to take forever to sort this lot out.

'And where were you thinking of taking all of this?' she asks, indicating the piles of paperwork. 'Please don't tell me you were going to throw it in the recycle bin.'

Her mother shakes her head, a look of amusement on her face. 'Of course I wasn't, dear. I was going to take it to the charity shop when I next go out.'

Despite herself, Teresa laughs. 'The charity shop is for your clothes. The ones that don't fit any more. Not this stuff. No one wants old papers.'

Her mum frowns. 'It's not just papers. There are other things as well.' Bending down, she searches in the pile nearest to her, scattering the papers until she finds what she's looking for. With a flourish, she presents it to Teresa. 'Here.'

Teresa takes her offering and looks at it, a wave of sadness threatening to cut her loose. Leaving her floating on a rising tide of helplessness.

'You can't get rid of this, Mum.'

The photograph is one she recognises, taken from the frame that's stood on the mantelpiece ever since she can remember. Smoothing the shiny surface with her fingertips, she traces the man's curly hair, remembering the feel of it when she sat on his shoulders as a child.

Her mother looks offended. 'Why ever not?'

Teresa swallows the lump that's formed in her throat. 'Because it's a picture of Dad.'

'Don't be ridiculous, Teresa.' Her mum frowns, but it's her next words that hurt her the most. 'I've never seen him before. You're making up stories just like you've always done. Why don't you just go home?'

Teresa covers her face with her hands, not knowing how she's going to cope. It's not her mum's fault; it's her dementia talking. She should just go home like she said, but she doesn't want to. Not just because she's worried about leaving her mum alone, but because she doesn't want to go back to Gary. She thinks of Stephen in his house on the cliff, wishing things were different.

If she told him she doesn't feel safe when she's alone with her husband, that she wants to leave him, he'd support her. Help her. Be there for her more than he is now.

Wouldn't he?

CHAPTER FOUR

Maya

It's warm tonight, the briny air still, the only sound the waves breaking on the shore. Maya stands at the water's edge, hands in the pockets of the light blue work tunic she hasn't changed out of, listening to the sea turning the shingle.

The moon is nearly full, sending a shimmering band of silver across the dark water, and the bone-white cliffs behind her make the perfect backdrop. It would be beautiful if only she could block out her dad's words.

A wave rushes in a little further than the others, hissing and fizzing, and Maya takes a step back so that her work trainers won't get soaked, watching as stones settle once more in its ebb. There's no one else on the beach, not surprising at this hour, and that's how she likes it… after the tourists and fossil hunters have left for the day and it's just her and the sea. The rock pools full of moonlight. It's the place she goes to think.

She guesses that anyone knowing her circumstances would think it morbid that she comes here, but she doesn't agree. How could it be morbid when the beach was the place her mother loved best in the world? The place she'd come when something was worrying her.

That's what her dad has always told her.

In fact, it was where he'd found her mum the day she went into labour – standing at the hem of the water about where

Maya's standing now, the bottom of her sundress wet, her hands cradling her belly. It had been a windy day, and her mother's hair had blown around her face, strands of it sticking to the tears on her cheeks. Her dad had said they were tears of bewilderment at the pain that tightened her stomach but also of love for the tiny baby she'd be meeting soon.

I've met someone, Maya.

Maya can't get his words out of her head. Who is this person who's made her dad so happy his eyes shone when he said it?

They were fine, weren't they, she and her dad? Since her mum died, it had been just the two of them looking out for each other, and for twelve years, her dad had told her it was enough. No one could replace her mother. He wasn't interested in meeting anyone else.

They don't need a stranger in their house, digging around into their past. Asking awkward questions about her mum's death that she can't answer – doesn't want to answer in case it upsets the delicate equilibrium that she and her dad have found. For then she might have to admit that at times when she can't sleep and the house is dark, the wind whistling down the great chimneys, she wonders what really happened the night her mother died… for she's seen how her father changes when his dark moods descend.

She knows he's never been honest with her.

'Why?'

She whispers the word to the night, the breeze carrying it away until it is swallowed by the fold of the waves.

Crossing her arms around her body, Maya turns and stares at the cliffs. The ones that shared their secrets with her when she was a child, offering up pieces of the past: the metallic curl of an ammonite or a bullet-shaped belemnite. Treasures she'd shown to her teacher on her first day of school. *Look! Mummy and I found these.*

She should hate those cliffs, stay away as people told her to, because it was, after all, the cliffs that had claimed her mum in the end and made her one of their secrets. Another treasure to be swallowed by the sea. She doesn't hate the cliffs, though… or the shingled beach.

What she feels is something she can't describe. A heightened sense of awareness. A certainty that she was loved like no other daughter was loved before.

'Maya!'

It's her dad, concern threaded through his voice, just like it was the day he found her curled up under the pylon on the cliff. Turning her head, she sees him on the concrete walkway that leads down to the Heritage Centre. Just a dark shape in the moonlight. Of course, he'd known she'd be here.

Maya doesn't go to him, but walks the other way, her feet crunching through the shingle. A part of her wants him to come after her, wrap her in his big arms and tell her it's all been a mistake, but it isn't going to happen. No, it would be better if he just went home without her. What would she say to him anyway? That he's making a mistake? That they're better off alone keeping their secrets safe?

But even to her own ears it sounds unreasonable. It's not as if she's a child any more, though sometimes she still feels like one. She knows she has no right to tell her dad what he can and can't do.

There are footsteps on the stones behind her. The sound of heavy breathing as her dad catches up with her.

'Maya.' He gasps for breath, bending forward with his hands on his thighs. His belly hanging over the belt of his trousers. 'We need to talk about this.'

Maya shoves her own hands deeper into her tunic pockets, tightening the material around her hips. 'Do we?'

He looks sideways at her, then straightens. 'Yes, we do. I didn't realise you'd be so upset.'

Out to sea, the wind catches the tops of the waves and plays with them, lacing them with silver moonlight. Maya watches them and sighs. 'You should have.'

'Why should I, love? You've been so settled lately… been doing just fine. I thought you'd be happy for me.'

His words hit her like a slap. Happy for him? How could he think that after the sacrifice she made last year? It's because of him she's stayed in this place with its fish and chip shop and pub full of locals. Why she works where she does, making beds, filling water jugs, lifting spoons to the mouths of those who can't do it for themselves.

'You'll like her, Maya. She's kind and funny, and it would be nice for you to have another woman to chat to.' He smiles, his eyes glinting in the moonlight. 'You know how I don't understand girls' stuff.'

Maya bites her cheek, forcing herself to make an effort. 'How did you meet her?'

His smile widens. 'I'd gone to the pub after work and she was sitting at the bar. Her friend had let her down and she was just about to go home. We got talking, and before I knew it, an hour had gone by. Please, love. Give her a chance.'

Maya digs deep. 'All right.'

Her dad holds out his hand to her. 'Come on, let's go home, it's getting cold.'

It's true. A breeze has blown up; she hadn't noticed it before. Goose pimples are forming on her arms. She wants to take his hand but doesn't. It would be a sign that she's softening, coming round to the idea of him having a love life. She knows what will happen. They'll go inside the warm house that the three of them used to share and he'll put the kettle on, or maybe open some wine. When they're settled in the conservatory facing the sea, he'll convince her that she overreacted. It's always been this way.

She shivers and, presuming it's from the cold, her dad puts his arm around her, turning her towards the concrete walkway. 'Please, Maya. I've brought the car down. We can talk on the way home.'

Although it was foolhardy, Maya had taken the zigzag steps that led down from the coastal path to the beach, lighting the way with her torch. It's dark and she doesn't fancy going back that way.

'Okay… but, Dad?'

She feels his soft grey curls brush against her cheek as he leans his head against hers. 'What is it, darling?'

'There *is* something I want to talk to you about.'

With her dad's arm around her, their sides pressed together, they start to make their way back along the beach, reminding Maya of the three-legged race they'd won at sports day when she was in primary school.

'What's that then?' he asks.

'The reason I reacted so badly…' she says, forcing herself to say the words. 'I want to talk about Mum.'

Her dad stops. Above their heads a seagull screams.

'What about Mum?'

'Every time I come to this beach, I feel her presence.' Maya points to the bluff, a dark shape against the moonlit sky. She draws in a breath of salty air, the words sticking in her throat. 'I want to know what happened when she died.'

Her father lifts a hand to his cheek and draws it down. She hears it rather than sees it… the soft drag of his fingers on his beard.

'You know what happened, Maya.'

Frustration mushrooms. 'No, I don't. Not really. You know I have no memories from that day, and you never talk about it. Why won't you tell me?'

'Because there's nothing to tell. It was a terrible, tragic accident.'

She stares at him defiantly. 'People say things about you, you know. Gossip about why she might have done it. Don't you think this woman is going to wonder too? Aren't you scared she'll want to know—'

His voice is frosty. 'Her name is Amy.'

Taking his arm from around her shoulders, he strides ahead, leaving her behind. The moon, so large and bright earlier, slips behind a cloud making it difficult to see him.

'Wait.' Suddenly Maya doesn't want to be alone on this beach. 'Dad, wait for me.'

She runs to catch up with him, but although she's desperate to ask about her mum again, she knows she shouldn't. She can see his mood has changed. She doesn't want the dark mist to descend on him as it does sometimes when he's under pressure. Causing him to close the curtains and take to his bed, all offers of food or conversation refused. She doesn't want to upset him, to force him to relive memories he would rather forget.

When he turns suddenly, it takes her by surprise. He takes her by the arms and bends close, his eyes level with hers.

'When Amy is in the house, I don't want you talking to her about your mum.' She feels the pressure of his fingers on her skin. 'Is that clear?'

CHAPTER FIVE

Teresa

Teresa puts the photograph of her dad on the hall table. 'Why don't you sit down in the living room, Mum? I'll make us both a cup of tea.'

She goes into the kitchen to fill the kettle and, ignoring her instruction, her mother follows her, nodding her satisfaction when she sees Teresa is using the teapot.

'Tea before the milk, Teresa,' she says, pointing to the delicate cups with their pattern of roses. 'That way you can see what colour it is.'

It's what she says every time as though Teresa hasn't ever made her tea before.

'How have you been, Mum?' She pulls a chair from under the kitchen table and guides her mum to it.

Her mum frowns. 'I've been fine. Why do you need to ask?'

'Because I care.' Teresa opens the fridge to get out the milk, then stops and frowns. 'Didn't the Tesco order come?'

Her mother's face remains impassive. 'Tesco order? No, I don't think so? When did you ask them to deliver it?'

Teresa puts the bottle of milk on the worktop. 'It should have come yesterday. Don't say there's been a cock-up.'

Her mother tuts. 'Language.'

Teresa feels a rush of irritation – not at her mum but at the incompetence of whoever it is that has mucked up the order. Now she's going to have to go out again and do a shop as she can't trust her mum to do it. Not since she returned with a box of Whiskers for a cat who hasn't been alive for over a year.

'I'll give them a ring. See if I can find out what happened. Maybe I selected the wrong day.'

Her mum nods absently. 'Yes, darling. I expect that's what happened.'

Teresa pours out the tea, then puts the two cups onto a tray. 'Have you eaten?'

Her mother smiles. 'Of course I have.'

'That's good. What did you have?'

'I had porridge like I always do.'

Teresa sighs and rests the flats of her hands on the kitchen table, rocking forward onto the balls of her feet. 'Not for breakfast, Mum, for dinner... or lunch even. Please tell me you've at least had lunch.' She scans the kitchen for evidence of a plate or cutlery, but all she can see is a bowl on the drainer and one lone spoon in the plastic cutlery holder.

Pressing the back of her palm to her forehead, Teresa looks at her mother. She seems smaller somehow, more vulnerable than she did even a week ago. Every time she sees her, it's like tiny pieces of the person she once knew have flaked away, and it scares her. It takes all of her energy these days to make sure she's safe.

'Mum,' she says, coming over to her and placing her hands either side of her shoulders. Her arms feel thin inside the rather worn M&S cardigan she insists on wearing because it's her favourite. 'This is important. Have you eaten anything today apart from the porridge?'

Frown lines appear between her eyes. 'I've told you before not to fuss, Teresa. I'll eat when I'm hungry.'

Teresa drops her hands in exasperation. 'But that's not good enough. If you don't eat properly, you'll get ill.' Tears form in her eyes as she pulls out a chair and sits next to her. Although

it was many years ago, it brings back memories of the last time
she'd lived in this house. She and her mum had sat at this same
table, a sheet of paper between then, making a list of what she'd
need to take with her to university. She remembers how her mum
had searched the cupboards to check for spare kitchen utensils
and tea towels and after they'd completed the list, had written
down Teresa's favourite recipes in a spiral folder to take with her.
Sitting opposite her now seems a million years away from that
time. Then it was her mum making sure she would be eating
properly. Checking that she knew how to keep safe. How the
tables have turned.

'Please don't do this to me, Mum,' she says.

Her mother looks shocked, her hand reaching out to touch
Teresa's cheek. 'Don't upset yourself. I'll try harder. Tomorrow I'll
make sure I have three proper meals. See, I'll even write a reminder
if it makes you happy.'

Reaching to the pad of sticky notes on the table, her mother
scrawls the word *eat* on it then sticks it next to several others,
reminders of hair appointments and Tesco delivery dates – many
out of date and which Teresa is certain she threw in the bin last
time she came. One has Teresa's son's name written on it.

Brushing the corner of her eye with the knuckle of her first
finger, she pulls herself together. Getting upset isn't going to make
things any better. Instead, she points to the sticky note. 'What's
this for, Mum? Why have you written Dale's name on here?'

Her mum bends closer and frowns. 'Maybe it's to remember
his birthday.'

'Dale's birthday isn't until next March.'

'Well, I don't know then.' Picking up the yellow sticky note,
she scrunches it in her hand, then goes over to the cupboard under
the sink. Pulling it open, she tosses the paper into the pedal bin.
'It obviously wasn't important, or I would remember. Why don't
I make us both a nice cup of tea?'

Teresa closes her eyes and takes a breath, picturing her diaphragm tightening and flattening, imagining the air filling her lungs, the oxygen moving through her bloodstream to reach every cell. Then she opens her eyes again and reaches for the tray, plastering a bright smile to her face as she picks it up.

'Lucky I made it already, Mum. I'll open a packet of biscuits to keep you going, then later I'll make you some dinner. How's that?'

'Whatever you like, dear.'

Going over to the cupboard where she knows she keeps the biscuits, Teresa opens it. What she sees there makes her fingers tighten around the door handle. On the shelf below the biscuits are neat rows of tins: baked beans, tomato soup, sweetcorn. Next to them are packets of rice and pasta, a new box of teabags and an unopened loaf of wholemeal bread. The ready meals, in their plastic trays, are neatly stacked one on top of the other, their cardboard sleeves showing what's inside. On the shelf below, next to a bag of sprouts, a pat of butter has started to ooze from its gold wrapper. All the things she ordered. The Tesco delivery came after all.

Teresa picks up the softened butter and takes it over to the kitchen bin, dropping it in with a soft thud. 'This should have been put in the fridge, Mum. The ready meals too. Now I'm going to have to do another shop for you.'

Her mum's face falls and immediately she feels guilty. Taking her arm, Teresa guides her into the living room and sits her in her favourite chair. She brings in the tea tray and takes the chair opposite that used to be her dad's. She looks around her, seeing to her relief, that the room looks tidy, the carpet hoovered and the television free of dust. At least her Mum's keeping on top of the housework.

She hands her mum her cup, watching as she sips from it before pointing to the mantelpiece. On it is a brass carriage clock flanked by two porcelain figurines, one with a wide-brimmed hat and crook, the other cradling a lamb. It's none of these she's looking at though; it's the empty silver frame that stands next to them.

'I was just wondering.' She looks at Teresa over her cup. 'Do you know what happened to the photograph of your father? The one that used to be there?'

Her mum's eyes are filled with such concern that Teresa's heart is in danger of breaking.

'It's all right, Mum,' she says. 'I know exactly where it is.'

It's then her mobile pings a message. She looks at the screen and sees it's from Gary.

Her mum leans forward. She's never got the hang of a mobile phone but is always fascinated when anyone contacts her daughter. 'Who's that, darling? Is it your lovely young man?'

Teresa looks at her mum. So trusting. So vulnerable. She closes her eyes feeling overwhelmed. Stephen is the only person she wants to speak to right now. He'd know what to do. She turns her phone over, so the screen is to the table, and takes her mum's hand.

'It's nobody important, Mum. Look, I've got to get home. Will you be all right?'

Her mum smiles, the brightening of the eyes and the lift at the corners of her mouth, reshaping her features to those of the woman she'd been before dementia took its hold.

'Of course I will,' she says.

The moment only lasts a second though before her face sags again and Teresa feels her gut clench. The time has come to act. If Stephen knew what was going on, he'd help her.

CHAPTER SIX

Maya

Maya stands at the bus stop and waits for the first bus of the morning, her mind on her mother and on her dad's reaction at the thought that she might talk about her in front of Amy. She rubs at her arms as though she's cold. Is he hiding something? Is that why he won't talk to her about what happened? Frustration prickles inside her. How can she protect him if she doesn't know the whole story?

She's impatient for the bus to arrive. It would be better if she could drive, but she's never got around to learning – apart from Three Elms, there's nowhere she needs to go. If the desire takes her to browse the clothes shops, which doesn't often happen, Bridport, where she works, fulfils most of her needs. She can pop out in her lunch hour or after work, if she's on an early shift, but, more often than not, she comes straight home, her need to check on her father greater than her need for a new pair of shoes.

The bus might be slow, but she's relieved she hadn't accepted the offer of a lift from Ailsa, one of the other care assistants, who also lives in Winmouth. It's not that she doesn't like her, it's just that Ailsa's the sort of girl who likes to pry and spending twenty minutes in the car with her would mean fending off questions about her life, and she couldn't cope with that.

The bus is usually on time, but still Maya leans forward, staring down the road for the first sign of it. Behind her, St Andrew's

Church looms grey and imposing behind its stone wall. She doesn't look at it, she never does, as although her mother wasn't buried, it makes her think of death, of loss, of the mother she never got to know…

Maya remembers standing beside her father in the church pew at the memorial service, her hand tightly clasped in his. It was a year on from the day her mother had died, and she was seven. As the words of a hymn she didn't know echoed around the lofty church, she'd looked up at her dad, intrigued by the snail-trail of tears that came to a stop when they reached his beard. When the hymn had finished and the church was silent again, he'd bent to her and whispered in her ear, his beard tickling her cheek.

'You must never forget your beautiful mother and what she meant to us.'

And, over the years, he'd made sure she never did. Instead of reading her bedtime stories, after he'd tucked her in, he'd bring the photo album up to her bedroom and look at it with her. Telling her tales from when she was younger. Smiling as he remembered.

Her mother's ashes were scattered out to sea one morning a month after it happened. Her father hadn't taken her with him as she was only little and wouldn't have understood. Instead, a family friend had come round to look after her, and they'd made chocolate chip cookies in the kitchen. Maya remembers how she'd been allowed to finish the bag of chocolate drops after she'd scattered them into the mixture. Can still taste the sweet paste that had stuck to the roof of her mouth once the chocolate had melted. She hasn't eaten a chocolate chip cookie since.

When her dad had come home, his waterproof jacket dripping onto the flagstone hallway, his beard jewelled with raindrops, he'd told her that her mum was happy now. That her spirit was as free as the seagulls that hovered on the thermals above the waves. He'd never told her where he'd stood to scatter her ashes or any of the details of that morning – even when she'd got older and pressed him. Instead, he'd told her stories of the things the three of them used to do together. The wonderful times their little family had shared when they were still a family of three... not two.

It was only when Maya was older and realised where her dad had been that morning, that she wondered why he hadn't chosen a better day to scatter her ashes. Her mum had hated the rain. Had liked to sit outside in the sunshine, Maya on her lap, making daisy chains, while below them, the restless sea pounded the cliffs.

She'd seen the photographs.

The church bell tolls seven, bringing her back to the present. Maya takes her phone out of her bag, ready to scan her ticket once the bus arrives, her eyes filmy with tears. In the end, after all the years keeping her mum's memory alive, it's her dad who's forgotten.

The events of the previous evening come back to her. How her dad had driven her back to the house from the beach in silence. How she hadn't known what to say. Unsettled by his sudden change of mood. But once he'd let them into the house, it was as if he'd forgotten his earlier sharpness with her. He'd gone to the kitchen, returning with a bottle of wine and two glasses and the two of them had sat together in the conservatory as they did every evening. She'd let him talk about Amy. What else could she have done? Hating how his voice had softened when he'd said her name. *A mee.* Lingering on the two syllables like a lovesick schoolboy. Worse than that was his nauseating attempt to sweeten the pill... *Amy loves cooking too and watching* Suits *and all that reality rubbish on TV that you can't get enough of.*

Finally, when he'd seen he wasn't winning her round, there had come the entreaty... *Please, sweetie, say you'll meet her. I can't be happy unless* you *are.*

Maya had sat on her favourite settee in the conservatory, a cushion crushed to her chest, staring out at the waves. As his words had tumbled out, all she could do was listen to him. Wondering how it was he couldn't see what he was doing to her. What Amy's presence could do to them.

The bus is here, pulling up inside the neat white box that's painted on the road. Picking up her bag, Maya gets on, pressing her phone to the scanner and finding her usual seat. The bus is half-full, and she doesn't look at the faces of the people who are already seated, their heads bent to phones and e-readers. It's how she likes it – everyone keeping themselves to themselves.

Hoping no one will sit beside her, Maya tips her head back and presses the white buds of her earphones into her ears. She closes her eyes, letting the vibration of the wheels on the road and the gentle rock of the vehicle, soothe her. Pretending she's invisible.

'Maya?'

The voice comes from the seat behind her. Maya shuts her eyes tighter in a vain attempt to kid herself this isn't happening. No one talks to anyone else on this bus. No one.

'I thought it was you. Do you mind if I sit here?'

The voice is next to her now. With no other option, Maya opens her eyes, her frown conveying her answer. But to her surprise, the person who has taken the seat beside her, shrugging off her jacket and folding it onto her lap, is one she's happy to see.

'Mrs Ellis!' Maya pulls the buds from her ears. 'You don't usually get this bus.'

The woman smiles. 'I'm meeting my sister in Bridport. She's taken the day off, so we thought we'd get an early start. That's the beauty of being a teacher, I can fit in with her in the holidays. Anyway, how have you been since you left Axe Valley? Are you liking being a student? I know medicine's a challenging career.'

Maya bites the inside of her cheek; she doesn't want to be having this conversation – even with one of her favourite teachers. Doesn't want to talk about the career path she never followed.

She stares at the back of the head of the person sitting in front of her, noticing the way her parting veers to the left as it leaves the crown.

'I didn't go,' Maya replies, and immediately she can sense Mrs Ellis's surprise.

'You didn't? But I thought it was all decided. You filled in the forms. I remember helping you with them.' Her forehead creases with confusion. 'You were my best student,' she says, pausing, thinking. 'Highest A level grades in the year. You had so much potential you probably could have applied to Oxbridge.'

Not knowing what to say, how to explain, Maya says nothing, just presses her arms against her body and grips the front of her seat, feeling the fibres move beneath her fingernails.

Mrs Ellis is looking at the hand nearest to her and Maya knows she's seen how the skin of her knuckles have whitened. Noticed too how her body has stiffened.

'I'm sorry, Maya.' Her teacher's eyes are filled with concern. 'I didn't mean to upset you. It's none of my business why you didn't go to university. I suppose it's just that I presumed you'd moved away and find it hard to imagine you still living in that large house on the hill. It's so isolated on that cliff path. So close to where your mum died.'

Maya's fingers dig deeper into the fibres of the seat. She knows her teacher's not meaning to be insensitive, but every word hurts. 'I like it there. It makes me feel close to her.'

'Of course it does.' Mrs Ellis looks at her with worried eyes. 'I'm just concerned for your welfare. Anyway, I'd love to know what you're doing now. Whatever it is, they'll be lucky to have you.'

There's a kindness to her voice that makes Maya want to cry. Instead, she keeps her eyes levelled at the back of the woman's head in front of her.

'I work as a care assistant at Three Elms. It's a home for the elderly in Bridport, specialising in people with dementia.'

If Mrs Ellis is surprised, she doesn't show it. 'You always had a caring nature. I'm sure you're a great asset. Not everyone can do a job like that.'

Maya turns to look at her to see if she's joking, but the warmth of her smile tells her she's not. That's what she always liked about her A level teacher, her sincerity. That and the way she taught her subject. The joy of maths spilling over to her students, making it hard for them not to love the subject too.

She has a sudden desire to confide in her.

'I did try to go, I even got as far as filling out the forms, but in the end, I just couldn't do it. It's difficult to explain the reason.'

'You don't have to tell me.' Mrs Ellis places a hand on her arm. 'Not if you don't want to.'

Now she's started, though, Maya can't stop. It comes out in a rush of words. 'I couldn't leave him. He'd have been all on his own.'

'Are you talking about your father, Maya?'

Maya nods. 'I was all he had. Who would look after him if I wasn't there?'

'How is he? I'm sorry, I should have asked earlier. It can't have been easy for him either after your mum died. Even though—' She stops, a flush coming to her cheeks.

'What, Mrs Ellis?'

She shifts in her seat. 'Really, it's nothing.' Mrs Ellis studies Maya's face as though wondering what to tell her. 'It's just I know they weren't always happy, and I did once wonder if they'd have stayed together… There was something my husband, George, said when you were first in my maths class. As you know, he taught the other year one class at your primary school and mentioned how once he'd had to break up an argument between your parents when they were waiting to pick you up from school. It must have been pretty heated for him to remember it after all that time – he wasn't one to gossip. Apparently, Mrs Lyons wouldn't let you out of your classroom until George had managed to calm them down.'

Maya feels her stomach clench. 'All couples argue.'

'I know.' Mrs Ellis pats her hand. 'And that's why you mustn't worry about it. It was a long time ago, anyway.' The bus is stopping. Bending to her bag, Mrs Ellis moves it so that it's not in the way of the people getting on. 'But if you ever feel you want to spread your wings, you mustn't feel your dad would be on his own. He's a grown man, and you can't make him your responsibility. I'm sure he has friends, neighbours, even work colleagues who would keep an eye on him. Doesn't he have his own private practice in Lyme Regis?'

'Yes, but it's not the same. He needs me.' Maya's voice slips away, so it's barely a whisper. 'Yes, he needs me. It's why I couldn't go to university.'

She doesn't want to talk about that time for, although her dad had been encouraging when she'd first told him she was applying, a week after the forms were filled in, a cloud had settled over him. One that was darker than previous ones. Maya had tempted him with his favourite food, enticed him out for healing walks along the clifftop, but nothing she'd done could lift it. Eventually, telling herself it was because of what she'd done, she'd deleted her application from the computer. When her dad had found out and asked why she'd done it, she'd told him it was because she couldn't face more studying. Would rather earn a living. Whether he'd believed her or not, she couldn't say. What she did know was that he'd never tried to change her mind.

'Do you like your job, Maya?'

Maya lowers her eyes and studies her hands. It's something she hasn't given much thought to. Her job is just something she does to get through the day. Something to black out the questions that swirl in her head. Questions her dad never answers.

'I suppose so. I like the residents… well, most of them anyway. It's just…' She turns to her old teacher. It feels right to tell her. 'Sometimes… some days… I don't feel fulfilled.'

Now she's admitted it to someone other than herself, it's a relief. But, almost at once, the guilt creeps in again to take its place. Maya straightens the material of her light blue tunic over her thighs, the polyester smooth under her fingers, and wonders what she'll say in reply.

'You're strong. I've always seen that in you… and your loyalty to your father and your job does you credit.' Mrs Ellis reaches out and covers her hand with her own. She gives it a maternal squeeze. 'It's never too late, you know. You can return to study at any age. It's something to bear in mind for the future.'

Bending to her bag, she takes out a notepad and pen, then scribbles a number on it. She hands it to Maya. 'Here. It's my number. If ever you change your mind and decide you want to apply to university again, I can help you with your application like I did before… and of course I'm more than happy to write you a reference. I still think you'd make a marvellous doctor but, of course, it needs to be when you're ready for it. When the time's right for you. You're only one decision away from a totally different life.'

Maya takes the note and puts it in her tunic pocket. 'That's kind of you, but I won't be needing it.'

'Keep it safe anyway.' She puts an arm into the sleeve of her jacket. 'This is my stop.'

The bus slows. Mrs Ellis waits for the doors to open before standing. She lifts the strap of her bag over her shoulder and smiles down at Maya. 'You look after yourself now and say hello to your father for me.'

'Thank you, I will.'

Maya watches her step onto the pavement and disappear down the road. As the bus pulls away and someone else takes the seat next to her, she turns her face to the window, feeling the cold, unyielding glass against her forehead.

She'll never go to university. She'll never leave the town where she lives, and she'll never leave her dad. She can't. Because of the thing she's never told anyone.

If she hadn't woken from a bad dream and walked into her father's bedroom, the week before her mum died, he might not be alive today.

CHAPTER SEVEN

Teresa

Teresa lets herself out of her house, closing the door as quietly as she can. It's only when she's in the safety of her car that her shoulders go down and her breathing slows. Another day at work. Another chance to see Stephen.

After fastening her seat belt, she looks back at the house. Remembering how excited she'd felt when she and Gary had bought it. A new house. A new start. No longer just her and Dale but a family again.

It's like a fist is around her heart, squeezing it. Gary had promised to love Dale as his own. That's what he'd said when he'd asked her to marry him. *Begged* her to marry him. But, of course, that was when Dale was still a child. Before he'd turned into a difficult sullen teenager. He'll be eighteen in a couple of months; his second-hand 125cc motorbike with its red L-plate parked in the side alley, and Teresa can't think how it happened. What spell has been cast over them to make the years pass so quickly?

How she misses her lovely boy. His infectious laugh. His jokes. Now he never smiles but wears his belligerence like a badge of honour. Hardly ever leaving his room unless he has to. The purple bruise of the black eye from his latest fight that he'd been sporting when he'd eventually come down last night, already fading to yellowy green in the centre.

When he was younger, she would never have dreamed he'd be capable of fighting… but what did she know? What did anyone?

Still, Gary could make more of an effort. She's seen how a good father acts, and he doesn't come close.

Dale's window is upstairs on the left, the blue curtains with their little white boats, which the two of them had chosen together the week they'd moved in, permanently closed. Teresa drags her eyes away from it. She hasn't been in Dale's room in months, telling herself it's because she respects his privacy. Deep down, though, she knows it's because she's scared of what she might see. Last time she'd gone in, it was to find he'd painted his room black – not just the walls but the ceiling too. She'd said nothing, but inside she'd been struggling to hold it together, not ready to face the thought that her son was no longer a child who stored Lego under his bed or stick insects in a glass tank on the floor. It's hard to think of Dale grown. Out of school. No job. No prospects.

It takes only a second for grief to overcome her, and she rests her head on the steering wheel, fighting the urge to cry. After a night worrying about her mother and tiptoeing around Gary's mood, is it any wonder she's bone-tired? What she'd wanted to do was talk to her husband about everything that was going on… starting with her mum. But when she'd tried to broach the subject, he'd just tapped the ash from his cigarette into his empty beer glass and turned the volume up on the TV.

Don't keep fucking going round there. It's not rocket science.

She turns the key in the ignition. She must stop feeling sorry for herself. It's just a bad time in her life, that's all, and she's not the only one who has to juggle ailing parents with children who are growing up. She'll get through it. After all, helping people get through things is what she does every day at work. She knows what advice she'd give her clients, but following her own advice is more difficult. Much more difficult.

When she's spoken to Stephen, it will make things easier. But when would be the best time? She taps her fingers on the steering wheel. She'll have to play that one by ear. Glad to be leaving, Teresa releases the handbrake and pulls away from the house that has felt like a prison these last few years. Things will get better. They must.

The drive to work is one she's always enjoyed, the road taking her through the Dorset countryside, cutting a path between the gentle swell of the hills. On both sides, a patchwork of green fields spread out, and in the distance she can see the sea. Some days it's a brooding grey, mirroring the clouds, but at other times, on mornings such as this one, it's a perfect sun-speckled blue.

She's nearing Lyme Regis now, and already the tension between her shoulders is easing. In just the few miles she's travelled between her house and the town, her breathing has become more even, her pulse slower. Sometimes, she wishes she could leave her whole life behind, but that would be the coward's way.

There's a small area behind the clinic with just enough spaces for the staff to park. No other cars are here. Feeling relieved, she locks the car and walks round to the front entrance, fishing her keys out of her bag as she goes. As soon as she's inside, the scent of jasmine drifts over from the diffuser on the reception desk and, instantly, she feels calmer. The clinic is her place of refuge. A tranquil oasis in a life that's spiralling out of control.

She's early, and the café round the corner from the clinic, where she's planned to grab something for breakfast, won't be open for at least half an hour. Teresa walks across to the coffee machine and gets herself an espresso. Normally, she'd have decaf, but today she has the feeling she'll be needing all the caffeine she can get.

She's just sliding the plastic cup from the ridged mat when the door opens and Stephen walks in, his clothes looking more rumpled than usual. His phone is in his hand, and he looks distracted.

Teresa puts her cup down, glad that he's come in early. She might have a chance to talk about things before his first client arrives. 'Hi.'

'Morning, Teresa. I was just…' He frowns and puts the phone away in his pocket. His eyes narrow slightly. 'Everything all right? You're not normally in this early.'

'Yes, I'm fine.'

'I'm glad. It's just that you look tired.' He pulls a face, shaking his head at what he's just said. 'Though of course that's the worst thing you could say to a woman if she's not feeling one hundred per cent. Or, even worse, if she *is* feeling one hundred per cent because then the last thing she'd want to look is tired. I'm a silly old fart. Forget I said anything.'

Teresa has to laugh. Stephen has a knack of saying the right thing even when it's the wrong thing. It's what he's always done and is probably why the clients like him so much. Why *she* does.

'Actually, you were right the first time,' she says. 'I didn't sleep particularly well last night.'

Stephen hangs his coat on the wooden coat stand. It's white like everything else in the clinic unless you count the green plants in their wicker pots.

'Is it Dale?'

'Amongst other things.' Teresa leans her back against the reception desk and takes a sip of her coffee, enjoying the bitter taste as it slips down her throat. This is her opportunity to say something. 'It's Mum as well. She's getting worse.'

Telling him about her family problems feels strangely unprofessional, but a part of her is relieved she has. She waits for him to ask her more, but he doesn't. He looks distracted, taking his phone out of his pocket and staring at the screen again.

Clearly, her mother and Dale aren't enough. Maybe this is the time to talk about Gary.

'Stephen, have you got a moment? I'd like to speak to you about something.'

He looks up at her, then shoves the phone back into his pocket, his face softening into its usual warm expression. 'Yes, yes, of course. Why don't we sit down?'

Stephen pushes back the cuff of his soft check shirt and looks at his watch, revealing a forearm covered in thick grey hair. 'We have another forty minutes before the first client is due. If anything's troubling you, you should tell me about it. We have to look after ourselves as well as our clients if we're to do our jobs properly.'

He indicates the settee at the side of the room. Its white cushions are made from a synthetic material that looks like leather. Teresa knows it's comfortable as she sometimes sits there when her day has finished, mustering up the energy and the enthusiasm to go home.

Her relief is huge. 'Are you sure you don't mind? Have you the time?'

'I always have time for my valued staff and my equally valued friends… and, of course, I count you as both.'

His words, as always, bring with them a warmth that she appreciates. She's grateful. After what happened, he doesn't need to be so nice. She pushes her self-doubt away. That was a long time ago.

Stephen gets himself a coffee. On his way back, he picks up Teresa's from the reception desk and carries it to the glass coffee table in front of the settee.

She follows him and sits down, feeling oddly disappointed when he doesn't sit next to her but takes the seat opposite. There's no time to dwell on this though as he's already asking her questions: How long has her mother been like this? Has she considered carers? Has Dale been given any career guidance from school?

She answers as best she can and as she talks, Stephen nods and strokes his shaggy beard with long, capable fingers. Teresa tears her eyes away from them and focuses on what he's saying. This feeling of release must be what his clients experience at the end of a session.

By the time Louise arrives, the open door bringing the sound of traffic and the smell of the sea, Teresa's back to her old self. Laughing at something Stephen has just told her. Ready to start her day. Grateful to him.

Louise raises a hand to them in greeting and throws her handbag onto the reception desk. 'Someone sounds happy.'

She doesn't answer, just smiles. Because she's correct. Right now, she *is* happy, and as she watches Stephen get up and walk to the stairs, she realises, with a jolt, that over the years she's known him, it's always been the same. It's how he's always made her feel.

And, hopefully, always will.

It's only as she gets up to go to her consulting room that she realises she hasn't told Stephen anything about Gary. She hasn't had to, but it's something to keep up her sleeve.

CHAPTER EIGHT

Maya

The house is empty when Maya gets home, an early shift meaning she has time on her own before her dad returns from work. Usually, she loves this time as it's a chance for her to tidy the house or sort the washing, but today she's restless. Picking things up and putting them down again. Flitting from job to job. Her mind returning again and again to what Mrs Ellis's husband had said. How her parents' argument must have been heated for him to have remembered it.

Finding herself in the kitchen, she decides to make a start on the evening meal. As usual, when she takes a knife from the block, the first thing she thinks about is how her mum would have prepared the same dish. How finely she would have chopped the onions. Whether she would have put crosses in the ends of the sprouts. How much of the fat she would have trimmed from the meat.

She knows her dad's uncomfortable with the role she's taken on – keeps telling her that she doesn't have to cook for him and is perfectly capable of rustling something up for them both when he comes in, but it's what she wants to do. What her mum would have wanted.

Her phone pings. As if reading her thoughts, her dad has sent her a message. *Might be a little late home tonight. Don't worry about food. I'll sort something out.* x

Quickly Maya types out a reply. *No problem if you're late. All under control.*

She isn't bothered. She's used to fitting in with his erratic hours. When her dad had first opened the clinic, he'd finished at five, but lately he's been staying later in order to fit in clients from the waiting list. Not wanting to let anyone down.

At least now there's no hurry to get the dinner on. Maya slides the knife back into the block, then, with her back against the worktop, views her domain. In front of her is the pine table where, as a young child, she'd sit and watch her mum cook. It's a story her dad has told her many times. One she never tires of.

Clutched in her small hand would be the crayon she liked to draw with. In front of her, a sheet of paper covered in bold markings. As her mum began to chop, or stir, or whisk, Maya would draw their house and the sea, every now and again stopping to pop pale curls of freshly grated cheese into her mouth. If any dropped onto the floor, her mum would just laugh. Then she'd bend and kiss the top of Maya's head, open the cheese packet and grate her some more.

She smiles as she turns her attention to the colourful drawing fixed to the fridge with an ammonite magnet. On it is the red shell of a house with a blue scribble of sea below it, the chimney all wonky. A smiling face at the window. The paper is stained and creased, but it's been there ever since she can remember.

Maya looks at the empty space where she'd sat, feeling the desire to reach out a hand to the child just as her mum would have done. Tell her that although the mother who loved her so much would soon be gone, she'd never be alone as she had a father who would fill all the empty spaces in her heart.

But it's too late. That little girl is no longer there, and in her place is a young woman whose life is yet to start.

Taking a tissue from her pocket, she dabs at her eyes. How she wishes she'd been older when they lost her. That she had her own memories and didn't have to rely on her dad's to conjure up the images she craves.

On the shelf above the microwave are her mum's recipe books. Maya slides one out and flips through the pages. She's hoping to find something different to do with the chicken breasts she bought at the butchers in town after she'd got off the bus. Thai maybe? It's a favourite of her dad's. Soon she's lost in thought, poring over recipes, deciding what spices she could use. She loves cooking; in that way she takes after her mum.

Amy loves cooking too. Her dad's words float into her head unbidden.

Maya's heart sinks. For one merciful moment she'd forgotten all about her. But now, instead of the picture she had of her mum at the cooker, a faceless woman has taken her place. She's not alone, though. No, Maya's dad is watching on from his seat at the kitchen table as the Amy woman flicks through one of their recipe books… bends to look in their fridge… rifles through their drawers… opens their cupboards.

Maya sees her hands on their food. Her hands on their cutlery. Her hands on her dad.

She puts the recipe book down. Now, instead of cooking, she wants to scream at the walls, put a chain and padlock around their life. But even as she's thinking this, she knows she's being irrational. It's how a child acts, and she's no longer a child. What is it she's so scared of? Is it that her mum's image will be erased by this woman who's taking her place?

Forcing herself to get her emotions in check, she slips the recipe book back on the shelf and makes her way to the living room. At the back of it is the conservatory that looks out to the sea. It's where she'd sat with her dad the previous evening, his happiness shining through his tiredness. While he'd talked, Maya had kept her face impassive. Hadn't commented on what he was saying but kept her eyes fixed on the cover of the photograph album on the glass coffee table. Ever since she can remember they've kept it there, the plastic pockets protecting the pictures that document the short time she and her mum spent together.

Last night was the first night in a long while they hadn't looked at it.

Maya picks it up and opens it. On the first page, there's a picture of her as a tiny baby in a carrycot, her little body swaddled in a cellular blanket. In another, she's in her mum's arms. Her mum's not smiling, but there's no doubt in Maya's mind that the look on her face as she bends her head to her child is one of love.

She'd sing you lullabies, Maya. And rock you until you slept.

Picking a page at random, Maya finds a photo she's always loved. It was taken on the coastal path that runs along the back of their garden before continuing its journey across the top of the Jurassic cliffs. Dipping and rising like the humps of a dinosaur's back.

Her mum is standing, her hand on Maya's shoulder. Behind them is a backdrop of rolling hills where a line of pylons, each one gaunt and skeletal like a giant's ribcage, march away into the distance. The ugly metal structures should spoil the scene, but strangely they don't. Whenever she looks at the photograph, she doesn't see their ugliness but sees instead what they represent. Safety. Security.

It's where they found her that day.

Just seeing them transports her back to that special place beneath their metal legs. The grass tickling her cheek. The white mist clearing to reveal a sky so blue it hurts her eyes. The waves folding onto the shore. Her mother whispering, *I love you.*

Through the conservatory window, she can see how the wind has whipped up the waves. Lines of them are rolling towards the unseen beach, and she pictures them crashing onto the shore in a spray of spume. She needs to get some fresh air to clear her head, help her get things into perspective, then when she's calmed down and her dad gets home, they can talk properly. She'll tell him the truth. Make sure he knows how she's really feeling.

Putting her phone in her pocket, Maya goes into the back garden and heads towards the gate at the end, the sea holly and waving heads of pink valerian that have taken over the borders brushing her legs as she walks past. Leaning her arms on the gate, she looks out at the sea, breathing in its scent. In the fading afternoon light, the gulls swoop and dive, and she watches them, thinking of the things she'll say to her dad when he gets home. Not straight away – first she'll ask if he's had a good day. Will check the slope of his shoulders and the way he's holding his body for signs that the dark mood has been kept at bay for another day, another week or, if she's lucky, another month. No, she won't ask him until later. First, she'll cook him his supper.

Maya turns and looks up at their solid, red-bricked house, taking in the conservatory and the large bay windows that look straight onto the sea. She knows it's too large for just her and her dad, a perfect family house, but neither of them have ever wanted to move. For that would mean moving away from her mum too and the memories that are so precious to them both.

She hears a car driving up the lane to their house; her dad isn't as late as she'd expected. Not wanting to go in straight away, Maya turns back to the sea and stares at the horizon, seeing how sea and sky are starting to merge as the light fades. Then, when she thinks she's given her dad enough time to come in and take off his coat, she straightens and walks back down the garden path.

As Maya walks past the conservatory, she sees it's empty, but her dad has clearly been in there as the cushions on the wicker settees are newly plumped, the photo album moved to a side table. What's brought on this bout of tidiness? She lets herself in through the back door and reaches down to take off a shoe. 'Where are you, Dad?'

His voice comes back to her from the other side of the house. 'We're in here, love.'

Maya stops, one hand resting on the tumble dryer for support, the other one holding her trainer. *We?* Surely, she's heard him wrong. Dropping the shoe, she places the flat of her hand against her chest, feeling the thump of her heart against her ribcage. Surely, he wouldn't have brought the woman home without telling her first.

Forcing her feet to move, Maya goes into the hall, and her heart sinks further. There are voices in the kitchen. One is her dad's, the other a woman's. At first, she thinks it's Teresa, and her eyes close with relief, but then the woman laughs, and she knows it was just wishful thinking. Teresa's laugh is light. This woman's is deeper. Throatier.

Maya steps closer. The door is open, the overhead light shining down on the kitchen table. Her dad is sitting there, his legs stretched in front of him. He's watching someone at the worktop… the owner of that laugh. Her back is to them both, and she's unwrapping fish and chips from a newspaper, her dark head bowed to her task.

Then, without warning, she turns, and Maya freezes, the blood draining from her face. She feels the room sway and clutches at the door handle to steady herself. She stares dumbly at the woman, and when at last she finds her voice, it comes out little louder than a whisper.

'Mum?'

CHAPTER NINE

Teresa

Teresa closes her laptop and pushes her chair under the table with her free hand. With her other hand, she presses her mobile to her ear. There's nothing but a dial tone. After two more rings, the phone switches onto answerphone, and she listens as her own voice tells her to leave a message or ring back later.

'Mum. When you get this, can you call me back, please?'

Cancelling the call, she goes to each window in turn and closes them, then files some notes in the filing cabinet. She looks at her phone again, willing it to ring. *Come on, Mum. What are you doing?*

Her mum knows she rings at this time every day. Deciding to give her another five minutes in case she's in the bathroom, Teresa wanders into the reception area and sits where she sat earlier that morning, on the white settee. The others have all left – even Stephen, which is unusual, or used to be, as recently she's noticed he's been leaving earlier and earlier. In the old days when they worked together, when the weather was fine, she'd suggest they go for a quick drink after work…

But that doesn't explain where he is as she's checked, and today he didn't have a late afternoon client. Usually when that happens, he spends that time getting on top of his paperwork. Not today, though, it seems. As soon as the young man he'd been treating for an eating disorder had left his consulting room, Stephen had hurried off. Just like that. With no word of where he was going.

Not that there's any reason he should inform her of his comings and goings – it's just that it's something he usually does. Also, she'd been hoping he might drop by her room before going home to continue the conversation they'd started that morning. Opening up to him about the things going on in her life had been a huge relief, bringing home to her how isolated she'd been feeling. Of course, she has her mum and Gary... Dale, even. But how can she confide in them when they all, in their various ways, have played a part in her growing anxiety?

She remembers the first time she and Stephen had met. How tongue-tied she'd been when he'd come up to her outside the lecture hall to discuss one of the questions she'd asked. Scared that her answers had sounded gauche. Her knowledge lacking in depth. But she needn't have worried. Instead of walking away, he'd asked her to clarify a few points and offered to get her a drink from the hospitality area. It wasn't long before she'd felt comfortable in his company.

If only she'd married Stephen instead of Gary, things would now be so different. She hadn't been given the chance, though.

This morning, when they'd sat together on the white settees, Stephen's voice had been just as calming as it had all those years ago. He'd left her a quiet space in which to reply to his questions, and, in the time before she answered, she'd found herself comparing him, as she always did, to her husband. Unlike Gary, he'd listened properly to her worries, and when offered solutions, she'd found her eyes slipping again and again to the greying hair that curled over the cuffs of his shirt. Wondering if she could reach out a hand and touch it. Remembering.

After all this time, the thought should shock her, but it doesn't. In an odd way, she finds it comforting.

Not wanting to analyse what's going on in her head, Teresa looks at her phone. Her mum still hasn't returned her call, and when she rings again, it goes once more onto answerphone. The next message she leaves is more urgent than the first. 'Ring me straight away, Mum. I need to know you're okay.' She stares at the screen. It's only been a day since she saw her, and she wouldn't visit again so soon, but the fact she hasn't picked up is worrying.

Teresa knows she should go and check on her, but if she does, what about Gary? It already annoys him the amount of time she spends there. Should she ring and tell him what she's doing? Or would it be better just to go?

Indecision is tearing her in two. If any of her clients saw her now, they'd be hard-pressed to reconcile this indecisive person with the professional one who sits opposite them in her consulting room. The one who works with them to help find a way out of their problems.

She looks at the clock on the wall. Five o'clock. If she leaves now, providing all is well, she can be there and back before seven. She tries not to think about what might happen if she isn't.

She's just closing the reception blinds when her mobile rings. Running back to the settee, she grabs it and reads the name on the screen. It's her mother.

After making sure she's okay, Teresa sinks back onto the white cushions. She covers her face with her hands and thinks she might weep with relief. She's free now of obligations. Her mum's safe, Gary won't be back for a couple of hours, and it won't matter to Dale if she's home or not as he's always in his room.

She goes to the window and parts the blinds, thinking of Stephen's house on the cliff. Wondering.

CHAPTER TEN

Maya

The woman is standing at the worktop, a bag of chips in her hand, and Maya stares at her, not caring that she's being rude.

Clearly not aware of the riot of emotions that are fighting for space inside her, the woman looks up and smiles at Maya. A warm smile that, under different circumstances, would take the edge off Maya's shock.

Those eyes, that hair, the way she's standing… they're just like the photograph of her mum that's on the wall next to the kitchen table. Positioned carefully so that she and her dad can look at her when they're eating their meals.

But how can it be her mum, when every day after work Maya walks the coastal path to Crewl Point and sits on her mother's memorial bench? A bench placed there because her mother is dead. She knows this, yet, even so, she can't tear her eyes away from the woman's beautiful face.

Aware of Maya's attention, the woman lifts a hand to her hair as though it might be out of place and, with that gesture, Maya feels her heart lurch. It's the hair that does it. Dark and waving to her shoulders like her mum's had been. She's slim like her mum was too, her blue eyes framed by dark lashes. Her lips delicately bowed as though drawn onto her pale face with a fine brush. Mid-forties maybe? It's hard to tell.

Her dad grins. 'Maya, I'd like you to meet Amy.'

Maya stares at her, then at the three pieces of battered fish that lie waiting on the plates in front of her, not knowing what to do or say. Her emotions are running wild, veering between anger and sadness. This woman, this Amy, is the person who has put the sparkle back into her dad's eyes. She knows she should be pleased for him, but how can she be when the person he's chosen is so much like her mother? Like his dead wife?

The bag Amy is holding is transparent with grease, and Maya watches as she shakes the chips onto the plate nearest to her before sharing it between the other two. She does it quickly and efficiently, then presses the pedal of the bin with the toe of her trainer and stuffs the wrappers inside. There's nothing awkward in her movements, no embarrassment at being caught in Maya's kitchen. It's as if she's meant to be there.

'Hi, you must be Maya.' She looks at her curiously, then holds up hands slick with grease and wiggles her fingers. 'I'd shake hands except then you'd end up smelling as bad as I do. Goodness knows how anyone could work in a fish shop.'

Maya can feel her dad watching her expectantly. Waiting for her to reply. What does he want her to say? It certainly won't be any of the things that are going around her head. That the woman's too young for him. That she doesn't want her in her kitchen… her house. That she'll never be able to forgive him for choosing someone who reminds her so much of her mother.

Instead of saying any of those things, she points at the cooling fish. 'I was going to do a Thai chicken curry tonight.'

Straight away, Amy's face falls. For the first time, she looks awkward. 'Really? Oh, I'm sorry, Maya. Your dad said he'd told you not to bother with cooking tonight.'

Maya thinks of the message her dad sent and realises what it was he'd been trying to say. She wants to think she'd misunderstood, but now she wonders if that's entirely true. Maybe a part of her wanted this outcome.

'I always cook for Dad when he gets home,' she replies.

Her dad considers what she's just said, a slight crease between his eyes. 'Well, thankfully you hadn't started, so no harm done.' Going to the worktop, he picks up two of the plates of food and takes them to the table before fetching the other.

Maya doesn't move from where she's standing but watches Amy who's at the sink washing the chip fat from her hands. When they're clean, she flicks her hands into the basin to get rid of the excess water, then dries them on the clean towel Maya had hung on the rail that morning. Her earlier composure has returned, and if she's aware of Maya's eyes on her, she gives no indication.

As she joins Maya's dad at the table, her hand rests for a second on his shoulder. 'Thank you for picking me up from the station, Steve.'

Maya stares at her. No one calls her dad Steve. Not even Teresa. It makes him seem like a stranger. He doesn't seem to mind, though. Far from it. In fact, he looks like the cat that's got the cream.

He grins. 'No problem. I couldn't expect you to get the bus.'

Why not? Maya thinks. *I have to get the bus to work every day, don't I?*

'Well, I just want you to know that I appreciate it.' Amy bends and kisses his cheek, then takes the seat opposite him.

Maya's stomach is a tight ball, any appetite she'd had before long since disappeared. Despite this, she walks to the table and sits down next to her dad. What else can she do? She picks up her knife and fork and starts to eat, but the fish turns to mush in her mouth. The chips stick in her throat.

They eat in silence. Maya keeps her head bowed to her plate, her shoulders rigid, unable to make eye contact with this stranger. But she can feel her dad's and Amy's eyes on her. Can imagine how they'll share a complicit look over her head, when they think she's not looking, wondering how they should handle the situation. How to make things easier.

In the end, it's Amy who speaks. 'So, Maya. I hear you work in a home for the elderly.'

Maya carries on chewing, her eyes glued to the cooling flesh of the fish. She doesn't want to answer, doesn't want to have any conversation with this woman, but knows she won't be able to avoid her questions forever.

She forces herself to look up. 'Yes. In Bridport.'

'I think that's amazing… *you're* amazing. I wouldn't be able to do that job. I'm much too impatient and heartless.' She laughs and her dad laughs too, but Maya doesn't. She doesn't want Amy's praise.

'I've never met anyone less heartless than you, darling.' Her dad reaches over and pats Amy's hand. 'And that's no lie.'

Darling? Maya looks from one to the other. That's not a word you use when you've only just met someone. She has to know. 'How long exactly have you known each other?'

This time Maya sees their eyes meet. Sees the thing that passes between them.

Her dad puts down his knife and fork and turns to her. 'It's actually been a few months now.'

Maya catches her breath. 'Months?'

'I know I should have said something, but I didn't know how you'd react.' He looks at Amy, then back at her, his expression turning serious. 'I needed to be sure it was going somewhere first. And when I was, I told you straight away.'

'All this time…' Maya stops, trying to get her head around it, the bitter taste of resentment in the back of her throat. 'All this time you've been seeing each other, and I never even knew.' A thought occurs to her. 'All those evenings you were late home, when you said you'd had to fit in an extra client, was that even true?'

Her dad looks sheepish. 'Sometimes. Not always. It was the only chance we had to see each other.'

Amy has been sitting silently, but now she speaks. 'Your dad just wanted to do the right thing by you, Maya, but it's obvious now that it wasn't. I'm really sorry if I've upset you. We've got off on the wrong foot, but if there's any way we can start again, I'd really like that.'

The plea is so heartfelt that Maya finds herself softening. Slowly, her anger creeps back into its cave, and the ball in her stomach loosens. Without realising it, she's nodding.

'All right.'

Before she knows what's happening, her dad gets up and pulls her into a bear hug, kissing the top of her head. 'That's my girl.'

They carry on eating and, when they've finished, Maya collects their plates and stacks them in the dishwasher. When she comes back, there's an open bottle of wine on the table.

Her dad holds it up. 'We're going to watch a film. *Pretty Woman*. Want to join us?'

'*Pretty Woman*?' Maya looks from one to the other. Her dad's often mentioned that her mum resembled Julia Roberts, with her brown wavy hair and her long legs.

She folds her arms and smiles tightly. 'Wasn't that Mum's favourite?'

'Well yes, but…'

'Then I don't want to watch it.' She turns away, not wanting to explain why. Hating that her dad's sharing her mum's special things with Amy.

Amy looks from one to the other. 'I'm sorry, it was me who chose it… I didn't know. You should have said something, Steve. Look, we can always choose a different one. Honestly, I really don't mind what we watch.'

Maya shakes her head. 'No. I'm tired. You two can watch it. I think I'll have an early night.'

She leaves them at the table and goes upstairs. Before she shuts her bedroom door, the movie's theme tune floats up to her, making her skin prickle. All these years she's avoided watching it, unsure of how it would make her feel if she did. Yet, Amy and her dad will be sitting side by side on the settee their eyes glued to the screen, more likely than not their fingers linked. Amy will laugh at the jokes her mum laughed at, cry in the places her mum did.

Maya lies on her bed and presses her pillow over her ears. Despite her earlier change of heart, it's too soon for her to be playing happy families. Amy being around is going to upset their equilibrium, and Maya knows she'll find it harder to look out for her dad if he's with her. What if he confides in this woman? What if Amy learns the secret of her mum's death before *she* does? Maya turns herself onto her stomach. If that happens, how will she be able to protect him?

CHAPTER ELEVEN

Teresa

Crewl House stands before her, its red-bricked chimneys looking too elaborate for the solid house that supports them. The curtains are all still drawn, although on the first floor, one of the sash windows is slightly raised. It's the first time Teresa's seen the house up close, and she's fascinated.

To be honest, she's not sure why she's here. What brought her to drive the twelve miles to Winmouth. Was it a magnetic pull from the past? Or something else? Either way, she knows it's wrong. Knows how it would look if either Stephen or Maya were to draw back a curtain and see her standing there, her head tipped to the windows on the first floor. Wondering what kind of life they'd led here when Maya's mother was still alive. Wondering what it might have been like if things had been different.

Despite her brain telling her otherwise, her heart knows very well why she's come. It's because there are two long days before she's back at the clinic. Two days before she'll be able to speak to Stephen. For when she'd woken up this morning, she'd had an overwhelming desire to confess to him her feelings, and, ridiculous as it might be under the circumstances, she'd known that because of what happened in the past, he'd understand. She'd been younger then, newly qualified and in awe of his greater knowledge. Dazzled by his senior position. His situation had been complicated then, but now it's different. They're equals, and he has no ties. If only *she* didn't either.

The kitchen is at the front of the house, the large main window facing the driveway where she can just see Stephen's car. At the side of the house, where she's standing, having left her own car in the lane, is a smaller window. It looks out onto the footpath that leads behind the house to join the clifftop path.

When she arrived at the house, with no thought other than that she needed to talk to Stephen, the kitchen had been empty, but now she sees a movement through the glass. Teresa can't see who it is as it's nothing more than a change of light and darkness behind glass that's patterned with a reflection of laurel leaves, but still she steps back. Ducking behind the laurel hedge that separates the house from the path. Hoping she hasn't been seen.

When she'd left her bed that morning, Gary had still been asleep, one arm crooked behind his head, the delicate veins beneath his eyelids visible in the light that spilt through the gap in the curtain. Leaning up on her elbow, she'd rested her head on her hand and studied him. He'd looked so peaceful, and it would have been easy to pretend he was the same man she'd married. The one who'd showered her with compliments and weekends away. The man who'd once made her feel as if all her birthdays had come at once.

But he wasn't.

Climbing out of bed, she'd prayed he wouldn't wake, for if he did, he'd roll over and circle her wrist with his hand. Would pull her back to bed and cover her body with the bulk of his own. Not caring whether or not it was what she wanted. As she'd lifted her dressing gown from the door, he'd rolled over and she'd held her breath, dreading that he'd open his eyes, but his gentle snore had signalled he was still asleep.

During her drive to Stephen's, what she was doing had seemed perfectly reasonable, but now, the reality of what she'd planned to do, the shock of it, has brought her to her senses.

Turning her back on the house, Teresa returns to her car. She's cross with herself. Coming here was a mistake and by allowing her emotions to take over, it's like she's crossed an invisible line – even if it's only one she's drawn herself.

She gets in and starts the engine, her hands shaky. Closing her eyes, she concentrates on her breathing, giving her heart rate time to return to normal.

As she drives away, she looks in the rear-view mirror and thinks she sees a curtain move at one of the upstairs windows. She glances away to navigate a parked car and when she looks again, sees that it's just the wind moving the net at the part-opened window.

Was she hoping Stephen had seen her?

Teresa shakes her head and indicates left before turning into the road that will take her into the village. She's had a narrow escape, but no one knows she's been here.

What she does know is that she must never let it happen again.

CHAPTER TWELVE

Maya

When Maya wakes, the sun is shining brightly through her thin curtains, and the worries of the evening before are just a memory. Pushing the curtains aside, she sees that it's going to be a beautiful day and as she looks out at the sparkling sea, feels foolish for having overreacted. For a moment, she thought her mother was alive… but how could she be? Very soon Amy will tire of her dad, with his paunch and overlong hair and find someone her own age.

Besides, Amy isn't here now, so she's not going to let the idea of her ruin the weekend that stretches out in front of her. Slipping on her dressing gown, she wonders what she and her dad will do to make the most of the fine weather. Maybe she can pack a picnic for the two of them, and they can take the coastal path to West Bay then catch the bus home. It's what her mum and dad used to do before she was born – the photos are in the album.

And while they walk, she'll talk to him about Amy. Ask him what he thinks he's doing and whether he's thought about the consequences of bringing someone into their lives. She opens the door and goes out onto the landing. Maybe, if the time feels right and with Amy gone, she can see if she can get any further with her questions. She'll even ask him about what Mrs Ellis said. See if he has a good explanation for his fight with her mum.

Liking her plan, she goes downstairs. The house is quiet, not unusual for a Saturday morning as her dad likes a lie in after a week at the clinic. The kitchen is filled with sunlight, and she picks up the kettle to fill it, wondering why the handle feels warm. Putting the kettle down again, she touches the plastic side with her hand, taking her fingers away quickly. The kettle has been boiled recently. That's certainly a first; her dad never gets up before her at the weekend.

Walking over to the sink, Maya turns on the tap and refills the kettle. When she turns, her free hand rises to her chest in surprise. She hadn't heard anyone come in and certainly hadn't been expecting someone to be standing there.

Lifting a hand, Amy draws her dark hair back from her face, holding it with her slim fingers behind her head before letting go and shaking the tresses free. Maya watches transfixed. The gesture is familiar, a memory…

'What are you doing here?' Maya asks. The words are out before she can stop them.

'I'm sorry, I didn't mean to startle you, Maya,' Amy replies. 'I thought your dad told you I was staying over.' She's wearing an overlarge check shirt that Maya recognises as her dad's. She pulls her eyes away from the woman's long tanned legs.

'No, he didn't say.' Maya feels awkward standing in her own kitchen in her faded towelling dressing gown. For some strange reason it's as if *she's* the stranger. 'I was just making Dad some tea.'

Amy smiles and leans back against the table. 'Oh, I made him one earlier. I was just coming down to rustle up something for breakfast. Your dad says there are some croissants in the cupboard.'

'I'll do it,' Maya replies. It comes out abruptly. Rudely. And even though it's what she's feeling, Maya hates the way she sounds. After all, it's not Amy's fault… it's her dad's. He should never have asked her to stay. Not so soon anyway.

As if reading her thoughts, Amy gives a small shake of her head. 'I feel really awkward about this, Maya. Sometimes, I just don't think. Like with the film last night. But please don't blame your

dad. If anything, you should blame me. I should have checked
the train times more carefully. I thought there was a late one, but
I was wrong. I really am very sorry if my being here has made you
uncomfortable in any way.'

Maya twists the tie of her dressing gown around her finger
– something she used to do when she was a child. The apology
sounds heartfelt, but she can't help how she's feeling. Upstairs, her
dad is lying in his bed, a mug of tea cooling on the bedside table
next to him. Tea that someone else has made for him.

'My dad and I will be going out later,' she says.

Amy looks puzzled. 'Oh, he never said.'

Just like he never said you were staying over.

'We walk if the weather's good. It's something we've always done.
I'm sure he won't mind driving you to the station before we leave.'

There's nothing ambiguous about what Maya's said, and a spot
of pink blooms on the apples of Amy's cheeks. Maya feels a flash
of guilt. She's just wondering if she's gone too far when her dad
walks into the kitchen.

Both women turn to look at him. He's holding an empty
mug in each hand. One has blue and white stripes on, the other
a cow. Neither is the mug with *Best Dad* written on that Maya
bought for him a few years ago and that he always uses for his
early morning tea.

He grins. 'Beautiful morning.'

Amy is the first to recover her composure. 'It most certainly
is. Maya says you always walk when it's fine.' She points at the
window. 'You couldn't ask for a better day for it.'

'Indeed.' He goes over to the window and looks out. 'That sky
is almost cloudless. You must come with us, Amy. The Dorset coast
is, in my opinion, the best place to be when the sun is shining.'

He's wearing his old plaid dressing gown and a pair of navy
pyjamas. His hair is dishevelled, his face still creased from the

pillow. He doesn't seem to care that it makes him look far older than his years.

He smiles at Amy. 'What do you say?'

Maya waits for her to say she can't, that she has things to do… but she doesn't. 'I'd love to, Steve. It's really lovely of you to invite me.' She turns to Maya. 'You don't mind, do you?'

Maya holds her anger tightly inside her. 'I suppose not.'

'Marvellous.' Her dad beams at them both.

Amy smiles and looks down at the check shirt she's wearing. 'Would you mind if I have a quick shower before we go?'

'Of course not. Make sure you turn the right-hand tap on fully or you'll be showering in freezing water. There are towels in the airing cupboard.'

'Thank you.'

Without saying anything more, Amy takes the mugs from him. As she puts them into the sink, she hums to herself, the tune sweet and soulful. A song designed to lull a child to sleep.

Maya knows this song. Knows the rise and fall of the melody but not the words. Closing her eyes, she sees a circle of gold and silver stars that give off glints of light as they turn above her head. Her arms reaching up to grasp them.

Unaware of Maya's attention, Amy pads out of the room, twisting her hair into a topknot and fastening it with the band that's around her wrist. As she walks through the hall, Maya's dad watches her, his eyes full of admiration. Seeing Maya's noticed, he covers it up with a yawn and a stretch.

'I suppose I'd better get myself dressed too. I'll just have a quick look at the paper first.' Picking up his reading glasses, he settles himself at the kitchen table and Maya watches as he licks his finger to turn the pages.

Upstairs on the landing Amy is still humming, the tune breaking when she opens and closes the airing cupboard door. Maya stands and listens. Wracked with confusion. What *is* that tune she's humming and why does it make her feel both sad and happy? She wants to ask her dad, but something is stopping her.

'You shouldn't have let her stay,' she says instead.

Her dad looks up from his paper, his brows pinched. 'What?'

'It's too soon to be sleeping together,' she blurts. 'You don't even know her.'

Slowly, her dad closes the newspaper. He folds it and sets it to one side. 'Not that it's any of your business, but Amy slept in the spare room last night.'

Maya feels a rush of hot blood to her face. 'Oh.'

'Although I shouldn't have to explain it to you, we thought, just as you did, that it wouldn't have been right so early on in our relationship. Not without checking it was okay with you first, anyway. It was something on which we were in total agreement.'

On hearing this, Maya dislikes Amy even more. Why hadn't she told her? 'I don't like her, and I don't think she's good for you.'

'You don't know her, Maya. You haven't even given her a chance.'

'She's too young for you, and one day she'll get bored and leave.' Maya knows she's behaving like a child, but she can't help it. Her anger is driving her. 'Have you thought about that? And if I leave you too, you'll have nobody.'

Her dad stares at her a moment, then shoving his hands in his pockets, he walks out into the hall. His movements slow. Troubled. She hears his heavy footsteps on the stairs, then the sound of his bedroom door opening and closing.

A knot forms in Maya's stomach. She knows what this could mean.

CHAPTER THIRTEEN

Maya

For the rest of that day and the next, although she tries not to make it obvious, Maya tiptoes around her father, knowing she should make amends but not knowing how. All the time, she's looking out for signs. Clues to his mental health: a deadness to his voice or a darkness in his eyes.

She should never have said what she did. In doing so, she could so easily have brought on the very thing that she's spent her life protecting him from. His dark mood. What she sees in his face though is nothing more than sadness tempered with acceptance. He'd clearly been excited by his new love, had hoped Maya would be too, and now, after what she'd said, it's as if he knows it was too good to be true.

In the end, none of them had gone for the clifftop walk. Her dad had told Amy he had a migraine coming on and would see her later in the week. She'd wanted to stay to make sure he was okay, but he'd kissed her on the cheek and said he needed to sleep. If Amy had thought his sudden change of mood was strange, she hadn't said.

Since then, it's as though her dad has forgotten Maya's cruel words, or maybe he's just forgiven her, for he's been as loving as always, and it makes her feel worse.

'Dad?' she calls.

She finds her father in the conservatory. He's sitting on one of the wicker settees, the family photo album open on his knee. His hand is resting on the page of plastic pockets, and his eyes are closed.

'Dad,' she says again gently.

He opens his eyes, and Maya thinks she sees tears in them. She looks away, guilt eating at her.

'I wondered where you were. Do you want some supper?'

Outside the window, dark clouds have blown over the sea, turning it a liquid pewter. As she waits for his reply, Maya tries to concentrate on the white caps that edge the waves, but they're too fast to keep track of, appearing and disappearing with the rise and fall of the sea.

'No, thank you. I think I'll give it a miss tonight.' He places a hand on his stomach and gives a small smile. 'Don't want to break the scales now, do I?'

The photos on his lap are of her parents on the beach. Her dad was younger then, trimmer, his beard no more than a dark graze on his chin. In the nearest photo, he's standing side on to the camera and the muscles of his stomach are taut, not yet showing the signs of middle age. Her mum isn't in this one, she must have been holding the camera, but she's in the next. She's wearing a striped halter-neck bikini and is sitting cross-legged on the stones, holding out a fossil to the camera. Her expression is guarded. Her dark hair falling around her shoulders.

Hair so much like Amy's.

Is that what it is? Is he comparing the man he is now to the one in the photograph and coming up short? Maybe, after what she'd said, he's thinking he's not good enough for Amy – not young enough, not fit enough. Is he thinking she's right and that eventually Amy will leave him?

Maya's heart gives a lurch. Her poor dad. But even as she's thinking it, a part of her is pleased.

'I'm sorry,' she says, knowing she has to say something.

'Sorry?'

'Yes, for what I said. I don't want us to be like this.'

A gust of wind rattles the conservatory door making them both look in that direction. The sky is darker now, the sea too, and Maya reaches across to the lamp and switches it on. Instantly, the sea disappears and only their reflections remain.

'Yesterday, when I was downstairs, Amy appeared in the kitchen and said she was making you some breakfast. She looked so much like the picture of Mum on the wall that I couldn't get past that. I wanted to hurt you for being so insensitive. For choosing someone who resembles Mum and bringing her into our lives. I'm sorry, Dad. I didn't know how upset you'd be at what I said. How sad. I didn't think about you... only me.'

She stops, not knowing how he's going to take it, but he doesn't look angry, just thoughtful. 'I'm glad you told me, Maya.'

'You're not cross?' She can bear anything but that.

'No, I'm not cross. Just disappointed.'

'I'm sorry.'

'No.' He gives a rueful smile. 'Not with you. With me. What I did was thoughtless.' He opens the album again, his face pained. 'Looking at the photographs now, I know what you're saying. Of course I see the likeness. It's probably what drew me to Amy in the first place. But I can't see why it upsets you so much. I would have thought it would be comforting.'

'But it's not. It makes me feel uncomfortable.' Maya's voice drops to a whisper. 'I just want Mum back.'

Her dad leans forward in his chair and studies her, a strange look on his face. 'I know you do... and maybe, subconsciously, that's why I did it.' He looks away again. 'We should have known it wouldn't work... or rather *I* should have,' he adds quickly. 'Maybe it's better if we break it off.'

Maya's heart sings, but then she sees the way her dad's eyes mist and her guilt returns.

'Why would you do that?'

'For the very reason you gave me. There have been many psychological studies about attraction over the years… I've even published one myself. When men are asked to rate a number of photographs of women on their desirability, the ones who receive the highest scores more often than not share the characteristics of an ex. The results aren't surprising, but the problem is that if you date someone because of this, your expectations will be higher. You'll want them to be like that person when the likelihood is, they won't be.'

Maya thinks of Amy. What her dad has said has given her hope. It's never going to work. Amy will never match up to her beautiful, loving mother. If she leaves them to it, it won't be long before their relationship runs its course.

She musters a smile. 'You might be a psychologist, Dad, but not everything's an experiment. I'm over it now,' she lies. 'Just go with your gut and do what makes you happy.'

'Then you don't mind if I ask her over for supper tomorrow?'

'It's fine,' she says, but of course she minds. Her words make her feel like she's inviting her dad to love her mother all over again. But she knows, for his own well-being, it has to be his choice. 'You sit here, and I'll make us both some supper.'

Maya gets up and leaves her dad to his thoughts. But as she goes into the living room, his words come back to her. That she shouldn't talk to Amy about her mother. The tune Amy was humming has been in her head. She has no real memory to support her theory, but she's becoming more and more sure it was a song her mum used to sing.

Maya stands in the middle of the living room her heart thudding. Her mind overthinking. To her right is the sideboard where they keep their photo albums, boxes full of old wedding invites, takeaway menus for eateries that no longer exist and pictures she drew for her dad when she was young. Things they should have sorted out but never have. Something is drawing her to it.

With a quick look over her shoulder to make sure she can't be seen, Maya goes over to the sideboard, bends and pulls open the doors. The box is where it's always been, the lid lifting away with the sheer number of things inside. She lifts the lid, smiling at the drawing that's on top, a picture of her family done in green felt pen: herself in the middle, her mum and dad either side, holding her hand.

It's not this she's looking for though, it's something else. Something she's never thought to look for before. In the conservatory, her dad is hidden from view by the large plant in the corner, but his foot is showing. From the jiggle of it, Maya can tell he's deep in thought.

Putting her hand into the box, Maya draws out a handful of items and sifts through them. She's searching for an order of service or a clipping from a newspaper. Anything from her mum's funeral. A funeral she didn't go to. A funeral her dad has never talked about.

She feels the need to know what songs he chose. What readings. Something that will give her proper closure and help her accept a new woman in their lives.

But there's nothing.

Then something catches her eye at the bottom of the box. Its bright colour calling to her. She pulls it out and sees it's a card with the word *SORRY* printed on the front in capital letters, the letter O turned into an eye, one teardrop hanging from it. Quickly, Maya opens it. Inside is one sentence. It's written in her dad's handwriting, and the words fill her with confusion.

Don't leave me. I didn't mean to hurt you.

CHAPTER FOURTEEN
Teresa

Teresa sits in her consulting room, her head in her hands, fingers raking through her fair hair. As soon as she got to the clinic that morning, she'd cancelled her early appointments, knowing she'd never be able to concentrate on someone else's troubles as well as her own.

Raising a hand to her throat, she touches it gingerly, wondering if there's a mark. Trying to ignore the tiny, secret part, buried somewhere deep inside, that's hoping there might be.

Now, though, she's wishing she hadn't cancelled her clients as without anything to occupy her mind, it keeps sliding back to the day before.

For what feels like the hundredth time, she tells herself she should never have married Gary. But after Pete, Dale's father, had died, Gary had made her feel safe, less lonely, alive. She remembers how he'd come over with his pint that day, pulling out a chair and swinging the full beam of his attention on her. Her friend, Jules, hadn't been impressed with her choice, had told her as much when they were in the ladies. She'd said she'd met his type before: the one where the smile never quite reaches their eyes. But she'd been lonely, and it had been an age since anyone had paid her any attention.

Teresa wonders what Jules is doing now. She hasn't seen her in a long time as it transpired Gary hadn't liked her any more than she'd liked him. *Jumped up tart* he'd called her. It's only now she realises how few friends she actually has. She misses someone to chat to over coffee. Someone to have a laugh with. If it's possible, she feels even lonelier than after Pete died. Poor Pete. He might not have been Stephen, but he was a good man nonetheless and Dale was the image of him. It was probably why, after his death, she'd agreed to marry Gary. His solid presence had been reassuring, for emerging from her grief, she'd had the strangest notion that unlike her fine-boned sensitive Pete, cancer wouldn't dare strike a man so robust.

Her mum's fond of Gary though and despite what she knows he thinks of her, Gary's always made an effort to be friendly when they've visited together… not that it happens often. In fact, her mother had been the one to encourage the marriage, making it clear she thought Gary would be a good father figure for Dale. Pointing out that he would give their little family a bit of security. Her dad hadn't been so sure about the match, but in her vulnerable state, Teresa had found the word *security* strangely seductive. She'd mistaken his control for concern. His obsession for love. Hardly surprising that she'd never introduced him to Stephen. She was too ashamed.

The photo on her desk is of Gary and Dale, taken a few years ago when they were still reasonably okay. Teresa pulls it towards her, and it's only now she sees how their body language is all wrong. Dale's face set, his shoulders tense. Gary's solid frame and tight smile making the blood draw away from her skin.

When was it she realised she'd never really loved him? Was it the first time he'd called her names? Or the first time he'd locked her in the house – refused to let her go out with friends?

Or was it when she compared him to Stephen?

She glances up at the ceiling, wondering if he's in yet. Would any of this have even happened if he hadn't distanced himself from her all those years ago? If she hadn't made her stupid mistake, forcing Stephen to tell her they could only be friends? She hadn't known about Cheryl, had never met her, but this woman who he said he loved had known about *her*.

Stephen had disappeared out of her life as quickly as he'd entered it. The friendship they'd shared just a memory. He'd married Cheryl and, a year later, she'd married Pete. If she'd known then what she knows now, how their lives would end up, she might have acted differently.

Then three years ago, out of the blue, Stephen had phoned her to ask if she'd be interested in a position at the clinic. Her job as a counsellor with the local health authority had not been as fulfilling as she'd been expecting, and he hadn't had to ask twice.

Positioned on the wall where her clients will see it when they come in, is a duck egg blue plaque. Teresa fixes her eyes on the white lettering. *Slow Down… Just Breathe.* As she concentrates on the words, she draws the air in through her nose and out again in an effort to still her thoughts. If she doesn't, she'll never get through the day.

Her breathing is interrupted by a sharp rap on the door.

'Knock, knock,' a voice says, and Stephen pokes his head around it. 'Can I have a word?'

Teresa lets out her breath and nods, knowing she looks a sight, her eyes bloodshot from lack of sleep. 'Of course.'

Stephen drags one of the chairs over to her desk and sits. He leans forward and fixes her with his brown eyes. 'Louise says you cancelled this morning's appointments. That's not like you, Teresa. Everything okay?'

Teresa thinks of how she'd stood outside his house, looking up at the window. Just the thought of it makes her feel embarrassed. What ridiculous notion had made her drive to Winmouth to get his attention when he's here, as concerned for her as he always is? How could she think he'd forgotten about her?

She rests her forehead against the palms of her hands. 'There's nothing you can do, Stephen.'

Stephen tilts his head. 'Try me. It worked last time, didn't it?'

On the drive here, Teresa had told herself she wouldn't say anything, would work things out herself, but now that Stephen is in front of her, all she wants to do is unburden herself like she did before. She wants him to tell her what to do. How to make things better.

Though she's practiced what she'll say to Stephen so many times in her head, saying the words is harder than she'd imagined, and she has to look away as she speaks them.

'The truth is, Stephen. I'm scared,' she says.

The enormity of what she's just said fills the room, and Teresa finds she's holding her breath. She can feel the strength of Stephen's gaze. Enveloping her. Calming her.

'Scared of what, Teresa?' he asks.

She turns her head, her eyes finally meeting his. 'Of what happened last night.' Without realising it, the fingers of her free hand have risen to her neck where the skin feels bruised and sore.

Stephen's eyes follow, but his voice remains neutral. 'Has Gary done something?'

'It's not what he's done.' Teresa closes her eyes, her throat aching. 'It's what I'm afraid he *might* do.'

She's imagined telling Stephen this for so long that she feels overwhelmed. Too shocked for the tears to come. By saying the words, she's started a chain of events that she might not be able to control, but it's too late to go back.

'Teresa?'

Stephen leans across the table and takes her hand in his and, despite her worry, she's shocked to find her body responding to his touch. Sending a small shiver through her.

'I think you should go to the police,' he says.

She shakes her head. 'What would I say? We'd been arguing, yes, but he didn't do anything.' Her fingers are at her throat again. 'It was about Dale. It usually is. Gary says he's doing drugs, but I don't believe it. If he was, I'd know. He's just irritated with him being in the house all day. Always there when he comes home from his shift, even though Dale doesn't leave his room unless we make him. I try to tell him it isn't Dale's fault he can't get a job, but he just calls him a loser. A waste of space. I tried to reason with him but—'

Stephen finishes her sentence for her. 'Gary doesn't like it when you try to defend your son. It makes him angry.'

'Something like that.'

Stephen shakes his head wearily. 'I wish I'd realised what was going on. Did you know I rang last night to check something with you? If only you'd answered your phone.'

'I couldn't.' She stares at her hands. 'It rang while Gary and I were eating, and it interrupted what he was saying. He snatched it from the table, and when he saw your name on the screen, he wouldn't give it to me.'

Stephen frowns. 'Why ever not?'

'Because he's suspicious of you. Even though I tell him he's wrong, he thinks there's something going on.'

'Between *us*?' Stephen's voice remains neutral.

'Yes.' She closes her eyes a second. 'I told him he was being ridiculous and that I needed the phone for work, and he said that if I behaved myself later, made sure I pleased him, he'd give the phone back.'

Stephen's face is serious. 'I see.'

Her skin crawls at the thought, but still she can't bring herself to say it.

Stephen gives an audible intake of breath. 'Whatever it is Gary has or hasn't done, it's affecting you and your son. You can't live your life in fear of what might happen. It will eat away at you until you don't recognise yourself.' He stops and gives her hand a reassuring squeeze. 'The only way to deal with this is by facing it head on. I can help you.' His voice is grave. 'What about Dale? He must know what's going on.'

Teresa's throat is dry, making it hard to swallow. 'He heard it all. Saw him…' The fingers that until now had still been at her throat, move to her lap and she swallows. Has she said too much?

'Saw him what?'

A cloud must have passed over the sun for the consulting room that had, up until now, been bright and welcoming, darkens. She has no choice but to go on.

'Gary tried to force himself on me after our argument, and Dale must have heard me shouting. If he hadn't come downstairs, I'm not sure I would have been able to make him stop.'

She squeezes her eyes shut, her mind conjuring up images. Sensations. Gary's hot breath on her skin. His knee forced between hers as he'd pushed her up against the kitchen units. His fingers as they grappled with the button of her jeans.

'Jesus, Teresa.' Stephen is visibly shocked. 'Are you telling me your husband tried to rape you?'

Stephen's voice brings her back to the present. 'No.' Her head is swirling. She can't think straight. 'It wasn't that. He was… He was just…'

He leans forward in his chair. 'Gary might be your husband, but that doesn't mean you have to make excuses for his behaviour. You know better than that, Teresa. What did Dale do when he saw what was happening?'

'Nothing. He didn't need to. He was holding a penknife to his wrist, and the threat of what he *could* do was enough.'

She tells him how she'd broken free of Gary's grip and run over to her son. How she'd grabbed his arm and pushed back his sleeve to find nothing but pale unbroken flesh. Her relief.

And, as she finishes telling him, Stephen's frown of concern is a balm. She leans her arms on the desk, mirroring him.

'Dale didn't say anything, not at first anyway, just stared at Gary with such hatred.' *Try something like that again, and I'll do it for real.* Those had been his words. 'I thought Gary would retaliate, but he didn't. Instead, he pushed past us and went out, slamming the front door behind him. Usually, Dale waits until we're in bed, then goes out, but last night he slept downstairs on the settee. He won't talk to me, Stephen. Why won't he?'

Teresa feels pressure from Stephen's fingers and looks down at their joined hands, wishing they could sit like this forever.

'It's how his worry manifests itself,' he says. 'I think you know that.'

She lowers her eyes, knowing he's right and how foolish she must look to him. 'I do. I've lost count of how many women I've counselled in my position. It makes a joke of what I do here.'

'Don't be too hard on yourself. It's one thing to give advice to others and another to heed it ourselves. I know that only too well. We might be therapists, but at the end of the day, we're human beings too, just like our clients. Living, feeling, human beings.' He lets go of her hand and sits back in his chair, a frown on his face. 'If you're not willing to go to the police, then you should consider leaving him.'

Teresa looks at her fingers, her skin receptors already mourning the loss of his hand. 'I've thought about it, of course I have, but I've nowhere to go.'

Stephen thinks for a minute, and Teresa watches for his reaction, relieved when his face brightens.

'I own a cottage in Winmouth,' he says. 'It's where we lived until we bought the big house, but now we rent it out to holidaymakers. It's the end of season, and there's no one in it at the moment. Why don't you and Dale move there until you've something sorted?'

He looks out of the window at the clouds that are gathering. 'You might hope things will change, but we both know the chances are they'll only get worse.' He stands and looks at her, his hands pushing deep in the pockets of his cord trousers. 'Do you trust me?' he asks her.

Teresa studies him. His shaggy beard. His greying hair. The soft check shirt and baggy cord trousers that are worn at the knee. He's one of her oldest friends. Of course she trusts him. He's the only one who can support her, and it's why she's told him.

'Yes,' she says, mustering a smile. 'You know I do.'

'Then you know what you have to do.' He leaves the room and comes back a moment or two later with a bunch of keys in his hand, which he drops onto her desk. 'I take it Gary's at work? Go home and get as much stuff into your car as you can. You can always collect the rest later. Make sure Dale comes with you, and when you get back here, I'll take you to the house.'

'But your clients—'

'Don't worry about that. I can rearrange. This is more important, Teresa. I hope you understand that. Especially with everything we've been through over the years.'

And she lets it all happen because she knows it must. She can't allow things to go on as they were. She needs things to change. Stephen's waiting for her to go, but her body won't respond. She's started to shake and wonders if it's delayed shock. Noticing, Stephen takes her coat off the back of the chair and drapes it over her shoulders.

'On second thoughts, I'll come with you, but first I'm going to make you a hot drink.'

He goes out, and Teresa hears the clunk of the coffee machine as it dispenses a cup. The woosh of the water as it fills. Then she hears Stephen telling Louise the two of them will be out until after lunch and to rearrange any appointments.

As she waits for him to come back, she thinks about what it will be like to be in the safety of his house. In his kitchen. In the bedroom he used to sleep in. Stephen has saved her as she knew he would.

When she moves to Winmouth with Dale, she'll be one step closer to him.

CHAPTER FIFTEEN
Maya

When Maya gets home from work the next day, there's a red Mini parked in the driveway. Cupping her hand to the window, she takes in the black leather seats and the Christmas tree air freshener that hangs from the rear-view mirror. It must be Amy's car. She frowns, remembering a photograph in the album of her mum leaning against the door of her Mini, tearing an L-plate in half.

At the thought of her mother, the card Maya had found in the box in the sideboard comes into her mind again. She pictures her dad hunched over the kitchen table as he wrote the words. His face pale and set as he wondered if his wife would accept his apology for what he'd done. Something so bad it had made her want to pack her bags.

Maya knows the card backs up what Mrs Ellis had told her, but still she doesn't want to believe it. Would rather think there's another explanation for what he wrote. But, whatever the truth, there's one thing she can't deny… There were things in her parents' marriage she knows nothing about.

She lets herself in and stands inside the hall, listening as she always does. Voices are coming from the living room. Her dad and Amy. Moving closer to the door, she waits.

'That was a very generous thing to do, Steve,' she hears Amy say. 'Offering her the cottage. Especially as you had to cancel some of the bookings.'

Maya rests her hand on the door frame. *Steve* again. It was what her mum used to call him.

'I didn't feel I could do anything else. The poor woman had nowhere else to go,' her dad replies. 'And of course there was Dale too. I invited her round for supper this evening, but she declined.'

'Maybe it's a good thing. She needs to settle in. And this husband? Is he really as bad as she says?'

'I've never met him.'

'Really? That's odd. Didn't you tell me you'd been friends for a long time?'

There's a pause, and Maya presses closer. She knows now they're talking about Teresa. She's never met Dale or her husband, but she doesn't like what she's hearing. It's clear something bad has happened. And so what if her dad hasn't met the guy either? What's it got to do with Amy and who is she to question Teresa?

'Yes, we've known each other a long time, but it was in more of a professional capacity.' There's a creak of a chair as he gets up, and Maya imagines him pacing as he speaks. 'What she's told me about Gary is very worrying. She was so lost, so vulnerable. I've never seen her like that before. When I offered to help her, she was clearly relieved. To be honest, I can't understand why she hasn't left him sooner.'

Through the gap in the door, Maya sees Amy's hand move to the glass of red wine that's on the side table next to her. A few seconds later, she puts it back down.

'I'm not the psychologist here, but I imagine it's because she needed you to sanction it. If she's telling the truth, she's done the right thing. No one should have to live under the influence of someone else.'

'Why do you think she wouldn't be telling the truth?'

Through the door, Maya sees the movement of Amy's shoulders as she leans forward.

'I don't know. I just think you should be careful, Stephen.'

Maya places the flat of her hand on the door. It's clear what Amy's doing here. Turning her dad against Teresa. Pushing everyone away. She needs to protect him from her. Can't let her continue like this.

Pushing the door open, Maya puts on her brightest smile. 'Hi.'

Amy's sitting on one of the chintzy settees, her feet tucked under her, and as Maya comes in, she looks up. Today, her dark hair is pulled behind her head in a messy bun, making her face look rounder. More homely. Despite having thought she'd got over her silly notion, Maya's heart gives a lurch. It could be her mum sitting there.

Her dad is leaning against the sideboard where heads of deep purple lilacs stand in a glass vase. Amy must have brought them with her as they hadn't been there when she'd gone out earlier. Their fragrance lingers in the room, stirring a faint memory of her mother. Had she liked them too?

Seeing her looking, Amy's cheeks dimple. 'Do you like them? I got them in town on my way here.' She twists in her seat and reaches for her glass again. 'Did you have a good day?'

With an effort, Maya smiles. 'It was okay. Tiring though. It always is.' She turns her attention to her dad. 'What were you talking about when I came in?'

'Just a bit of a crisis at work. Nothing for you to worry about.' She recognises the tone of his voice. It's the soothing one he uses when he's with one of his clients, and she's irritated by it.

'It was about Teresa, wasn't it?' She shifts her feet uncomfortably. 'I heard you say her name.'

Once, her dad would have discussed any problems, work or otherwise, with her, but now Amy's here, it's clear she's to take a back seat. It shouldn't bother her, but it does.

'Maya's right,' Amy says. 'Don't shut her out, Steve. She needs to know, especially as Teresa will be living in the same village.' She takes a sip of her wine and turns to Maya. 'You've met her, I presume?'

'A few times, yes,' Maya answers. 'But I don't know her that well.'

'Well, apparently she's been having a rough time at home, and she and her son have moved into your dad's rental cottage in the high street until she can decide what to do.'

Maya stands with her arms folded. 'What sort of rough time?'

Amy is about to speak, but her dad is quicker. 'Just marital stuff.'

'What's that supposed to mean?' She's seen the look her dad and Amy exchanged. It makes her feel excluded. 'Tell me…'

'It's not that I don't want you to know, love. Just that it isn't my place to say. Amy thinks Teresa might not like me discussing her private business.'

Yet you told *her*, she thinks. 'I'm going upstairs to change.'

Maya leaves them to it. She can't help but think about how quickly things have moved on. How influenced her dad is by Amy. How long will it be before she becomes more important to him than her?

Her bedroom is at the back of the house, looking out onto the sea. On days when the weather's bad, she likes to throw the window wide open and sit on the windowsill, half in, half out of the world, and cup her hand to the rain. And through the veils that blur the headland, she'll sometimes see her mum on the cliff path beyond the garden. See her beckon to her. Maya's smart enough to know that the woman with the long dark hair blowing in the breeze is just someone her imagination has conjured up, but still it's a comfort. The urge to follow strong.

When she draws back the curtain and opens the window this evening, though, the path beyond the garden is empty as she knew it would be. The air still. The horizon clear. She pushes the window wider. Out there, somewhere across the ocean, there are countries she's never been to. Ones she's never considered visiting, knowing her life is here with her dad. She's seen the photos her old classmates post on Facebook and Instagram. The places they've been, the people they've met and the fun they're having. Lots of them have gone on to university, making new friends and moving on with their lives. But she's stayed here with her dad, her ambitions pushed to one side.

It hadn't bothered her before, but now it does. All these years with her life put on hold because she's been worried about how her dad might be without her. Now, suddenly, she's been made redundant.

Maya unzips her tunic and steps out of it. She rolls off her tights, then sits on her bed to pull on her jeans and a T-shirt. Her feet are aching. Lifting one foot, she presses her thumb into the soft skin of her instep to massage it.

Downstairs, her dad and Amy are talking, and she wonders what they're saying now she's gone. The familiar ache fills her chest as she thinks of Amy curled up on the settee, her glass in her hand, her dark head on his shoulder. Her dad and Amy. Her dad and her mum. Like the two of them are the same person. She knows it's ridiculous to think like this, but she can't help it.

Maya presses the heels of her hands to her temples to stop the thoughts. *No!*

She shakes her head, making herself focus. She can't live her life like this, forever scared that any secrets her parents had might come out at any moment. The words on the card she found are tormenting her. *Don't leave me. I didn't mean to hurt you.* What she needs to do is face the past and find out more about her mum's death.

Her laptop is on the dresser next to her mum's photograph. She's just opening it when there's a knock on the door. Guessing it's her dad come to talk to her about Teresa, she quickly closes the cover. It's not her dad though, it's Amy.

'Maya. Do you mind if I come in?' She sounds hesitant as though uncertain of Maya's response. 'I'd like to talk to you.'

Maya doesn't want to speak to her, but what can she do? 'Okay.'

Amy comes in. She looks around her. 'This is a nice room.' She touches a finger to the pale blue wallpaper covered in tiny white clouds, her face wistful. 'I love this.'

Maya watches as her finger traces the edge of a cloud, remembering how her mum had done the same. The wallpaper has been there forever, and she's never let her dad change it. Even when she was old enough to do it herself, something had stopped her. Some strange loyalty to the past.

'Mum got it for me when I was little,' she says. 'She took me shopping in Bridport when I was about three or four, and when I saw the book with the wallpaper samples in, I kept shouting, *this one*. Whenever she suggested anything else, I cried.'

'Bless you.' Amy smiles at Maya. 'I'm surprised you remember that far back. I don't remember much before primary school.'

'I don't remember. Dad must have told me. Sometimes, when I was little, instead of a bedtime story we'd look at old family photographs and he'd tell me stories of the things we used to do... The things I'd do with my mum.' She looks at Amy. Her dad's told her not to talk about her mum, but she doesn't care.

Amy gives no reaction, just nods. 'Well, anyway, it's a lovely memory.' She points to the bed. 'May I?'

'I don't mind,' Maya replies, shrugging slightly. Being so close to Amy, seeing close up just how dark her hair is, just how young her face looks, makes her uncomfortable.

Amy sits on the bed next to Maya. 'I know you don't like me, Maya, but I'd dearly love you to give me a chance. I understand how difficult it must be for you having someone come into your dad's life after all these years, but I'm nice... honestly.'

Maya folds her arms. She's no intention of liking Amy, but if she's going to get to the bottom of what she's doing here, protect her dad from her, she'll need to get to know her at least.

Maya looks at Amy's lovely face, and the tendril of dark hair that's escaped from the clasp at the back of her head and once more the odd feeling of familiarity hits her. She lifts a hand to the strand of hair, then drops it again. 'Do you know you look like my mum?'

Amy sighs. 'I didn't until your dad told me. When I came to your house the first time, he said he wanted to show me something that would help me understand why you might not be comfortable with me being here. It was your family album. He knew it was a risk showing me, but he also knew it was important if we were to move forward.'

Maya turns and looks at her. 'Why was it a risk?'

'Because he honestly thought that I'd take one look at your mum's photo and get back in my car. Your dad's not stupid and would have known what I was thinking... that a person who's passed on is often romanticised. More intriguing than the living, breathing person who stands before them.' She takes a deep breath, letting it out slowly. 'It's hard to live up to a memory.'

'Yet you *didn't* leave. Why not?' Maya's interested to hear the answer.

'I was tempted it's true, but I really like your dad. He's been through such a lot and deserves another chance at happiness. We both do.'

Maya's going to ask what she means, but Amy's got up again, her attention caught by her mother's photograph that stands on the chest of drawers. Going over to it, she picks it up and studies it, a small smile hovering on her lips.

'But neither of us are prepared to give love another go unless we know you're happy about it.'

The air in the room feels a little thinner. What does Amy mean? '*Another* go?' she whispers.

From the photograph in Amy's hand, her mother's eyes look up at her. Eyes just like Amy's. Without realising it, Maya's hand reaches for hers, her fingertips remembering. For a second, she could almost believe...

'Are you all right, Maya. You're very pale.'

Maya pulls back her hand, tucking it under her armpit. Whatever was she thinking?

'I'm fine. I just wasn't sure what you meant when you said…' She trails off, unable to explain why the simple words have shaken her.

Amy replaces the photograph on the shiny wooden surface and sits next to her again. 'I just meant that both your dad and I know what it's like to feel the pain of lost love. Neither of us want to go into it again lightly.'

Maya pulls herself together, ashamed at where her imaginings have taken her. How ridiculous and immature they would sound if she voiced them… like a child believing in the tooth fairy.

'No, I suppose not.'

'And you're all right with us? Me and your dad?'

Maya shrugs. 'It's not up to me what Dad does.'

'That's true, but it's not what I'm asking, Maya.'

'I want whatever makes Dad happy.'

Amy smiles. 'I'm glad. As long as you're certain.'

'I am.'

Amy gives Maya's hand a squeeze and stands. 'Then I'll tell your dad the good news.'

After Amy has gone, Maya sits for a few more minutes, her eyes fixed on her mum's photograph, trying to compose herself. When she's ready, she goes to the door, but doesn't go downstairs straight away. Instead, she stands in the doorway listening to the voices in the kitchen below. Amy's is light and melodic, her father's lower. From where she's standing, she can't hear what they're saying, but they sound happy, their conversation punctuated by laughter.

Something is niggling at her. Some doubt she can't dispel, and she knows what it is. There's a question she should have asked Amy but didn't. Has her dad been honest with her? Has he told her about his episodes… and if not, why not? When his moods can affect them all.

Whatever he's said, she's more certain than ever that her father needs protecting from himself. And she's the only one who can do that. What she needs to do is find out more about the woman who's infiltrated their lives. For despite her hopes, it seems that Amy's going nowhere.

CHAPTER SIXTEEN
Teresa

It's four days since Teresa moved their things into the little cottage on the high street. Four days of looking at her phone. Four nights of lying in Stephen's bed, listening to the wind whistle through the gaps in the sash windows and down the chimney, wondering.

She's never stayed in a cottage with a fireplace in the bedroom before and at any other time she'd admire the black iron grate and the delicately patterned tiles. Smile at the wonky floor, the sloping eaves, and the tiny-paned window. But she's not one of the holidaymakers who usually rent this place. She's fearful that along with all the problems Dale already has, she's brought another into his life.

Her plan could make them safe for the first time in years, protected for once in their lives. But she's taking a risk and has no idea if it will pay off…

She looks at her mobile. It's been eerily silent since she moved here: no calls or messages from anyone. She'd expected Gary to be in contact, had even worked out what she'd say in reply, but there's been nothing. Without contact, she can't know what he's thinking or planning, and that's worse.

He wouldn't know where she'd be living now, but he does of course know where she works. Every day when she goes in, she's petrified she'll see him walk up the front path. And if he did, would he make a scene? Louise on reception has been primed to ring the police immediately, but would that be enough? What if he said something to Stephen?

The only thing that's positive in this whole mess is being in the same village as Stephen. Of course she sees him every day at work, but just knowing he's nearby helps to make things bearable. Makes her feel stronger. More in control.

She's been home an hour and knows Dale's in as his motorbike is parked round the back. She hasn't seen him, just heard him moving about upstairs. Going to the window, Teresa parts the curtain and looks out. If she presses her cheek against the glass, she can just see Crewl House on the clifftop. Is Stephen lonely without his wife? If she'd lost someone she loved in such terrible circumstances, she wouldn't want to continue living so close to the place where they died.

As she thinks of Stephen and Maya in their isolated house on the exposed clifftop, she's consumed with a sudden desire to see inside it. Would it be like she imagines? The wind whistling down the chimneys, the large empty rooms lying dormant, waiting for something, or somebody, to bring them back to life? She'd had the chance to see it the day she'd moved in as Stephen had invited her and Dale to supper, but how could she have accepted when, from one day to the next, she has no idea what mood her son will be in? So, instead, she'd made her excuses and stayed in the cottage, parting the curtains occasionally and looking at the tiny squares of light that were the windows of Crewl House. Wishing she was there.

'Dale, I'm going out,' she shouts.

Her call goes unanswered, so she drops the curtain, gets her coat and lets herself out of the house. She could do with some fresh air and a walk along the coastal path will do her good.

As she walks, she tries to persuade herself she isn't going this way because she's hoping Stephen might be in his garden or that he might catch sight of her and ask her in for a cup of tea or a glass of wine. For if she lets herself accept the truth, she'd have to question her motives. So, instead of glancing into Stephen's conservatory as she passes behind his house to meet the coastal path, she keeps her eyes firmly on the view, enjoying the sweep of undulating clifftop in front of her and the waves that race towards the hidden shore. The tide must be in, and once she's safely out of view of the house, she stops a moment, imagining the build-up of the waves before they separate and run up the shingle. Listening to them break against the base of the cliff, in an explosion of white foam. Then she lets her feet take her onwards. Treading the same path Cheryl had taken all those years ago. Knowing where she's going. Feeling the pull of it.

At the time of the tragedy, she hadn't wanted to read the news-papers for fear of seeing a photograph of Stephen. Hadn't known if she could stand to see his grief or the love he'd felt for his wife. But it's different now. The mild curiosity she'd had when she'd started working with Stephen again has turned into something more insis-tent. A relentless itch that's calling to be scratched. And now, living in the same town as him, and with nothing to do in the evenings, googling the past has turned into something of an obsession.

If only she could get inside Cheryl's mind, for then she'd know what she'd been thinking that morning when she'd set out along the cliff path. What had made her head out towards the bluff? The papers had called it misadventure. A simple accident. She'd misjudged the path in the fog and plunged to her death on the stones below the cliff before the sea had swallowed up her body and dragged it away... but how could they know? Over the years in her job, she's gained a good understanding of the workings of a woman's mind. She knows how powerful emotions can be... what they can make you do.

And what of Maya found curled up alone on the cliffs? When a distraught Stephen had carried her back to the house, along the path she's walking now, had the psychologist in him stopped to analyse his feelings? Not that he could have known his wife was dead. Not then anyway.

Teresa shakes her head. How could anyone move on from something like that?

She buttons her coat higher up her neck and walks quicker, knowing the answer. Sometimes, you have no choice but to move on when you have children to consider. She thinks of Dale. Sometimes, the universe offers you no other choice.

She's nearly at the place where the path divides and considers turning back, but ahead of her, surrounded on three sides by the sea, is the bluff covered in scrubby grass.

A smaller track, little more than a ribbon of trodden grass, leads to it and at the end she sees what she came for – a wooden bench. Her feet carry on moving, taking her towards it along the chalky trail. A sudden gust of wind catches her hair, blowing it into her face, but she keeps walking until she reaches it.

She stops, a hand resting on the bench's wind-scoured back and looks out at the choppy sea. This is the place where Stephen's wife died, and if she were to walk to the edge, she'd be standing directly above the place where Cheryl's body had lain, broken and alone, before the sea had taken it. She shivers and sits down, trying to push the image away, but there's no ignoring the press of the brass plaque against her back and eventually she turns to read the inscription.

In loving memory of Cheryl a cherished wife and mother.

A lump forms in Teresa's throat, and she swallows. As the papers said, it was indeed a tragedy. Cheryl was a young woman when she died, with a wonderful husband and a daughter who was too young to lose her mother. It makes her think of Dale. How would he react if something happened to her? She owes it to Dale to make his future a brighter, happier one.

She stands again. She's seen what she came to see, and all it's done is fill her with both sadness and something else she can't analyse. Despite being a beautiful spot, she feels as if she's intruding. After all, the bench wasn't put there for her but for the family Cheryl left behind. A place for them to remember.

Without looking back at the bench, Teresa rejoins the main path and retraces her steps along the cliff path, her eyes fixed on the distant house. She's unsettled by the lonely, barren place she's just visited and walks quicker, trying not to think of the rumours she's heard. People who've claimed to have seen a dark-haired woman walking the path. One who's looking for her little girl.

As she hurries on, the line of pylons in the field to her left accompany her and to her right, the sea stretches out as far as she can see. Navy in the early evening light, seagulls screaming above the white-peaked crests. She's more aware now of how solitary the path is. Not a soul on it since she came out.

So many emotions fill her as she walks: emptiness, sadness, guilt, concern. Rather than sate her curiosity, coming here has piqued it. While she'd been sitting on Cheryl's bench, imagining the waves below her sucking at the bare rocks before pulling away again, a thought had come to her. Having lived in the house for many years, wouldn't Stephen's wife have known the path like the back of her hand? Is it likely she'd stumble onto the wrong track? She doesn't think so, but it's possible. Why, though, had she been out walking in the fog with a small child? It's a question the papers didn't ask. But *she* does.

It's getting cold, and she wants to be back now, instead of being out here with the wind blowing the hawthorns. But the laces on her trainer have come undone and as she bends to retie them, she sees someone standing on the path. They're some distance ahead of her and are on their own. Although Stephen had told her the occasional walker comes here to look at the steep drops, a shiver runs through her.

She hesitates, not knowing whether to walk on or not. The person who stands on the windswept path between her and Crewl House is too far away to tell if they're male or female, but it's not this that bothers her. It's the fact they're just standing there.

She shouldn't find it unnerving, but she does.

Suddenly, a terrible thought comes to her. What if it's Gary? How could it be though, when he doesn't know she's moved to the village? Teresa pushes her hands into her pockets and closes her eyes, concentrating on the feel of the wind on her cheeks. The rise of her chest as she takes in the salty air and the fall of it as she expels it. Even if Gary knew she was in Winmouth, he wouldn't know she'd be out here on the cliff.

Opening her eyes again, she looks to see if the person ahead of her has started to walk, hoping they'll be heading back to the village, but there's no longer anyone on the path. The red-bricked house in the distance is the only thing she can see.

Maybe they were never there at all.

CHAPTER SEVENTEEN

Maya

It feels to Maya that Amy seems to be at their house all the time now, but there's little she can do about it, so mostly, when she's not at Three Elms, she stays upstairs in her bedroom or walks the cliff path to her mum's bench.

She doesn't want Amy there and yet there's no doubting the difference in her dad since she entered their lives and there's been no sign of him dipping into his dark place. In fact, she's never seen him so cheerful.

Also, Amy has taken to bringing her car so that she doesn't need to stay over, and Maya can't help wondering whose idea that had been. She should feel grateful to whoever it was that has been sensitive to her feelings, but she isn't. And that lack of gratitude only makes her guilt grow as she knows she should be making more effort herself for her dad's sake.

What she does know is that Amy and her father are becoming closer with every day that passes, and it's inevitable that at some point things will change. She's dreading the day she'll wake up to see Amy's red Mini still parked in the driveway, the bed in the spare room not slept in, her dad's bedroom door closed. It's going to happen, and there will be nothing she can do about it.

It's Sunday morning, and she's taken the coastal path behind their house, as she often does, and navigated the steep wooden steps to the beach. It is windy today, the sails on the yachts out at sea billowing. She pushes her hands deep into her pockets, feeling the cold, hard shapes of the fossils she's collected. Taking pleasure in the dips and ridges created millions of years ago. She won't keep them, she never does, but will scatter them back onto the beach at the end of her walk for she doesn't need them. The important fossils are at home, in a box under her bed. Fossils her mum collected with her in the days before she died.

As Maya walks, she scuffs her feet along the shoreline, loosening the pebbles, looking out for a hint of fool's gold or the telltale corrugation of rock that will point to a find. She feels relaxed, as though a weight has been lifted from her shoulders, and she knows why. It's because, for the first time since she can remember, she doesn't feel completely responsible for her dad and his well-being. She's been able to relinquish some of the responsibility to Amy, and it's a surprising relief.

The tide's pulling back, leaving a stretch of glistening sand between its lacy edge and the ragged line where the stones begin. She presses her trainer to the damp sand then lifts it, watching as her print slowly vanishes. It's then the truth hits her. If she carries on with her life as she is, she'll leave no mark. She'll be invisible. Is that really what she wants?

Maya looks at the horizon. There is another way she could live her life, but could she do it? Is she brave enough? In the pocket of her coat is the piece of paper Mrs Ellis gave her that day on the bus. The one with her contact number on. Although she never thought she'd need it, she hasn't thrown it away. Could it be that deep down she's known the day might come when she'd consider using it? Could this be the day?

Taking her mobile from her pocket, she looks at it, wondering if she has the courage. If she does, it will be the first time she's done something for herself in an age. Different emotions crowd in, vying with each other to confuse her further: excitement, anxiety and guilt. The promise of something different is exhilarating, but what if her dad does something like before? What if this time she's not there to stop him?

An image comes to her of the pills lined up on the dressing table in her dad's bedroom. Some big. Some small. She's only young in the memory and doesn't know what they are of course – guesses they're sweets. Her dad stands in front of them, his hands pressing down on the dark wood surface, his anguished face reflected in the mirror. Even though she'd been too little to understand, it hadn't stopped her being frightened. She'd sensed his desperation. Seen it in those tormented eyes. Where had her mum been, she wonders.

As he'd stared into the mirror, her dad had seen her standing in the doorway, her comforter in her hand, and his eyes had locked with hers. Slowly, he'd turned, and she'd heard his sharp inhalation of breath. The sob that caught in his throat. Reaching out an arm, he'd swept the pills into his hand and gone into their en suite. She'd heard the toilet flush, and the next thing she'd known he was striding over to her, bending to pull her into a hug that had taken her breath away. And when she'd reached out a hand to his face, it was damp with tears.

It was only as she'd got older that she'd realised the significance of what she'd seen. They'd never talked about it, it was just another thing he bottled up inside him, and she'd never pushed him. If she didn't talk about it, then she could pretend it had never happened. Maybe it's the same reason that stops her dad from wanting to talk about the day her mum died.

But her dad is in a better place now. He has his own practice and a girlfriend who's just like the wife he loved and lost. More importantly, there's been no sign of his inner demons coming back to torment him. She looks at her phone and then at the number written on the page. What would he care if she did something for herself for a change?

Her eyes turn to the cliff. Taking in its folds and shadows. The lines of strata running horizontally across its chalk face. Looking higher, she sees where the rock ends and the sky starts, the perfect blue punctuated by the line of pylons. Just the tops visible.

As it always does, the sight of them fills her with a perfect peace, its warmth spreading outwards from her core to reach every part of her being. The sun that is now flooding the beach is the same one that sent sunbeams glinting off the pylon's metal legs. Its warmth on her face bringing with it the happiness she'd felt lying under their metal cradle. And the sea that now curls towards her in a hiss of foam, before drawing back to leave a ribbon of dark glistening seaweed, is the same sea she heard as she lay there, her cheek tickled by the grass.

But the inner peace that's come over her is short-lived. For she knows that when she gets back to the house, nothing will have changed. Her dad will still be behaving like a lovesick schoolboy, and Amy will still be a factor in their lives.

Mrs Ellis's words are in her head. *You're only one decision away from a totally different life*. At the minute, a different life is what she needs. Before she can change her mind, she punches in the number and waits for her old teacher to answer. She'd always feared that something bad would happen if she tried to leave, but now she doesn't care. It's happened anyway.

When she gets back to the house, her heart is racing with the enormity of what she's done. Down at the beach she'd been so sure, but now uncertainty has edged its way in again. What if her dad says she's making a mistake? He'd been in the garden when she'd left, but now it's empty. She can't see him in the house either.

'Dad, I'm back,' she calls.

A voice comes from upstairs. 'I'm in here.'

She finds him in his bedroom and is surprised to see his bed covered with clothes.

'What are you doing?'

Her dad finishes folding the shirt that's in his hands and adds it to a pile that looks in danger of toppling onto the floor. 'I'm having a clear-out. It's about time as most of this stuff I haven't worn since prehistoric times.' He picks up a T-shirt with a picture of Iron Maiden on it, the transfer rubbing off in places, and frowns. 'Not my best moment.'

'Good grief, Dad. I never had you down as a headbanger.'

He laughs. 'I wasn't… not really. I bought it when they did a gig when I was at university back in the day. Your mum found it and gave me an ultimatum, this T-shirt or our marriage.' He studies the faces on the black cotton, then chuckles. 'She thought I'd thrown it away, but, well, it has sentimental value. It reminds me of my long-lost youth.'

'You're not that old.'

'Why thank you.' Picking up one of his jumpers, he throws it at her. 'Here you can help me.' He places his hand on top of the pile. 'I thought you could have a sort through and see if any of these would be suitable for the bring and buy at the old folks' home. That's if they haven't got too much stuff already.'

'No, there's no such thing as too much. Three Elms is always in need of some extra help so sort away.' Maya looks at the open wardrobe doors, the half-empty chest of drawers. 'Anyway, what's it all in aid of? You'll be walking around naked if you carry on like this.'

A flush of colour comes to her dad's neck. 'I'm just making a bit of room.' He runs his fingers through his thick hair. 'Just in case.'

'Just in case?' Maya frowns, then it dawns on her what her dad is talking about. She takes a moment to decide how she feels about it. The part of her who's always been the number one in his life feels betrayed, but the part that is considering stepping into a new life feels relief.

'You're going to ask Amy to move in, aren't you?'

Her dad looks at her. 'Would you mind if I did?'

'Do I have a choice?' She sits heavily on the bed, and looks at the piles of clothes.

'Of course you do,' he answers. 'I wouldn't do anything unless I knew you were okay with it.'

Maya looks up at him, shocked by his blindness. Can't he see? Can't he tell?

She doesn't answer his question. Doesn't want to. Instead, she asks him one of her own. 'Why do you make it sound as though you've known Amy for years rather than a few months?'

'Do I?' Her dad frowns.

'Yes, whenever you talk about her.'

'I suppose it's because she makes me feel that way.'

Maya absorbs what he's saying. 'But how did you know?'

'Know what?'

'That she was the right one after all this time alone?'

'I haven't been alone. I have you.'

'You know what I mean, Dad.'

He sucks at his top lip. 'I'm not sure. Call it a sixth sense, but as soon as I walked into the pub and saw Amy sitting there, I felt something good was going to happen. We started talking at the bar and had this immediate connection, despite the difference in our ages.'

Maya considers this. The age difference couldn't be much different to the one between him and her mum. This fact seems to have evaded him, though.

'I'm not getting any younger, Maya,' he continues. 'And when you get to my age, you don't want to let a second chance of happiness slip through your fingers. I know to my cost that you can never be sure what's going to happen in your life. When the rug might be pulled out from under your feet. I'd never have considered this when you were a child, but you're all grown up now.'

Maya looks at her hands, at the nails that have always gone unpainted because she's never had anyone she's wanted to impress.

Then she looks at the empty hangers in her dad's wardrobe waiting for Amy's clothes.

'But how can you be so sure it's the right thing to do, Dad? You haven't known her any time at all.'

He sits next to her. 'I've never been surer about anything in my life. I think I knew the first time I set eyes on her that she would be my soulmate.'

'But what about Mum?'

He looks at her sharply. 'What about her?'

'You always said *she* was your soulmate.' She tries to push away Mrs Ellis's words and the card that lies at the bottom of the box in the living room. She could always get it... ask him about it. But what if his explanation for it isn't one she's ready to hear?

'It's possible to find that special love again.' Her dad shifts, so one of the piles of shirts topples and he has to reach out a hand to catch it. 'I know I've been lucky.'

'But you weren't lucky to lose her, were you?' Maya presses her knuckles to her cheeks. 'There's something you've never told me, Dad. Where Mum's body was found. Where it was washed up.'

He stands so suddenly it takes her by surprise. His hand rakes through his hair, his frustration with her etched on his face. 'Don't do this to me, Maya. Not now. Do you *never* want me to be happy?'

'Of course I do. It's just that—'

'Then do this one thing for me and leave the past where it is.'

Maya sits looking at the open wardrobe. The space where Amy's clothes will soon hang. There's no doubt in her mind now that she's doing the right thing.

'I need to tell you something, Dad.'

Her dad closes the wardrobe door. 'What's that?'

She thinks of the phone call she'd made on the beach. How pleased Mrs Ellis had been at her change of mind. She's suggested that they meet tomorrow to talk about her application and discuss the tests she'll need to take before sending it.

'I've made a decision. I'm going to have another go. I'm going to try again to get a place at uni to study medicine.'

A shadow passes over her dad's face, and Maya wishes she hadn't said anything.

'Dad? Say something.'

Just as quickly, the shadow disappears, and he forces a smile. 'Are you sure that's what you want to do?'

'I wasn't at first, but now I am.'

He turns away. 'Then there's clearly nothing more to be said.'

Maya watches as he puts the jumper he's holding into a black bin liner and picks up another. His movements are heavy, weighed down with an emotion she can't read.

'I won't do it if you don't want me to,' she says hastily, 'but I thought you wouldn't mind. You said yourself that I'm an adult now.' She feels her frustration rising. 'And it's not like last time. Things are different.'

Her dad turns worried eyes to her. 'Different? How so?'

'You've got Amy now.'

'Amy?' For a moment it's as if he'd forgotten her. He looks down at the jumper in his hands, then at the half-empty wardrobe. 'Yes... Yes, of course I have.'

CHAPTER EIGHTEEN
Teresa

The girl who's sitting in front of Teresa is young, not yet out of her teens. Her beautiful blue eyes are large in her small face and her jeans are loose on her slim frame. With her long legs and slender wrists, she looks like a catwalk model, but from her answers to her questions, Teresa knows she has an eating problem. Not that the girl agrees with her. It was her mum who made the appointment, and it's clear she doesn't want to be here – the way she checks her phone and answers Teresa's questions betray the way she feels. Teresa desperately wants to help her, but she knows it's not going to be easy.

The session is nearing an end, and she's spent the time trying to build up a rapport with the girl: not pushing her for answers, letting her know that she can trust her. In the next session, she can go further. You must never push anyone too far. You need to be patient.

'I want you to know, Kiera, that I'm always on your side. We'll work through this together, and you'll come out stronger.'

The girl looks up from her phone. 'There's nothing to work through.'

Teresa smiles. 'Positivity is a good emotion, but denial can overshadow that. It's something we can talk about in your session next week.' She pushes an A4-sized piece of paper towards her. 'In the meantime, I'd like you to do something for me before I see you next time. Every time you have a meal, I want you to jot down how you feel before and after you have it. Anything you like. Just a word will do. It will be something to work on next week.'

The girl looks at it doubtfully but folds it up and puts it in her bag. She stands and peers out of the window, the tendons of her slim neck pronounced.

'My mum's here.'

The car is parked outside, and Teresa knows she's keen to leave. 'I'll see you at the same time next week then, Kiera.' She gets up too and opens the door for her. 'Look after yourself.'

It's what she says to all her clients and she means it. If she could help each and every one of them, she would.

Teresa waits until Kiera has left, then shuts the door. Immediately, she feels her heart sink and her confidence drain away. What right does she have to help these people with their problems when she can't even solve her own? She thinks of Dale. How she's worried that something is festering inside him, eating away at him so that she barely recognises anything of the happy boy he once was. She'd hoped that once they'd moved away from Gary, things would change but they haven't. He won't come down for meals and only talks to her when he has to.

After she'd come back from the cliffs, she'd found the cottage freezing – colder than it should have been on a late summer's evening. A crow had cawed, the sound too loud, and she'd crossed to the kitchen to find out why. As soon as she'd walked in it had been obvious, as the back door was wide open, the mat covered with leaves the wind had blown in. She'd stepped outside and looked up and down the footpath that ran behind the cottages, but there had been nothing to be seen.

She'd called Dale's name and when she'd got no reply had climbed the stairs, hesitating outside his room before going in. The room was empty, but his bedcover was rumpled as though he'd just got up. Beside the bed were the bags and holdalls containing the clothes he'd brought from the house. Apart from that, the bedroom had looked unlived in. Teresa had been just about to leave the room when she'd noticed the dressing table on the other side of the room. It was made of stripped pine and had a bevelled mirror attached that had seen better days. She'd stared at it, not knowing how she could have missed it earlier. Not the mirror itself but the writing. For scrawled across the black, spotted glass in marker pen, were words that had filled her with sadness.

Fuck. You.

Her phone rings, startling her, and she answers it, expecting it to be someone wanting to make an appointment, but it's not.

'Mrs Davies?'

'Yes?'

'This is Police Constable Lamb. I wonder if I could have a word.'

Teresa's heart gives a lurch and immediately she thinks of Dale. Something's happened to him. Drugs. Another fight. Who knows what?

It's not Dale they're ringing about though, it's her mum.

'We thought you should know, Mrs Davies. Your mother's had a burglary.'

Teresa grips the edge of the table. 'A burglary? Is she all right? Was anything taken?' She looks at her watch, wondering how long it will take her to get there in the rush hour.

'Yes, she's all right. We're with her now, and her neighbour, Mr Tiber, is sitting with her while we try to ascertain what, if anything, has been taken. He was the one who gave us your number. She'd been having tea with him and his wife when it happened. When she came home, she said the place had been ransacked.'

'Oh, Lord. Can I speak to her?'

'Yes, of course.'

There's a silence, and then her mum comes on the phone. 'Oh, Teresa. Why did they do it? What did they want?'

'It was probably kids, Mum. Looking for cash. Are you okay? I'll drive over straight away.' She lifts her coat from the hook on the door and threads her free arm through the sleeve. 'Then we'll pack a bag, and you can come back with me.'

'I'll be fine, Teresa. You don't need to fuss. Anyway, what would Gary think?'

Teresa raises her eyes heavenward even though her mum can't see. 'I'm not with Gary any more. Don't you remember? I told you last time I spoke to you. Look, Mum, let's not waste time talking on the phone. I need to leave now, and I'll be with you as soon as I can. Just try and think what might have been taken.'

She puts the phone down and leaves her office. As she passes the reception desk, Louise looks up. 'Are you off?'

'I have to go to my mum's. There's been a break-in.'

'Oh, goodness. That's awful.'

'I know. Is Stephen still here?'

'As far as I know… I haven't seen him leave.' Louise checks on the computer. 'Yes. He's got a client in half an hour.'

'That's good.' Still wound up from the phone call, and feeling relieved that she can tell Stephen, Teresa takes the stairs to the first floor and knocks on his door. When he says come in, she pokes her head around it. 'Have you got a minute?'

He's sitting in one of the comfy chairs that are carefully arranged around a low coffee table. He's looking at his phone and as she steps inside the room, he transfers the smile he has on his face to her.

'I've got more than a minute.' He looks at his watch. 'Everything all right at the house? I know the shower can sometimes be a bit temperamental, but I'll get it fixed as soon as I can. Scouts honour.' He scratches his head and his smile changes to a look of concern. 'Are you all right, Teresa? Has something happened? Is it Gary?'

Teresa shakes her head. 'No, nothing like that. As far as I know, he doesn't know where I am. It's my mum. She's had a break-in, and I'm going to need to go early. I'm sorry, I really am.' She searches his face for a reaction.

'For goodness' sake, Teresa, this is your mother we're talking about. There's nothing to apologise for. You must be worried sick.' Stephen puts down his phone, stands and comes over to her.

Teresa steps into his open arms, feeling the softness of his brushed cotton shirt against her cheek. Hearing his heartbeat inside his ribcage. Her heart is racing, and she leans her head against his chest, wishing they could stay like this for longer.

But then his mobile rings, and he steps away.

CHAPTER NINETEEN
Teresa

By the time Teresa reaches her mother's house, it's nearly an hour later. Despite her worry about her mum, Stephen's hug has made her feel less anxious about what she'll find when she goes in. It had been frustrating to be interrupted by his phone ringing, but he'd been right to answer it. She would have done if it had been *her* child calling.

Her mum is in the living room, sitting on the settee next to her neighbour. A female police officer is in the chair opposite, a notebook on her lap.

'I'm PC Lamb,' she says. 'It's good of you to come.'

Teresa tucks a strand of hair behind her ear. 'I'm glad you called me.'

She goes over to her mum and bends to kiss her cheek. Apart from looking a little startled, she seems none the worse for her ordeal.

'There are so many people in my house, Teresa. What do they all want?'

Teresa places a hand on her shoulder. 'They're here to find out what happened, Mum. To see what was taken and how they got in.'

Her mum looks at her, eyes wide. 'Who, dear?'

She tries to keep her voice calm. 'The burglar. The person who broke into the house.'

PC Lamb taps her pen on her notebook. 'To be perfectly honest, we're not actually sure what happened. There's no sign of a break-in, we've just your mother's word for what happened.'

'I don't know what you mean. I had a phone call. You said—'

'Oh, we're pretty sure someone's been in the house and had a look around. Drawers were open and things were scattered everywhere… that's what you said, isn't it, Jean? It's just that there doesn't seem to have been a forced entry. My colleague is in the back garden doing a final check, but from what we've seen, it's pretty definite.' She leans forward, her elbows on her knees. 'Are you sure you didn't let anyone in, Jean?'

Teresa's mum raises her eyes to hers. 'Did I?'

'I don't know, Mum. I wasn't here.' She bites back her frustration. This is not the best day for her mum to be having one of her memory lapses. 'Try and think. Did you open the door to anyone?'

Her mum raises her hand and counts off on her fingers. 'I got my coat. I put on my shoes. I made sure I had my key, then I went over to Roger and Kath's.' There's one finger left, and she looks more doubtful. 'I didn't let anyone in. I'm sure I didn't.'

Her eyes fill with tears, and Roger Tiber reaches over and pats her hand. 'It's all right, Jean. No one's suggesting it's your fault.'

Teresa looks around the room. Surprised that nothing seems out of place. 'Has anything been taken?' she asks the officer.

'As far as we can establish, just some cash.' PC Lamb looks around her. There's a duster and some spray polish lying on the sideboard and, with sinking heart, Teresa knows what she's going to say. 'The crime scene investigator should be with us soon to dust for prints, but I'm not sure what he'll find. Unfortunately, your mother had a bit of a clean-up after she called us.'

Her mother nods. 'I couldn't let you see it in the state it was in. What would you think of me?'

Roger turns to Teresa. 'I tried to stop her but…' He shrugs helplessly and she feels sorry for him. She knows how hard it is to stop her mum once she's got a bee in her bonnet about something.

She closes her eyes and sighs. 'Oh dear, I'm sorry. Today of all days, Mum decides to be house proud.' Getting up, she goes to the window and looks out, turning when another uniformed police officer comes into the room.

'This is PC Cole, Mrs Davies,' the policewoman says. 'Anything to report?'

PC Cole shakes his head. 'There's definitely no sign of a break-in? All the windows and doors are secure.'

There's a cup of tea next to Jean that she hasn't touched. Teresa picks it up. 'I'll make you a fresh one, Mum, then I'll help you pack a bag.'

'Where are we going?'

'To mine. You can't stay here on your own.'

Her mum's chin tips defiantly. 'I can and I will.'

'No, you can't, Mum. Not after what's happened.'

PC Lamb nods in agreement. 'It would be for the best, Jean. For tonight at least.'

Jean's shoulders slump. 'Just for one night then. No longer.' Reaching out a hand she grips at the fabric of Teresa's blouse. 'What *did* happen, dear? Can you remind me?'

Tears prick the back of her eyes. 'Someone's been in your house, Mum. You can't have forgotten already.'

Her face brightens. 'Was it Dale?'

'What? No, of course it wasn't. He's at home. You'll see him soon.'

PC Lamb makes some notes. 'And Dale is…?'

'He's my son. He lives with me.'

'And how old is he?'

Teresa's unsure where this is going. 'He's seventeen, nearly eighteen. Why are you asking?'

'As no one broke in, we need to know who else might have access to your mother's house. It's just routine.'

'My son's only got a 125cc motorbike. Much as he loves his gran, there's no way he'd spend precious petrol money coming all the way up here.'

Roger leans forward. 'Could it have been an opportunist at the door? I've heard of people asking for glasses of water and nipping inside while the owner's back is turned. Makes me a bit worried for me and Kath.'

'Yes, that's something we'll be pursuing,' PC Lamb says. 'We'll be doing some house-to-house enquiries to see if anything of the sort has happened to anyone else. They use many tricks to gain access, masquerading as someone from one of the utilities is another one.' She turns to Teresa's mum. 'No one asked to read your meter, did they, Jean?'

She frowns. 'I don't remember. I don't think so.'

PC Lamb directs the next question to Teresa. 'Your mother says she lives alone.'

Teresa searches her words for traces of criticism, immediately feeling defensive. Should she have allowed her mum to continue living on her own when it was clear her dementia was getting worse?

'She's been coping fine, otherwise I'd have organised some care for her. It's only recently her memory's started to deteriorate.' But she knows that's not true. She's been worried about her for a while now. Teresa feels the cold twist of guilt. What if something had happened to her? Something worse? As soon as the police have gone, she's going to phone the doctor and have him assess her. If she tells him it's urgent and explains the situation, with any luck, he'll be able to do it today.

'I'll get you some things, Mum. It will only be for a short while until we can get something sorted.' She can't meet her eyes. They can't carry on like this. She's going to have to start looking for somewhere for her mother to live.

As she sees the police constables out, she feels her anxiety rise again. She makes herself remember the comfort of Stephen's arms as he'd embraced her. Using the memory to calm her before she goes back in.

Terrible as the situation is, there is one silver lining. Her plight might bring her closer to Stephen.

CHAPTER TWENTY
Maya

Maya lies on her bed, her laptop open. Over the last day or so she's been doing some research into her mother's death. Looking up newspaper articles and anything else that might help her understand what happened, but there's little to go on. She's found a couple of bits in the local papers, but they haven't said much. Little more than that a woman from Winmouth had gone missing after falling from the clifftop path at Crewl Point. A photograph attached to the report shows the fossil beach with its outcrop of rocks, their house perched above it. In the second article, her dad looks out at her, his face solemn, the caption beneath stating he's Stephen McKenzie, husband of Cheryl McKenzie, the woman who fell to her death. It also mentions their six-year-old daughter, Maya, who was found next to the cliff path beneath an electricity pylon.

Neither of the news items had been on the front page, and it saddens her to think that the death of a young woman had been considered less important than a school closure and a local MP who had been questioned for indecent assault.

She frowns at the screen. What *is* interesting is that at the time it was written a body had not yet been found. Her heart beats faster. She needs to find something else.

There's a knock at the door, and Maya looks up. It's Amy, a mug of coffee in her hand. She comes over and puts it on Maya's bedside table. 'I thought you might like this. You look busy.'

Maya shifts round on the bed so Amy can't see the screen. 'I'm just working on my personal statement. I'll need it for my uni application.'

'You've been up here for so long your father and I were beginning to forget what you looked like.'

Maya knows Amy's trying to be nice, but she can't be bothered to fake a laugh. 'I just need to get it done. The application has to be in by mid-October, and that doesn't give me long if I'm to impress them. But that's the next stage. First I have to pass the UCAT test.'

'Goodness, what on earth is that?' Amy sits on the bed next to her, and Maya wishes she hadn't elaborated. She wants to tell her to go back downstairs, but she obviously can't. Was it her dad who sent her up here?

'It's a test to measure your mental ability,' she says eventually. 'Verbal reasoning, decision-making… that sort of thing. The test is next Wednesday at a centre in Weymouth. It's something I need to pass before I can send my application.'

Amy points to Maya's laptop. 'Applications are hard. Do you want me to take a look? Maybe I can help.'

'No, it's fine. I can manage.' She shuts the lid. 'I just need some space to think.'

This time Amy takes the hint. She stands and smiles. 'Well, I think it's a very brave thing that you're doing. I wish I'd done more with my life. Don't let anyone take this chance away from you.'

As she speaks, her fingers tap out a rhythm on her thigh, and Maya watches them, thinking about what she's just said.

'Are you talking about my dad?'

Amy's fingers stop their tapping. 'Not him specifically. I mean anybody. This is *your* time. You don't want to end up like Teresa spending your life worrying about your parent.'

'Teresa? Why, has something happened?'

'She rang your dad earlier this evening. Apparently, someone got into her mother's house – I don't think they took anything, but it's shaken Teresa up. She's brought her mum back to the cottage, and your father was on the phone to her for ages…'

Maya watches Amy, wondering if her concern is genuine. 'Poor Teresa. That's a worry.'

Amy nods. 'I know.'

She draws the cardigan she's wearing around her. It's an unusual shade of blue, but Maya can see that the colour suits her. It matches her eyes.

'Come down for supper when you're ready,' Amy says. 'I've made a green Thai curry. I know it's your favourite.'

Maya's not that hungry and has the beginnings of a headache, but she doesn't want to appear rude. 'Okay.'

'I'll see you downstairs then.' Amy points to the mug of coffee on the bedside table. 'Don't let that get cold now.'

She goes out, shutting the door behind her.

What Maya should be doing is writing some more of her application, but the whole process is like a ball rolling away from her. The application, the test, the interview. It's not just that though, it's everything that will come after, and she doesn't know if she's ready for it.

Instead, she continues searching for information about her mum, but behind her eyes, a band of pain tightens. What she probably needs more than anything is a break from the screen and food.

Although she doesn't want to, Maya closes the computer and goes downstairs. Amy and her dad are in the kitchen, and as she walks through the hall, the smell of the fragrant curry makes her stomach rumble. The sandwich she ate in the staff room at Three Elms seems a long time ago now.

In the kitchen, Amy is at the sink, rinsing a pan under the tap. As she bends to place it in the dishwasher, she sings to herself. It's the song she was humming the first time she stayed over, but this time there are words.

Maya stops in her tracks, aware of no other sound except this one: not the rain against the window, the soft whir of the washing machine or the tap of her dad's pen on the table as he attempts to do the crossword.

Her breathing becomes shorter and her heartbeat thumps against the confines of her ribcage.

As Amy pulls up the sleeves of her blue cardigan, exposing her delicate wrists, Maya's dad looks up at his girlfriend and smiles, but Maya doesn't.

'What are you singing?' she asks, panic rising in her.

Amy straightens. Seeing her standing in the doorway, she smiles. 'Oh good. You came down. I was going to call you.'

'What's that song?' Maya repeats.

'I don't know. It's just something that came into my head. I couldn't tell you what it is. Do you know it?'

Maya searches her memory for something, but the only thing she can find is the hazy image of silver and gold stars rotating above her head.

She turns to her father. 'Dad, when I was little, did I have a mobile above my bed?'

Her dad looks up. 'A mobile? Yes, I think so.' He glances at Maya. 'Why do you want to know?'

Maya doesn't answer him. Her head feels as if it's bursting. 'And did Mum sing to me when she put me to bed?'

'I suppose so. I really don't remember,' he replies.

The words of the song come to her now. *Sail away. Sail far away.* As she remembers them, her lips move silently, forming the words. It's the song her mother would sing to her to get her to sleep. She's certain it is.

'How do you know it?' She stares at Amy, her voice rising. The pain in her head worsening. 'Why would you sing that song when there are a million others you could choose?'

'Maya!' Her dad shoots her a warning look, but she doesn't care. All she can hear are her mother's words. Her mother's voice. It's the first time she's remembered it. Amy's face swims in and out of focus.

'Tell me!'

'I don't know, Maya. Maybe it's something I heard on the radio.' Amy's hand is at her throat, her fingers fiddling with the fine gold necklace that she wears. 'Please... sit down and tell me what it is I've done.'

Maya grips the door frame for support as images fade in and out: she sees her seven-year-old self, gripping the hand of her father at her mum's memorial service. Remembers her dad's face when he came home from scattering her mother's ashes... *if* he scattered them. But this isn't evidence. What if her body had never been found and he's not told her? She wasn't there with him on that clifftop any more than she was there at the funeral. A funeral no one ever talks about. *Maybe it had just been close family* was what Shirley in the 7-Eleven had said, even though her dad had told her that she and her mum had once been quite pally.

There's a hollow pain in her chest as she looks from one to the other. She's only got her dad's word for everything. What if there never was a funeral? Maya's mind races. People have memorial services for relatives who are missing, presumed dead. Could this be what happened? Could it be that the body had never been found and that he's been lying to her all this time, making her believe her mum had passed on when she hadn't?

'Maya, what is it?' Her dad is frowning. He gets up from his chair and comes towards her, but she takes a step back. Her eyes are not on him, they're on Amy.

The woman looks back at her with eyes she sees every night when she kisses her mum's photograph goodnight.

She feels sick.

The words come out before she's thought them through.

'You've got to tell me, Amy. Are you my mother?'

CHAPTER TWENTY-ONE

Maya

'Maya! What's got into you?'

Her dad is staring at her as though she's gone mad, and Amy's face registers her shock.

Maya covers her eyes with her hands, not bearing to see it. 'Just tell me the truth,' she shouts in desperation.

Her dad's arm is around her, leading her to a chair at the kitchen table. 'What truth, Maya? You're talking in riddles. Of course Amy's not your mother. How could you think she is?'

Maya gulps back a sob. 'The songs she sings, the way she looks, even the film on her first evening here was Mum's favourite.'

'Coincidence, darling. Nothing more.' He holds her to him, stroking her hair to calm her. 'How could you think otherwise?'

Amy says nothing, but her face is white. Unconsciously, she twists a strand of dark hair around her fingers. Maya watches her, then drags her eyes away.

'Where was the funeral?'

'The funeral?'

'Yes, where was it held? When?'

Her dad's voice holds a warning. 'You're being ridiculous, Maya.'

He glances at Amy, and Maya remembers his words on the beach. *When Amy is in the house, I don't want you talking to her about your mum.*

But she's beyond caring.

'Tell me, Dad. How do I even know there *was* one? I've looked everywhere and there's nothing. No order of service. No condolence cards. Nothing. The newspaper articles from that day only say she fell from the cliff. That she was missing.'

Stephen steps away from her. His voice panicked. 'Please, don't do this, Maya.'

'I want proof.' Maya swipes at the tears that are running down her face with the back of her fingers. 'Proof that she's dead.'

There's a silence in the room, but it's Amy who breaks it. 'What's going on, Steve?'

He looks at her, then his face sets. He draws himself up as if mustering the strength for what he must do. 'All right.'

Maya watches as her dad leaves the room and goes upstairs, already fearful of what he'll bring back down. She can't look at Amy. Can't let her see how much she wanted to be right.

After five or so slow minutes, her dad returns with a slim white envelope. Without speaking, he hands it to her, then sits heavily at the table.

Maya lifts the flap and draws out the page, already knowing what she'll find when she unfolds it. It's all there: her mum's name, the date, the place, the cause.

Her death certificate.

'Cervical fracture,' Maya says, her voice no louder than a whisper. The truth pressing down on her. It's the first time she's seen it in writing. The paper is smooth under her fingers. Seeing it in black and white has made it real.

'She broke her neck during the fall,' her dad says gently. 'You know that… I never hid it from you.' The hurt in his voice is impossible to ignore. 'I'll find the order of service from the funeral for you if you want.'

Maya stares at Amy with eyes blurred with tears. The colour of her cardigan is taunting her. Drawing her back to somewhere else.

'Where did you get your cardigan?'

Amy runs her arm down the sleeve, a slight flush coming to her cheeks.

'I'm not sure, I—'

'I gave it to her,' Stephen answers quickly. 'Is that a problem?'

His arms are folded across his stomach, and the confrontation in his voice is unmistakeable.

Maya stares at him. 'Why did you have a woman's cardigan?'

His eyes flick to Amy then back again. 'It was one of your mum's. Amy forgot to bring a jumper with her, and it's bloody cold this evening.'

Amy looks uncomfortable, but Maya doesn't care. She can't take her eyes off the blue cardigan. Recognising it now. She feels light-headed, disassociated from her body. The last time she saw the cardigan was in the photo album. In the picture, her mum is sitting on a rock at the foot of the Jurassic cliff below their house. the cardigan partially covering the swimsuit she's wearing.

'You kept Mum's clothes?' Maya can't believe it. As far as she knew, her dad had given them all away.

'Not all of them… just some.'

She can't get her head around it. 'All the time they've been here in the house and you've never shown me.' Tears are gathering. Her throat constricting. 'How could you keep them from me? She was my *mum*.'

'I'm sorry.'

Maya stares at him as though he's a stranger.

'But why? Why would you keep them if not to give to me?'

Her dad picks up his glass of wine and swirls the red liquid around it. 'I just thought they might come in handy one day.'

Maya can't believe what she's hearing. 'Come in handy for what?' She looks at him, horrified, then points at Amy. 'For if Mum comes back from the fucking dead?'

She feels his hand before she sees it. The sting of his slap on her cheek. The room goes silent. Out of the corner of her eye, she sees Amy's hand rise to her mouth.

It's as though time has stopped, and as Maya touches her cheek with her fingertips, a distant memory stirs. Another slap. Another moment frozen in time.

'Oh God.' Dropping to his knees, her dad pulls her head to his lips and kisses her forehead over and over. 'What have I done?'

Maya can't speak. It's as if the world is tipping away from her, and it takes all her effort to stop herself from crying.

Amy stands stock-still, her fingers grasping the wooden spoon with which she's been stirring the curry. She's staring at the two of them, her face white. Slowly, she puts the spoon down, then slips her arms out of the cardigan. She folds it neatly and places it on the worktop. 'That was unforgiveable, Steve.'

'It was, and I don't expect Maya to forgive me... or you for having to witness it.' He rocks back on his haunches and looks up at Amy with anguished eyes. 'I certainly will never forgive myself.'

Amy turns off the gas under the curry. 'I think it would be better if I went home. The two of you need to have a talk. Will you be all right, Maya?'

Maya nods. Her head throbs, and she's started to shiver uncontrollably.

She rubs the tops of her arms. 'Yes. I'll be all right.'

Looking uncertain, Amy picks up her bag. 'I think we all need some space to think about what's happened here tonight and decide the best way forward.' Maya sees her eyes slip to the blue cardigan. 'We'll talk about this tomorrow. I'll see myself out, Steve.'

The front door shuts, and Maya hears the sound of Amy's car as it crunches out of the drive. She sits mute, her eyes staring into the distance, unsure of what she should say or do.

It's her dad who speaks first. 'I'm truly, truly sorry, Maya. I don't know what else I can say.'

Maya touches her fingertips to her cheek, the skin still tender. Her eyes brim with tears. 'How could you?'

He shakes his shaggy head. 'I don't know. It was what you said about your mother, the way you implied I'd done it deliberately. Given Amy the cardigan to bring her memory back. I don't know what happened, but something just snapped. I've never hurt you before, Maya. You know that. You're the most important person in my life, and I would never have got through the years after your mother's death if it weren't for you.'

Maya pushes back her chair and stands. 'I'm tired. I'm going to bed,' she says.

Leaving him standing at the table, his head bowed, she goes upstairs to her room. Her cheek is still smarting, and she walks over to the mirror, turning her face to the side to see better. Relieved that there's only a slight redness.

But as she takes off her make-up, the cotton pad drawing across her cheek, making it sting, a little voice is in her head vying for her attention. A voice that is telling her something important.

Her dad's wrong. This is not the first time.

CHAPTER TWENTY-TWO
Teresa

Teresa's sitting at the little dining table in the living room with her mother when Dale comes down the stairs. It's a long time since he's got up this early. He's dressed in his usual uniform of low-slung jeans and hoodie, and she notices his skin has erupted in a cluster of spots around the corner of his mouth. At the front door, he bends and forces his trainers on.

Teresa stretches and presses her fingers into the small of her back, trying to relieve the ache of a night lying on the settee. 'Where are you going, Dale?'

'Out,' he says.

'I can see that but where?'

'Does it matter?' He draws the sleeve of his hoodie across his mouth as though wiping away the words he wants to say, then looks at his grandmother. 'All right, Gran?'

She puts the piece of toast she's been eating back on the plate. 'No, I'm not all right. I don't know why we all have to be here when we have perfectly good houses to live in.'

Teresa closes her eyes for a second, then opens them again. 'You know why you can't be at your house, Mum. It's not a good idea until the police find out what went on.'

'What went on? Nothing went on. Too many people making a fuss about nothing. Where's Gary?' She looks around her as though he might suddenly appear. 'Where's your husband?'

Dale's face closes in on itself. 'Give it a rest, Gran. He's not here. Three cheers for that.'

Teresa stands so her back is blocking Dale from her mum's sight and lowers her voice. 'I won't have you talking to your gran like that. I don't want her upset.'

Reaching behind him, Dale pulls the hood of his sweatshirt over his head. He points a finger at Teresa's chest. 'Yes, play happy families, Mum. Just like we've always done. Except this family isn't happy, is it? It's fucked up.'

He pulls the front door open and steps outside, slamming it behind him.

'It was nice to see him the other day,' Jean says, still staring at the place where Dale was just standing.

Teresa frowns. 'Who?'

'That person at my door.'

'You said there wasn't anyone.'

'Maybe there was. Maybe there wasn't.' She dabs at her chin with the square of kitchen roll Teresa's given her in lieu of a napkin. 'I don't remember. Why do you always have to go on and on about things?'

Teresa can't hide her frustration any longer. 'Because sometimes, Mum, it's necessary to remember things. Please. Try and think. Did someone come to the door or not? It's important that the police know.'

Her mum's fingers flutter at the neck of her blouse, and she closes her eyes. Teresa wills her to remember, but when she opens them again, it's as though someone has pulled down a blind. Teresa wants to be annoyed with her, but she can't. It's not her fault. What she does know though is she needs to start thinking about her mum's care. The more time she spends with her, the more certain she is she can't live alone and she can't expect Stephen to be responsible for the safety of all three of them in his little rental house. Not that she'd be able to look after her mum long-term.

Bending to her, Teresa puts an arm around her shoulders. 'Don't worry, Mum. It doesn't matter.'

She's taken a few days off as annual leave, but she can't stay home with her mum forever. Reaching for her iPad, she opens the email the doctor sent with the list of care homes in the local area. One catches her eye. Three Elms. Isn't that the place where Stephen's daughter, Maya, works? The one specialising in dementia? She looks at her watch. If Maya's on a late shift, she might be able to catch her before she leaves for work.

Taking her phone into the kitchen, she closes the door and rings Stephen's number. It takes a while for him to answer and, when he does, he sounds strange. As though he's ill.

'Stephen, it's Teresa.'

She thinks she hears him sigh. 'Oh, hi, Teresa. What can I do for you?'

'Actually, it was Maya I was after. Is she there or has she left for work?'

'She's gone for a walk along the coastal path. Do you want me to get her to call you back?'

'If you wouldn't mind.' Teresa lowers her voice. 'It's about my mum.'

'Ah, yes. How is she?' She'd phoned him yesterday to tell him what happened, but his enquiry today lacks his usual empathy. It's as if he's just going through the motions, and Teresa wonders if he's okay.

She leans her elbows on the worktop and, with the first finger of her free hand, traces a heart shape on the shiny surface. 'She's fine. Can't even remember what happened and thinks I'm making a fuss over nothing, but are *you* okay, Stephen? You sound a bit off.'

He clears his throat. 'What? Oh yes. I'm just feeling a little under the weather. In fact, I might stay at home myself today.'

'Is there anything I can do?' She hates the thought of Stephen ill and alone in the house when Maya goes to work. 'Would you like me to pop over later?'

'There's no need. It's just a migraine.'

Alarm bells ring but sorting out her mum is what's important right now. 'Well, take care. I think I might see if I can catch up with Maya. To be honest, I could do with the fresh air, but if I don't manage to see her, I'll ring her tonight. And Stephen...'

His voice seems to come from far away. 'Yes?'

'Are you sure you'll be all right?'

'Completely.'

She ends the call, feeling doubtful. Going back into the living room, she sits down next to her mother and takes her hands, her fingers rubbing the thin skin of her knuckles.

'I need to go out. I shouldn't be gone long. Will you be okay?'

Her mother looks at her as though she's said something stupid. 'Why wouldn't I be? What do you think I'm going to do, burn the house down?'

She feels guilty for admitting it, but all sorts of things had crossed her mind, this being one of them. 'Of course not. It's just that you don't know the house or the area. I don't want you wandering off.'

'Like that son of yours?'

Her eyebrows arch as she says it, and in that one gesture, Teresa recognises the smart, intuitive woman she used to be. She knows though that in another ten minutes she could have forgotten who he is again.

Teresa turns from her, blinking back tears. There once was a time when her mum would have been the one she'd talk to about Dale but not now. She's confused enough as it is, and she doesn't want to give her anything else to worry about.

Instead, she gives her hands a squeeze. 'Exactly that. There are some magazines in the rack over there, and I'll turn the TV on for you. Just don't go out, and if anyone comes to the door, don't open it. If it's important, they'll call back.'

'Like Dale did, you mean? When he came to my house?'

'No, Mum. It wasn't Dale. Don't you remember, we had this conversation yesterday, didn't we? Dale was here. Your house is almost an hour away, and he doesn't have a car.'

Her mum is far away again. Remembering something from weeks ago, months even. 'Always so nice to me. Lovely boy.'

Teresa sighs, knowing it's easier to go along with her. 'Yes, of course he is. He takes after me.'

Helping her mum up from the table, she offers up her arm and leads her to the chair opposite the television, flicking through the channels until she finds something her mum will be interested in.

'*Celebrity Antiques Road Trip*. You like that.' She kneels beside her. 'Look, Mum. I'll be back before you know it. Just stay here.'

Her mother looks up at her with innocent eyes. 'Where else would I go? I live here, don't I?'

The words are like a knife in Teresa's heart. How will she ever tell her? But there's no point dwelling on the reason she's going to try to find Maya because if she does, she'll never be able to live with the guilt. As her daughter, she should be able to look after her. But she can't.

Teresa forces the muscles of her face into a smile. 'Okay, Mum. If you're sure. And don't worry about Dale. He has a key and can let himself in when his sulk's worn off and he decides to come back.'

'Dale?' Teresa's mum looks at her, confusion written across her face. 'You'll have to remind me. Which one is he?'

'Forget it, Mum. I'll see you in a bit.'

She lets herself out and heads to the centre of the village where she'll take the steep lane that will eventually lead her past Stephen's house.

As she walks, she shakes her head. She'd told her mum to *forget it*. The irony of the words is not lost on her. But she's going to see Stephen's daughter and hopefully things will get sorted out. Who knows? It might even bring them all closer together.

CHAPTER TWENTY-THREE
Teresa

As Teresa had guessed, Maya is sitting on her mother's bench, staring out at the sea. She looks lost in thought, and Teresa wonders if she'll mind being disturbed. From the few times she's met Maya, she's found her to be a lovely, if solitary, girl. A pleasure to have around the clinic on the days Stephen had brought her in. A daughter like Maya is something she's always longed for.

'Maya?'

The girl turns her head, her face registering her surprise. 'Oh, hi, Teresa. What are you doing here? Hardly anyone comes this way except me.'

'Your dad said you'd gone for a walk, and I guessed this was where you'd be,' Teresa replies, hoping that it doesn't seem strange that she'd seek Maya out. She walks up to the bench and runs her hand along the wooden back. 'This is a lovely memorial to your mum. May I join you?'

Maya nods but doesn't answer. Her eyes are fixed on the water.

Teresa sits beside her. 'Do you come here a lot?'

'Most days if I can,' Maya replies, then adds almost as an afterthought. 'I feel close to her here. It's where she died.'

Teresa finds it strange that she needed to state this fact, and her eyes follow Maya's gaze to the sea. Today, with no wind to whip it, the waves are calm. They look dark and motionless, languid even. As though waiting for something to happen. A storm perhaps.

'Did your dad tell you that I'm staying at your other cottage?'

'Yes, he did,' Maya replies.

'And did he tell you why?' Teresa asks, knowing it's likely that Stephen had been discreet, that he's not the type to gossip or overshare. It's a good quality he has. One of many.

'Not really. He just said you were having some family problems. I'm sorry.' Maya turns to look at her, and Teresa sees how like Stephen she is. The curly hair. The brown eyes filled with compassion. She looks nothing like her mother.

'The fact is I've left my husband, Maya. The reasons are many and complicated, but it was the right thing to do both for me and for Dale. If I'm honest, I should have done it a long time ago. I don't think I would have had the nerve if it hadn't been for your dad.'

Maya says nothing but looks into the distance, her forehead creased as though trying to work out a difficult problem. 'Sometimes leaving what you know is hard.'

'Yes, it is.' Teresa knows what she's talking about. 'But it's my mother I wanted to speak to you about. I know I could have just phoned, but it's a conversation I'd prefer to have face to face. You see, she had a break-in recently, or rather she let someone into the house, and is very confused about what happened. It's not just that, though. Sometimes, she thinks my father is still alive, and at other times she can't even recognise his photograph. I've suspected her dementia is getting worse for a while now but what happened brought it to a head. Made me realise she can't live on her own any longer. I'd dearly love to have her live with us, but the cottage is barely big enough for me and my son and I…' Teresa lets the sentence drift, trying to regain her composure.

'And you thought of Three Elms?' Maya straightens her tunic.

'Yes.'

'Knowing what's best for our loved ones is always difficult. But if it makes it any easier, from what you've said it sounds like you're making the right decision. You really mustn't feel guilty.'

Teresa nods, blinking back the tears that have formed. 'Yes, Three Elms was on the list her doctor gave me. I knew you worked there, and I remembered your dad telling me it specialises in caring for residents with memory problems.' Her fingers tighten around the arm of the bench. 'I couldn't bear to have her living somewhere where she wasn't looked after properly. It's a parent's job to look after their child, but there comes a time when the roles reverse.'

Maya twists her body and runs a fingertip over the engraving on the metal plaque. 'Sometimes, it happens sooner than you think.'

The girl's finger stops on the word *mother,* and Teresa's heart goes out to her. But at least she still has Stephen. A loving father is better than no parent at all.

'Your dad is a super father, but I realise how much you must miss her, Maya. I'm so sorry for your loss.'

Maya looks mildly surprised. 'I didn't know her. Not really.' Her hand drops to her lap. 'Anyway, it's *your* mum we were talking about, and you've asked at a good time as just last week a room became vacant. Why don't you come to the home tomorrow and I'll give you a tour? If you like it, we can take it from there. I can let the manager know you're coming when I go in later.'

'That would be great. Thank you so much.' Teresa tries not to let her mind ponder the reason why the room has become free. She's just grateful it has. 'Tomorrow would be perfect.'

Maya's eyes stray to the plaque on the bench again. 'Only you should know I might not be working there next year. I'm hoping to study medicine at uni. I'd be lying if I said I wasn't nervous, though.'

'I'm sure you've no need to be,' Teresa says.

'You're probably right. It's just that I get anxious going to new places... after what happened to Mum.'

Maya looks down at her hands, and Teresa takes in her small frame and the sad eyes that are the same colour as Stephen's, feeling a strange desire to be closer to her.

She leans forward, her elbows on her knees.

'Have you ever considered talking to someone, Maya? About what happened and how it's affected you? You never know, it might help.'

'No, I haven't,' Maya replies. 'I don't really have any friends.'

'I'm talking about a professional… but obviously not your dad. It would have to be someone who's not so close to you.'

Maya's face closes and she folds her arms across her body. 'Thank you but there's no need. My dad told me there was an inquest, and it was decided my mother's death was an accident.'

She stops and despite her bravado, Teresa can see she's struggling with herself.

'I sense there's a but, Maya,' she says.

Maya pushes a strand of hair behind her ear. 'Maybe. I don't know why but, recently, I've been struggling with the idea of what happened. I feel there's so much more to the story, and it's eating me up.'

'Then talking to someone might be a good thing.'

Maya shakes her head. 'What would I even talk about? I've no memory of what happened except for when dad found me under the pylon. That part I remember vividly even though I was only little. I hate not remembering but that's how it is. Talking to a therapist would be a waste of everyone's time.'

'It's not just about remembering. A good therapist would look at the whole picture and help you discover if you've been dealing with things okay.'

'I'm fine,' Maya says. 'And I'd be grateful if you didn't say anything about this to Dad.'

The words are said with such finality that Teresa sits back. She hates that she's made her feel uncomfortable. She gives a careful smile. 'I'm sorry if I've upset you, Maya. But, if ever you change your mind and feel you want to speak to someone, I'd be very happy to be that person. The past is sometimes hidden just under the surface of the present. With help, if you peel that layer away, it can come back to life.'

'I said I'm fine.' Maya forces a smile. 'But thank you.'

Teresa nods. 'Well, I must get back to Mum. I've left her way too long as it is. Are you going back now? If you are, we can walk together.'

Maya lifts her hand to her cheek. 'No, I'll stay here for a bit. There are things I need to think about.'

'Okay, if you're sure. I'll see you tomorrow… and thank you. Before I go though, there's just one thing. Is your dad all right? When I spoke to him this morning, he didn't seem himself. In fact, he said he was taking the day off.'

Maya looks worried. 'Really? I didn't know. I left before he was up.'

'I can call in on him on my way past, if you like.'

'No, there's no need. I'll be going back myself soon.'

Teresa doesn't like leaving Maya on the clifftop, but then she reminds herself that she must know the path like the back of her hand. Walks it every day. A thought comes to her. One that fills her with disquiet. It's the same path her mother took. The one that eventually led to her death. Is it normal to want to keep revisiting the spot where the tragedy unfolded? Maybe, instead of remaining here with all its sad memories, Maya and Stephen should have moved away. It's what *she* would have done. But, if they had, she'd never have had the chance to reacquaint herself with Stephen.

Teresa stands and puts her bag over her shoulder. She's just walking away from the bench when she stops, her eyes frozen to a spot someway off along the path. She can't be certain, but it looks like someone's standing there, in the same place as before near the pylons, halfway between where she and Maya have been sitting and the house.

A kernel of uncertainty settles inside her and she grips the back of the bench. Who is it that's standing watching them?

'Seems like we're not the only ones enjoying the good weather this morning.'

Maya turns her head to look. 'I don't see anyone.'

'There, where the path opens up.' She points. 'Next to the pylon.'

Maya shields her eyes so she can see better, her hands rubbing the tops of her arms as though she's cold. 'I still don't see.'

'No?'

But though she strains her eyes, Teresa can no longer see anyone either. Just the green sweep of the clifftop and the line of pylons braced like cowboys.

She grips the back of the bench harder, Cheryl's metal plaque cold against her palm, as an unexpected gust of wind buffets her. Despite the clear sky and the calm sea, the bluff is exposed, the vast ocean on either side making her feel small and vulnerable. As if she's being watched.

CHAPTER TWENTY-FOUR
Maya

As Maya walks back to the house, she's unable to get what Teresa had said at her mum's bench out of her head. *Your dad is a super father.* If she'd said it last week, she would have agreed as he'd always been supportive and loving towards her, but what about the slap? Whenever she thinks of it, she still gets the unsettling feeling that it isn't the first time it's happened.

Mrs Ellis had said the argument he'd had with her mum had been so bad her husband had needed to intervene. She'd thought her dad's black moods had been brought on by her mum's death, but maybe he'd always had them. Maybe, back then, they'd manifested themselves in outbursts of temper. What has her dad been hiding from her all these years? Might it be something that could be connected to her mum's death?

When Maya reaches the house, Amy's car is parked in the drive and she stands looking at it, trying to gauge her thoughts. Although she hadn't expected her to, Amy has come back as she said she would, to talk about what happened the previous night.

Emotions bombard her as she looks from the car to the house – shame at what her dad did, embarrassment at what she'd said to Amy. But most of all relief. Things in her life are changing and her attitude needs to change too. After what happened last night, she's started to see things more clearly. Even though it means she'll no longer have her dad to herself, having another adult in the house could be a good thing. The atmosphere in the large house with its big windows and high ceilings is undoubtedly a happier one with Amy in it.

She's made a decision. If Amy will let her, she'll try to explain why she acted so emotionally. So childishly. Try to make things better again.

But she doesn't get the chance. As soon as she lets herself in, she can see something's wrong. Amy's standing in the hallway, her face pinched with concern. It looks as if she's been waiting for her.

'Your dad's in his bedroom,' she says before Maya's even closed the front door. 'He's locked himself inside, and I can't get him to open the door.'

A wave of fear washes over Maya. 'How long have you been here?'

'Half an hour or so. When no one answered, I let myself in with the key he gave me. I hope you don't mind. I'm worried about him, Maya? Has he done this before?'

Without answering, Maya walks past Amy and takes the stairs two at a time. This is exactly what she'd feared might happen if a new person came into their lives: that their stability, their safety, their routine would be ruined. That her father would do something like this and put himself in danger. It's one of the things she's tried to protect him from.

Maya runs across the landing and, when she reaches her dad's room, thumps on the door with her fist. 'Dad. Are you in there?' She presses her ear to the door but can hear nothing.

Amy's behind her. 'Do you think he's all right?' she asks. 'Should I call someone?'

'No, I'll deal with it.' Maya bangs again. 'Dad. Dad. It's me, Maya. Let me in.'

Her heart is racing so fast and so loud she's surprised Amy can't hear it. She's just wondering what to do when the key turns in the lock and her dad stands there, his hair awry, his face creased.

Reaching out a hand, Maya touches his arm. 'Are you all right?'

Her dad massages his forehead with the heel of his hand. 'Go to work, Maya. I just need some sleep,' he says, and Maya can see that he doesn't want to look at Amy.

The room is dark, the curtains drawn, even though it's after nine. Maya hesitates, unsure what to do. Sometimes, when he's like this it's best to leave him, other times, he wants her to stay near him as though scared he'll lose her if she goes back downstairs. Each time is different, and she's learnt from an early age that an episode can come on with no warning often after he's been drinking or is overtired. Her guess, though, is that the darkness descends when he's got maudlin about her mother.

Before she can think what to do, Amy has moved past her into the bedroom. She goes to the window and pulls open the curtains. Bright sunlight floods in and Maya uses it as an opportunity to check the top of her dad's chest of drawers and the bedside table for tablet boxes or anything else she should be worried about. Terrified he might try again. That this time, there'd been no little daughter to stop him from taking anything. Thankfully, there's nothing out of the ordinary in his room except for his unmade bed.

Her dad raises a hand to his eyes as though the light is hurting them. 'No, don't.' But there's no conviction behind his words. 'Just leave me… please.'

It's a long time since he's been this way. His voice flat, his movements heavy. And after last night, Maya doesn't know if she has the strength to get him out of it.

Amy is by her side. She takes her arm. 'Come on, Maya. I think what your dad needs is rest. We'll leave you to sleep, Steve, and you can come down when you're feeling better.'

Maya watches as her dad sinks onto the bed, his head in his hands. 'Thank you,' he says. 'But please, close the curtains again.'

Maya does what he asks, then follows Amy to the door. She looks less anxious now that she's seen him.

'Don't you need to get to work, Maya?' Amy asks when they get downstairs. 'Would you like a drink first?'

Picking up the kettle, she walks to the sink and fills it before spooning coffee into two mugs even though Maya hasn't answered.

'I don't think I'm going to go in today,' Maya replies, watching Amy pour boiling water into the waiting mugs. 'I'd rather be here… just in case.'

Amy hands her the coffee. 'You're worried about him, aren't you?'

'Of course.' It's clear now that his dark moods are something that her dad has kept from Amy. Now she knows, it's going to be harder for her to protect him from himself. 'He gets like this sometimes. Says it's a migraine but—'

'You know different.'

Maya nods and sits at the kitchen table. She looks at the woman she was desperate to believe was her mother and sighs. 'He's never got over what happened to Mum and when he's down, this is how it always comes out. It's worse when he thinks he's going to lose someone. It brings it all back. You know… what happened to her.'

'And you think what happened last night, and my leaving, brought on one of his,' she searches for the word, 'attacks.'

'Maybe.' Maya wraps her arms around herself. 'That's why I've never been able to leave him. Why I'm concerned about going to university. You understand that, don't you?'

'Of course I understand, but you're not on your own now, Maya.'

'Surely you can't want to stay after everything I said last night?' She's scared of Amy's answer, remembering again the cardigan and the ridiculous way she'd behaved towards her. None of this is her fault.

Amy takes her coffee to the table and sits. 'Last night I thought long and hard about this question. I'll be honest with you that my head was telling me that I should stay away.'

'But your heart?'

She smiles. 'My heart was saying the opposite. I've never been one to back away from a problem, and this is hardly a good time to be jumping ship. That would be hard on you both. And if I did, I'd be making myself unhappy as well. I want to be with the two of you, to help make life a little easier if I can. That's if you'd like me to, of course.'

Amy holds out her hand to her across the table, and Maya finds herself taking it. She nods, realising that it's true. After her dad's slap, having someone else in the house is comforting. She no longer feels comfortable being alone with him, especially when he's like he is today.

Yet… he's her dad, and she loves him. His black moods are not his fault. It's an illness.

As if reading her mind, Amy speaks again. 'Grief can manifest itself in strange ways. You must see it a lot at the care home. When I came back here this morning, it was to tell you that you don't have to do this on your own any more.' She gives Maya's hand a squeeze. 'If you've made up your mind not to go into work today, why not spend it on some last-minute revision for the test?'

'So you think I should still do it?'

Amy smiles. 'I think you should do whatever it takes to make your future better. It's what I'd do.'

'Then I will.' Maya looks at her watch. 'I'd better call work, though I hate letting them down.'

Amy takes a sip of her coffee. 'Go in if you want to and I'll stay here. In fact, I might even take the week off. I'd been thinking of handing in my notice anyway as I've not been enjoying my job for a while. I was hoping I might be able to get something a bit more local to here.'

A blush has crept into her cheeks, and Maya knows what she's saying.

'Does that mean you're moving in?' She's surprised at how pleased she is.

Amy smiles. 'It was something your dad and I talked about last night, while you were revising. Before—' She stops, and Maya knows she's remembering her outburst. The slap. 'Anyway, I'm coming to the end of the tenancy agreement on my flat, and we thought we'd see how it goes. It has to be something we're all happy with, and then we need to take it one day at a time. It will be a change for all of us, and if you're unsure, I'd rather you say now, Maya.'

The kitchen is silent. The only sound the ticking of the kitchen clock. Amy is waiting for her to reply.

Eventually, Maya looks up and their eyes meet. She's made up her mind.

'Welcome to the family,' she says.

CHAPTER TWENTY-FIVE
Teresa

By the time Teresa gets home, her worry about her mum is not nearly so all-encompassing as it had been before she spoke to Maya. She can now make progress with finding a suitable place for her mother and, in an odd way, the conversation with Stephen's daughter has made her feel a little closer to her.

When she lets herself in, she's relieved to see her mum is sitting in the exact same spot she left her. Her eyes glued to the TV.

She looks up as Teresa shuts the door and smiles. 'I'm glad you're home, dear.'

Teresa bends and kisses the top of her head, feeling the soft fine hair against her lips. 'I'm glad to be home too. I'm sorry I was so long.'

Above their heads, there's a loud bang, footsteps moving across sparsely furnished rooms. Teresa realises that Dale must be home, and she resists the urge to see what he's doing.

Her mum follows her gaze to the ceiling. 'It's so nice to see him after all this time. I told him I didn't know how long you'd be. Was that right?'

'You only saw him an hour ago, Mum.'

She looks puzzled. 'No,' she says. 'I don't think so. I haven't seen him since the day you came to my house.'

A sliver of fear lodges itself in her chest. 'Who are you talking about, Mum?'

'Oh, you silly thing. You know who.'

Teresa stands rigid, bracing herself for whatever it is she's going to say next. Unable to take control of the dread that's mushrooming.

'No, Mum. I don't.'

'Gary,' she says, with a smile. 'Who did you think I meant?'

Teresa waits for the footsteps on the stairs that will tell her he's coming down, her chest so tight she can barely breathe. She can't believe he's found them so soon.

With hands clasped in front of her, her nails digging into her skin, she raises her eyes to the ceiling. He'll be angry. Incensed that she's had the audacity to leave him. He'll use the word *disrespect* – as though it's possible she could ever respect a man with such low regard for her and Dale.

When the footfall on the stairs comes, Teresa's worked herself up into such a state of anxiety that it's almost a relief. At least this way, she'll know what he wants, and it will be over sooner. The door opens and, not wanting to alarm her mum, she presses the back of her hand to her mouth to stop the sound of her fear from escaping.

Then he's standing in front of them, and Teresa thinks she'll collapse with relief.

'Dale!'

He's wearing a pair of baggy jeans, the crotch halfway to his knees and an inch of Calvin Klein underwear showing above his waistband. He's bare-chested and Teresa's surprised to see that the biceps of his lean arms are well defined, a dark shadow of hair running down the centre of his pale chest. She could have sworn that the last time she saw him without his shirt, he still had the body of a boy. Now a man stands before her. His hair is wet from the shower, and Teresa averts her eyes from the yellowing bruises above his kidneys that she hasn't seen before.

He rubs the side of his pale face and glares at her. 'What?'

Teresa points to the ceiling. 'Was someone up there with you?'

He looks at her as though she's mad. 'What are you on about?'

'Is your dad up there?'

'Of course not.' He turns to go back up the stairs, but she catches him by the arm.

'I mean it, Dale. I'm not joking. Is he here?'

Dale shakes his arm free. 'For fuck's sake! Why would I lie about something like that?'

Teresa turns to her mum, unable to hide her anger. 'You said it was Gary! Christ, Mum, I thought he was here. Do you know how scared I was?'

Her mother doesn't look at her but continues to stare at the television. 'He said he hadn't seen me for a long time. He made me a nice cup of tea.'

Teresa looks at the mug on the small table by the side of her chair, the contents long since gone cold. It looks like the one she made her earlier. What is she talking about?

'You're losing it.' Dale's words are said with contempt, and at first Teresa thinks he's referring to his gran. But he isn't.

'Don't talk to me like that, Dale.'

'Why not?' He makes a circle at his temple with his finger. 'You're going crazy. Gaga like her.' He points to his grandmother.

Her face hardens. 'Stephen's daughter would never dream of speaking to her father the way you speak to me.'

'What the fucking hell has Stephen got to do with it?' Dale throws up his hands. 'Christ, you're obsessed with him.'

'That's enough!'

Suddenly, it's all too much. Gary, her mother, Dale. In fact, her whole bloody life. She turns on him, spitting out the words. 'Don't you see that everything I do is for you? Why can't you just do something rather than skulk about the house? Get a job. Go to college and get some qualifications. I don't care.' The words rush out, hot and cruel. All her frustration at her mum, directed at him.

'Why can't you get your bloody arse into gear and do something? I'm sick of spending my life worrying. I'm sick of everything. Sick of you. You're no better than your stepfather.'

On the television, an auctioneer is giving his estimate for an ugly china vase in the shape of a frog. Her mum's no longer looking at the screen, but at Teresa, her face giving away her shock.

Teresa sinks down onto the settee and covers her eyes, but not before she's seen the look on Dale's face. A tightening around the jaw. The slow disbelieving shake of his head.

Too late, she realises what she's done. Lowering her hands, she looks at her son, her eyes brimming with tears. 'Oh, God, I'm sorry, Dale.'

He says nothing, but his expression tells her everything. Turning his back, he goes upstairs, and she hears him banging about in his room. She aches to follow him, to tell him she's sorry and that she didn't mean what she said, but she's afraid that if she does, she'll make it a hundred times worse.

Her mum turns to her. 'Is the boy all right?'

'No, Mum. Not really.'

The two of them sit in silence, the only sound the auctioneer's gavel as it hits the table. The whoop of delight as the team realise they've made a profit. Neither of them is really watching, though. Instead, they're listening. Waiting. They don't have to wait long as within minutes Dale is thumping down the stairs, a rucksack on his back.

Teresa stands. 'What are you doing?'

Dale doesn't answer but instead goes over to his grandmother and kisses her on the cheek. He won't look at Teresa and when she tries to take his arm, he shakes it off. His hurt is like an aura around him. His anger tightly wound.

She wants to ask where he's going to stay. How he's going to get there. She wants to ask him to forgive her. But the look on his face tells her there's no point. He's made up his mind.

Dale opens the back door and goes out, slamming it behind him, and a few seconds later, Teresa sees him wheel his motorbike past the window. She stands immobile in the middle of the room, guilt and loss and all manner of other emotions pushing in on her, until her mother speaks.

'Are you going to let him go like that?'

Her words break the spell. 'No… no, of course not.'

She hurries to the front door, hoping to stop him, but she's too late. He's already on his bike and as she runs after him, anything she'd wanted to say is drowned out by the thrum of the engine. She watches, helplessly, as the bike disappears down the street and turns the corner, taking with it not her little boy but a troubled young man.

She stands a moment longer, her eyes trained on the place where she last saw him, then turns and goes back inside. Hoping that everything she is doing will be worth it.

CHAPTER TWENTY-SIX

Maya

Maya hasn't been home long. She's joined her dad in the conservatory and is watching a tanker move slowly across the horizon, trying to calm her thoughts. At this time tomorrow, she'll be in Weymouth. She'll have taken her test and will be making her way back to the station. But even though she's worked through the revision links Mrs Ellis sent and feels as ready as she can be, a niggling doubt remains. She looks at her dad, his head bent to the photo album on his lap and wonders again if she can leave him.

'What time will Amy be coming home tonight?'

He looks up. 'Sorry, what?'

'Amy. When will she be home?'

Slowly, he lifts his wrist and studies his watch. 'Soon.'

'That's good.'

When she'd first met Amy, she could never have imagined it, but now she looks forward to hearing the crunch of the Mini's tyres on the drive. The sound of her key in the lock. When Amy's here, things are easier, the atmosphere less strained. She breathes life into the old house, and it stops the onus being constantly on her to make conversation with someone who doesn't want to talk. Recently, they've taken to cooking the evening meal together and when they've eaten and cleared away, Maya revises while Amy jollies her dad along, telling him about her day. Acting as though there's nothing wrong with him.

She watches as her dad shuts the photo album. There's a strange atmosphere in the conservatory, and she doesn't like it.

Eventually, he speaks and there's a new frostiness in his voice. 'What have you been asking people?'

She knows what he's talking about. It's obvious from the look on his face that someone in town has said something to him.

'Don't pretend you don't know what I'm talking about, Maya. You've been bothering people… prying into the past. Asking stupid questions and making us look ridiculous. Did you think I wouldn't hear about it? Shirley at the 7-Eleven couldn't wait to tell me you'd been in.'

She feels her cheeks flush. 'It wasn't anything, Dad. All I did was ask them about Mum. What they remembered.'

Her dad thumps his fist on the table, making her jump. 'It's none of their damn business. It wasn't then and it isn't now.'

Maya holds her ground. 'But it *is mine*. Cheryl might have been your wife, but she was *my* mother. I have a right to know.'

'How many times do I have to tell you?' He sinks his head into his hands, his fingers massaging his scalp. 'There's nothing *to* know.'

They're interrupted by the sound of Amy's voice and her footsteps moving from the hallway to the living room. 'Anyone home?'

Maya closes her eyes in relief. 'We're in the conservatory.'

Amy comes in. She walks behind Stephen's chair and crosses her arms around his neck, resting her chin on the top of his head. 'Good news, Steve. I've handed in my notice. Should have done it months ago, but I don't like to let people down. Tomorrow, I can bring the rest of my stuff over from the flat.'

He looks up, and Maya sees how his mood has changed. How he's pretending everything's all right. 'I'm glad.'

From the way he smiles at Amy, it's clear how much happier he is when she's with him. More like his old self. She doesn't know whether to be hurt or pleased.

Amy straightens up. 'So how was your day, Maya?'

'All right. Teresa's mum moved in today.' Maya turns to her dad, glad that the conversation has moved on from her investigations. 'Did you see her at the clinic this afternoon? It's always hard when you have to leave someone for the first time, and she was pretty upset when she left Three Elms.'

'We were hellishly busy today. I saw her just as I was leaving but didn't have time to ask.' Two lines deepen between his brows. 'Oh, dear. That was thoughtless of me. I really should have. Perhaps I should go round and see her.'

Amy takes off her coat. 'Not now, Steve. We'll be having dinner soon. You'll see her tomorrow, won't you?'

'Of course, but I know how worried she was about it. I can't believe I forgot.'

Amy puts her hand on his shoulder. 'Poor Teresa. Has she been having more trouble from the husband?'

He shakes his head. 'Not as far as I know, but she's right to be wary.'

Amy goes to the window and looks out across the back garden. 'I'd be too. It must be horrible to spend your life looking over your shoulder. At least he doesn't know where she's living.'

'That's something, I suppose. I think she should tell the police though, don't you?'

Amy turns to look at him. 'And tell them what? As far as we know, he hasn't actually done anything.'

Maya looks at them both and frowns. 'Yet.'

That morning when Teresa had dropped her mother off at Three Elms and settled her in, she'd looked tired. Her face gaunt. Maya had been worried about her. 'She was telling me today how concerned she is about her son too.'

Her dad looks up. 'Dale?'

'Yes. From what she was telling me, he's a bit of a strange one. Anyway, they had an argument the other day and he stormed out. She's no idea where he's gone, whether he's sleeping rough or what.'

'That's a worry.'

Maya nods in agreement. 'I know, but he's nearly eighteen and there isn't much she can do about it.'

'An ailing mother, a troubled son and an abusive husband. She's really not in a good place at the moment. No wonder she's worried.'

Amy is standing by the conservatory window, her hand pressed to the glass. She looks uneasy. 'I didn't tell you before, but when I was out walking on the cliff path the other day, I saw someone.'

'What?' Stephen asks. 'Someone you knew?'

She frowns. 'I don't know. They were too far away to see. They were just standing on the path, a way ahead. For some reason it unnerved me, and I turned back.'

'It was probably just a walker.'

'Yes probably.' She gives an involuntary shudder. 'Stupid, I know.'

'When was this, Amy?' Maya doesn't like what she's hearing. Teresa saw someone too up on the cliff path.

'It was a couple of days ago, before you got a key cut for me. I'd got to the house before either of you had come back from work... Do you remember, Steve, I phoned you? Anyway, I thought I'd take a walk while I was waiting for one of you to come home. I hadn't planned on going far.' She looks at Maya. 'Only to your mum's bench and back, but then I saw them on the path ahead of me. Not walking or looking out to sea, just standing. It was odd.'

Cold fingers flutter at the back of Maya's neck. 'What did they look like?'

Amy turns to face them. 'I don't know. Like I said, they weren't close enough for me to see. Then they just disappeared, and I guessed they'd pushed through the hawthorns into the field with the pylons. All I know is I didn't want to be there any more.'

Maya looks at her dad. A shadow has passed over his face. 'Why didn't you say something at the time?' he says.

Amy shrugs. 'It didn't seem important but maybe it was Teresa I saw.'

'Or her husband,' Maya adds.

Stephen frowns. 'I honestly don't know what to think. It's probably nothing at all. You haven't seen anything strange have you, Maya?'

A knot of anxiety forms in Maya's chest. She could tell them about the person who stands on the path below her window. The one who smiles and beckons to her, how tempted she is to follow, but she knows they are just her imaginings.

Instead, she tells them something they'll understand.

'Teresa's seen someone too.'

Her dad's jaw tightens. 'She never mentioned it to me. Why ever not? It was me who suggested she move here and if something's bothering her, I'd rather I knew about it.'

Amy leaves the window and sits next to him. 'She probably didn't want to worry you.'

Maya knows why she's said this. It's because of how her dad's been recently. Teresa must have noticed too – she'd hinted as much when she saw her this morning.

'Maybe I'll just give her a quick ring.' Taking his phone out of his pocket, Stephen squints at the screen. 'Just to make sure she's all right.'

Amy reaches out her hand, lowering his mobile to his lap. 'Teresa might not thank you for interfering. Think about it, Steve, she's been in a marriage where she's had no control and has broken free. Do you want to take the independence she's gained away from her?'

He thinks about this, then turns questioning eyes to Maya. 'What do you think?'

Maya frowns. It's strange to be asked. Only a week ago, it would have been him who would have come up with this reasoning, but recently it's seemed to her that he's lost his way. Forever doubting his own judgement.

If she goes to see Teresa, she can get a second opinion. Find out whether she's been concerned about him too.

'I think you're both right,' she says. 'Why don't *I* go and see Teresa rather than you, Dad? I want to talk to her about how her mum is settling in at Three Elms anyway.'

'Yes, you go, Maya,' Amy says with a smile. 'It makes more sense.'

'Okay then. I'll go after we've eaten.'

She gets up and goes to the kitchen to think about supper and as she looks in the fridge, she wonders how much she should tell Teresa.

CHAPTER TWENTY-SEVEN

Maya

It's later than Maya had been expecting when she finally sets out to see Teresa. The street lights are on and the pavements are shiny with the rain that had thrashed at the windows while they'd been eating.

There aren't many people about. There never are in the evening, even in the height of the tourist season when tourists flock to the village for pub meals and fossil hunting. As she walks, she's aware of how the shadows pool between the glow of the street lamps. It's never bothered her before, but tonight a nub of disquiet has lodged in her chest, and whenever the wind rustles the branches of the trees, she has to tell herself it's nothing. What Amy said has spooked her. She doesn't like the idea of someone out on the cliff path but would have dismissed it had it not been for Teresa having seen them too.

She can't help wondering though, whether the chill she feels this evening is because of everything that's happened recently or because she fears she knows who it is out there on the cliff. Knows it's the same person who calls to her on days when the mist surrounds her house, swallowing everything in its path. Merging sea and clifftop into one. Someone conjured up by her loneliness.

Her mum.

Maya shivers. She knows it's *her* she's waiting for. Wanting to show her the truth. Not Amy or Teresa… or the dogwalkers who no longer choose to walk there because they consider it dangerous.

The flint wall of the churchyard is to her left and Maya pictures the tombstones standing like sentries, their cold, hard stone engraved with the names of those who are buried there. Those who have lost their lives like her mum. She shivers and hurries on. Past the bus stop. Past the shops with their blank closed faces. When she's opposite the row of thatched cottages that hunker down as if bracing themselves for the next onslaught of rain to begin to fall, Maya crosses. Teresa's house is near the end and it's only as she gets closer that she sees hers is the only one that spills light from around the edge of its curtains.

A car's behind her. She can hear the shush of its tyres on the wet asphalt, its headlights lighting the road in front of her. She expects it to pass, but it doesn't. Maya glances back, unease tightening her scalp, uncertain as to why it's moving so slowly. She walks faster, head bent against the rain that's started again, relieved when she reaches Teresa's front door. But the car has stopped too, and her body tenses as she hears the soft hum of a window being lowered.

'Excuse me. Could you tell me where Orchard Close is?'

The rush of relief makes Maya dizzy. What's the matter with her? She's lived in this town all her life and never felt on edge like this before. She gives the woman directions and watches the car drive away, berating herself for how stupid she's been. It must be worry about the test tomorrow that's caused her to be so jumpy.

She's just about to turn back to the cottage, has even raised her hand to lift the knocker, when something catches her eye. A way down the street, at the place where the road cuts down to the beach and the Heritage Centre, someone is standing watching her, their outline blurred by the rain that's heavier now. A chill runs down her spine, and she lifts the knocker quickly, bringing it down onto the shiny wood. Once. Twice. Three times. Praying for Teresa to open the door. She wants to be inside not out on the street where she feels so exposed.

The door opens a little way, and Teresa peers out.

'Who is it?'

'It's me.'

Teresa looks wary. 'Maya?'

'Yes.' Maya steps out of the shadows and into the light. 'I'm sorry it's so late.'

'No, it's fine, honestly. I'm just surprised to see you, that's all.'

'I thought I'd come over and let you know how your mum got on today. It seemed more personal than ringing you.'

'That's really thoughtful.' Teresa opens the door wider. 'Goodness, you're soaked. Come in, and I'll make you a hot drink.'

She stands back to let Maya in, looking up and down the street before closing the door behind her.

'What would you like? Tea? Coffee? A glass of wine?' She looks nervous, glancing behind her as if checking the room. 'Here, let me take your coat.'

Maya shrugs out of her wet mac. 'Thank you, but I won't have anything. I can't stay long as I've still got some last-minute revision to do before tomorrow.'

'Oh, the test. Yes, of course. Are you feeling confident?'

'As I'll ever be, I suppose.' She looks around the room. Despite having only moved in a short while ago, Teresa's managed to make it look homely.

Teresa gestures to a chair. 'Please, sit down.'

Maya goes over to the settee beneath the window, and Teresa takes the chair opposite.

'Although it's only her first day, your mum's settling in well.' She folds her hands in her lap and gives a reassuring smile. 'She's taken a shine to one of the other residents, Jill, and at tea she was telling her all about the break-in. Have you heard anything back from the police?'

'Yes, but there's nothing new. They think it's pretty definite she let someone into the house. The problem is that her memory is so bad she doesn't remember who. They couldn't get any prints and, without that, there's little they can do. I'm just glad she's not on her own any more.' She glances at the window where rose-printed curtains hide the night and gives an almost imperceptible shiver. 'Very glad.'

Maya nods. 'We'll take good care of her.'

'Thank you. I know you will and I'm very grateful.' She looks as if she's about to say something then stops.

'Was there anything else you wanted to ask me?' Maya asks.

Teresa looks as if she's deciding whether or not to say something. 'As a matter of fact there is, but it's not about my mum.' She hesitates and her fingers rub at her throat where a red patch has appeared. 'It's about your dad.'

'My dad?'

'Yes. To be perfectly honest, I'm worried about him. He hasn't seemed himself recently and I was wondering if everything's all right at home.'

Maya hesitates, wondering how much to tell her. 'There have been some changes.'

'Really?'

'Good changes,' Maya adds quickly. 'But Dad always takes a while to adjust to new things. He's like me I guess.'

She thinks of Amy and wonders what Teresa would make of her. Clearly, she doesn't know about her or she would have said something. But, however much she'd like to talk to someone about it, it's not her place to put Teresa in the picture.

'Every so often, ever since I've been old enough to understand, Dad's had periods where he gets low. It hasn't happened for a while, but over the last week or so, he's been... well... different.' Her fingertips trace the place where he slapped her. 'Has done things that are out of character.'

Teresa frowns. 'What sort of things?'

'It doesn't matter.' She lowers her hand. 'When I go to uni next year, that's presuming I get in, of course, you'll keep an eye on him, won't you?'

She knows Amy will be with him, but two pairs of eyes have to be better than one.

Teresa smiles, clearly pleased to have been asked. 'Of course I will. And I'm sorry to have brought this up. I'm sure your dad's fine, but I want you to put your mind at rest that, when you're away, I'll make sure all's okay.'

'Thank you.'

On the mantelpiece is a photograph of a smiling boy with eyes like Teresa's.

'Is that your son?' Maya asks.

'Dale? Yes. It was taken before his dad died.'

It's hard to think that this happy boy is the same difficult youth her dad described to her earlier. 'You must be really worried about him.'

'I am worried. I just hope he's safe, that's all.'

'Have you tried ringing his friends?'

'He didn't really have any. I know he's my son, but he's a strange boy. A loner. Every day, after work, I walk the streets looking for him... but nothing. When the police rang about my mum, I thought about telling them, but Dale left of his own free will, so they wouldn't class him as a missing person. He's nearly eighteen after all.'

Teresa's sorrow resonates with Maya. She knows only too well what it's like to lose someone. 'I hope he comes back soon.'

A gust of wind rattles the windows and Teresa looks towards them, her face a picture of misery.

'I do too.'

CHAPTER TWENTY-EIGHT
Teresa

Teresa's exhausted. Although she knows she must have, it feels as if she hasn't slept for days. Without her mother there, or Dale, she lies awake at night listening to every creak of the floorboards. Every rattle of the sash windows. Her imagination running wild, imagining someone's trying to get in or, worse still, already in her house seeking revenge. Even when she does drift off, her restless dreams are of Dale, either sleeping in a doorway under a layer of cardboard or lying bloodied at the foot of Crewl Point. The place where Maya's mother had fallen to her death.

When Stephen had knocked on her door at eight to see if she wanted a lift to the clinic, she'd imagined it to be the police. Had readied herself for the worst. And even the relief at seeing him hadn't been enough to calm her anxiety.

They're sitting now on the white settee in reception, cups of coffee in their hands. She watches, with sympathy, as Stephen leans forward and pinches the soft skin between his eyes. He looks tired, dark circles under his eyes. She knows how he feels.

'Headache? I've some paracetamol somewhere.' She reaches for her bag and unzips a side pocket. When she locates the packet, she pushes a couple of tablets from their foil blisters and holds them out to him. 'There.'

'Thank you.' He takes the tablets from her and goes over to the water dispenser next to the reception desk. He comes back with a plastic cup and swallows the pills down with a backward jerk of his head. 'Though I don't know if they'll help.'

'It's worth a try.'

Stephen puts the cup down on the table, twisting it one way then the other between finger and thumb. He looks troubled. 'Do you think she's ready for this, Teresa?'

Teresa's eyebrows draw together. 'Who are you talking about?'

'Maya. Should I let her go?' He turns anxious eyes to her. 'I've no doubt she'll pass the test this afternoon, and the interview when the time comes, but what if something should happen to her when she leaves home for good? I won't be there to protect her. It feels as if I'm losing my little girl. We've been as close as father and daughter can be, and I've tried to share with her everything I love: the sea, walking, fossil hunting. Can we exist without each other?'

'Of course you can.' Teresa thinks of Maya's visit to her house. How she'd opened up to her a little about Stephen and had asked her to keep a watchful eye on him when she goes to university. It's somehow made her feel closer to the two of them.

'You're a good father, Stephen, but it would be wrong to stop Maya from living a life outside your protection.' She leans forward and touches his arm. 'I hope you don't think I'm talking out of turn, but she needs to live and being in this small town, doing what she does, isn't living. Not when you're an intelligent, young woman with your whole life ahead of you. She's young. She should be having fun.'

He smiles tightly. 'Then you don't think I should be worried?'

'You have to let her go sometime. Nothing is going to happen to her. She isn't Cheryl.' Teresa stops, realising what she's said. As if by some tacit agreement, they've never talked about his wife.

Stephen's smile drops away, and he stares at some place in the distance. 'No, she isn't.'

With dismay, she sees a tear slip down his face. It runs around the crease of his nose and drops into his beard. Teresa's hand rises to her mouth. 'Oh, Stephen. I'm sorry. I shouldn't have mentioned her.'

'No.' In that one word she hears so many things: condemnation, bewilderment but, above all, pain.

Without thinking, she gets up and goes around the coffee table. Takes a seat next to him. She slips an arm around his shoulders and when he turns to face her, rests her forehead against his. It should feel wrong, but it doesn't. He's shown her so much attention since he found out about her family troubles that she's started to feel that there could be something more to it than just friendship. It reminds her of the early days before she knew about Cheryl.

'I'm so sorry,' she says again.

He takes her hand, his eyes misted. 'You're a good woman, Teresa. Remember that.'

Teresa doesn't know what it is about the moment: the smell of him, the warmth of his skin, but she can't help but feel closer to him. Taking his face between her hands, she presses her lips to his.

But before she can do anything more, he jerks away from her. The softness of his mouth lingering on hers.

'No, Teresa,' he says in a low voice. 'This isn't right.'

Even in his rejection he is calm and loving, but the room swims as the terrible reality of what she's just done hits her. How could she have been so stupid? How could she have made this mistake again? She moves away from him, pressing her fingers to her lips. 'Oh, Stephen. I'm so sorry. I shouldn't have done that. I didn't mean...'

Teresa's cheeks burn, and she wishes the floor would open up. Before he can say anything, she picks up her bag and runs to the sanctuary of her consulting room, leaving him alone on the settee.

As she leans her back against the closed door, she tries to blot out the look in Stephen's eyes when he broke away. But she can't. She should be thankful it wasn't disgust she saw in them. What had been there though was almost as bad. Pity.

She knows Stephen won't hold this against her. Knows that he can sweep this under the carpet and move on… but *she* can't.

She'd had a plan. She'd thought it would be different this time. Now she knows that just like before, she has ruined everything.

CHAPTER TWENTY-NINE
Teresa

By the time she's seen her last client of the day, driven to Three Elms to visit her mum, then gone back home to change, it's gone seven. But Teresa knows she needs to do this, to see Stephen face to face and deal with the mistake she's made. She'd tried to see him earlier, had been about to go upstairs to his consulting room to explain herself, but Louise had told her he'd left after lunch with a migraine.

Stephen's car is in the drive, and the lights are on at the front of the house. She can see him through the window, sitting at the table with his head in his hands, a tumbler of whisky in front of him. What she wants to do is turn around and walk back the way she's come but knows she can't. What if she no longer has his support? What if he no longer wants her to stay in the house? God, it's a mess.

She presses the doorbell and waits, listening to the sound of the waves, thinking how lucky Stephen is to live in a house in such a position: how wonderful it would be to wake up to that sound. She knows now that will never happen for her.

It takes a while for him to come to the door, but when he does, he doesn't look surprised to see her. Instead, he looks distracted. Jumpy. 'Teresa.'

'I had to see you. I couldn't leave things as they were. Can I come in?'

Stephen nods and stands back, the whisky in his hand glinting in the hall light. 'Of course.'

Teresa steps into the hall, trying to take it in before following him into the kitchen. It's large and homely, the dark tiled floor setting off the wooden cabinets and farmhouse-style table.

'I came here to talk about what happened at the clinic, Stephen. To try and explain.'

Stephen leans back against the counter, his check shirt straining against his stomach. 'Really, there's no need. Please, sit down.'

He gestures for Teresa to sit, and she pulls a chair out from under the kitchen table. 'There *is* a need. What I did was stupid and unprofessional. It should never have happened, and I just hope we can get past it. That it doesn't spoil our friendship.'

'It's not going to spoil it. I'd hate you to think that.'

'It did before.'

He doesn't answer. He looks distracted, taking out his phone and staring at it before putting it back in his pocket and moving his gaze to the window.

Teresa waits until she can stand the silence no longer. 'Stephen?'

With a smile of apology, he turns his attention back to her. 'That's all in the past. And even then, things might have been different if it hadn't been for Cheryl. Look, I think I know what happened.'

Teresa feels wrong-footed by how magnanimous he's being. How lovely. 'You do?'

'Yes, but before I explain, can I get you a drink?'

'Thank you. Wine would be lovely.'

Teresa watches as Stephen bends to the fridge and pulls out a bottle of Chablis. He unscrews the lid and pours her a glass, downing the remains of his whisky before pouring one for himself.

He carries the two glasses to the table and hands one to Teresa. 'Your good health,' he says, taking a mouthful.

Teresa raises her glass back to him. 'You too.'

Stephen settles back in his chair. 'Look, Teresa. You've had a hard time of it recently.' He twists the stem of his glass thoughtfully. 'And it's understandable you'd need reassurance. All you did was to take things a little too far. I don't think you should give it any more thought.'

Teresa feels herself blushing. 'That's easier said than done. I just don't want things to be awkward between us at work.'

He cups his hands around the bowl of his wineglass and smiles. 'It won't be. We've worked well together up until recently and there's no reason for that to change. I value your friendship and wouldn't have asked you to come and join me at the clinic if I hadn't thought you a damn good psychologist. You believe me, don't you?'

Teresa checks his face for evidence that he's being genuine and finds it in the frankness of his gaze. The warmth of his smile. She smiles back at him with relief. She hasn't ruined things after all. He hadn't repelled her advances because he didn't like her, but because he'd thought the timing wasn't right. It's as simple as that.

She settles back in her chair and has another sip of her wine. 'Have you heard anything from Maya yet?'

'Maya?' His eyes narrow slightly as though she's asked him a trick question.

'Yes… the test. Has she told you how it went? I know how nervous she was.'

He runs a hand down his face and glances at the window. 'No, I haven't heard anything.'

'I'm not surprised. She's probably waiting to tell you herself, rather than over the phone.'

'Maybe.'

She looks at him, taking in the tense shoulders. The set of his mouth.

'Are you all right, Stephen?'

'Yes, yes, of course.' She sees the attempt he makes to pull himself together. 'Just a lot on my mind, that's all.'

That much is obvious. It pains her to think she's contributed to it.

'Are you picking Maya up from the station?'

'No. She said she'd get a taxi as she wasn't sure what train she'd be getting.'

He's pacing now, stopping every so often to look out of the window, and she wonders what's bothering him.

'Stephen…?'

But he isn't listening. Instead, he's gone over to the window and is looking out again. Headlights flash through the window, then sweep across the ceiling before the glass goes dark once more. It must be the taxi. Maya must be back.

Teresa waits for Maya to come into the kitchen, a question ready for her on her lips, but the words die when she sees that the person who walks through the door, a carrier bag in each hand, isn't Maya at all. It's a woman. Slim. Attractive. Her dark hair falling to the shoulders of her belted raincoat.

When she sees Teresa, she looks just as surprised, but covers it with a smile. 'Hello.'

'Hi,' Teresa returns, the word coming out too loud in her attempt to hide her shock. Her bewilderment.

She expects Stephen to introduce them, but he doesn't. Instead, he walks over to the woman and smooths the hair from her face before placing a kiss on her lips. Teresa turns away, feeling sick to her stomach. Now everything is clear.

The woman looks uncomfortable. 'Aren't you going to introduce us, Steve?'

Teresa stares. The shortened name is laced with familiarity. *She's* never called him that.

'I'm sorry. You're right, that was very rude of me. Please forgive me, Teresa. This is Amy.' He puts an arm around her and smiles at Teresa as though showing off a prized possession.

The woman has the decency to look embarrassed. She pulls away from his embrace and walks towards Teresa with outstretched hand. 'It's lovely to meet you at last, Teresa. I've heard a lot about you from Steve. From Maya too.'

Teresa shifts uncomfortably, wondering what they've said about her.

Stephen smiles. 'Teresa came over to fill me in on what happened at the clinic this afternoon. I came home early as I had a hell of a migraine starting.'

Something changes in Amy's expression. 'But you're all right now?'

'A lot better for seeing you.'

Teresa picks up her bag, feeling like a gooseberry. 'Look, I really should go.'

'Absolutely not.' Stephen shakes his head. 'We wouldn't hear of it. You must stay for supper.'

It's like he's a different man. Younger. All the tension and nervous energy that had been there earlier, gone. She can't understand it.

'No really, I don't want to impose. Anyway, Maya will be back soon. You'll have a lot to talk about.'

'Don't be silly, we insist, don't we, Amy?'

There's a fraction of a second's pause before Amy answers. 'Of course. You'd be very welcome. I've bought plenty.'

'Well, if you're sure.' Although she feels painfully out of place, she doesn't know how to extricate herself.

'I am.' Amy tucks her dark hair behind her ear. 'I'll just get the last bag out of the car.'

As the front door shuts behind her, Teresa closes her eyes, trying to think how she's going to get through the meal. She tries to imagine sitting at the table with Stephen and Amy, making conversation with the weight of what she did hovering between them. The elephant in the room. Will Stephen tell Amy after she's gone? When they're lying in his bed after making love? Will they laugh at how she practically threw herself at him, dismissing it as the action of a needy woman?

Worse still... Will he tell her it isn't the first time?

She shouldn't have agreed to stay, should have made up some excuse and left, but they'd both been so insistent she hadn't known how.

'Stephen. If this is awkward...'

Stephen regards her, his thumb and index finger stroking his beard. 'I don't feel awkward and neither should you. In particularly stressful times, the mind can make you believe things, feelings, that aren't real. If I did anything to contribute to those thoughts, I sincerely apologise, Teresa.'

Teresa looks down at her hand. The diamond engagement ring Gary presented to her glints in the overhead spotlight. She really should take it off. Her wedding ring too.

'No. You did nothing to encourage me. You're right, though. What with everything that's been going on at home, I haven't been thinking straight.'

Stephen pushes his hands into the pockets of his cords, jiggling his car keys. 'Then as far as I'm concerned, nothing happened. You mustn't give it another thought.'

Amy comes back in with another carrier bag. She places it on the worktop, taking things out and putting then in the fridge as though she's lived in Stephen's house for years. When Teresa asks if there's anything she can do to help, she just shakes her head. 'No, Teresa. You're the guest.'

She's certainly lovely to look at. A number of years younger than Stephen, her heart-shaped face framed by the long dark hair that falls to her shoulders. After being on his own for so many years, he certainly hit the jackpot when he met her. No wonder he's besotted. She wonders how long they've been together. But, more importantly, she wonders what Maya thinks? It can't be easy sharing her father with someone else after all this time.

Someone who looks just like her dead mother.

For only a fool would miss the likeness. And if they did, the evidence is in the photograph of Cheryl that hangs on the wall next to the one of Maya.

Stephen pulls out a chair for her and she sits down, allowing Stephen to refill her glass. As she sips it, she thinks how little she knows him, despite their lives having converged several times over the years before dividing again.

At the clinic, the man she's always held in high regard is the softly spoken therapist who makes his clients feel valued and understood. Here, though, at Crewl House, she feels as if she's seeing another Stephen. The one with a past she knows little about. One whose changing moods are hard to keep up with.

She's just finishing her drink when there's a pounding on the front door.

'Could that be Maya?' Amy asks. 'Didn't she have her key with her, Steve?'

'Maybe she forgot it.' The pounding comes again. 'All right. All right. I'm coming.'

He gets up from his chair and goes through to the hall. Amy puts down the baking tray she's holding and follows him, but Teresa remains seated at the kitchen table. She's no wish to interfere.

There's the sound of the front door opening then silence. Does Stephen gasp? She can't be sure. She waits, wondering what's happening, and it's only when Amy's urgent voice comes through from the hallway *For God's sake, Steve. Help me get her inside*, that she pushes her chair back and runs to the door.

The three of them are like a tableau, Maya in the middle, Amy and Stephen either side of her. The girl's head is bent, her fair curls covering her face.

'Maya.' Stephen's face is ashen. 'Darling. What's happened?'

At first sight, Teresa can't see what the problem is, but when Maya raises her head, her pupils are dilated, and mascara has pooled beneath her eyes. She stands rigid in the light of the hall, her fingers balled into fists, the knuckles white.

Teresa takes a step forward. 'Is she hurt?'

Maya remains silent. Mannequin still. On many occasions, Teresa's seen young girls in her consulting room who have suffered trauma. Witnessed their tears, their anger… but never a blankness such as this.

'She's shivering,' she says. 'You need to get her into the warm. I'll call the police.'

It's Amy who speaks first. 'Yes, of course. I'll take her into the conservatory.' She puts an arm around Maya, but as her fingers make contact with her arm, Maya cries out and jerks away.

Amy looks from Stephen to Teresa. Reaching out a hand, she carefully pushes up the sleeve of the girl's jumper. She lets out a long breath then pushes up the other sleeve.

Teresa stares, her mobile pressed to her ear, for circling the soft flesh of each of Maya's arms, is a pattern of dark bruises.

CHAPTER THIRTY

Maya

Maya sits on one of the settees in the conservatory, her eyes fixed on her reflection in the window. Wishing she was anywhere, but in this glass room answering the police officer's questions. She can't stop shaking, her body still reacting to whatever it is that has happened.

'Would you mind me taking a look at the bruises, Maya?'

PC Bailey looks kindly at her. Since he and his colleague arrived, they've been nothing but considerate and courteous. They haven't pushed her too hard – and that's good, as she can't remember much of what happened.

Slowly, Maya pushes up the sleeve of the cardigan she threw on to reveal the dark marks, now more purple than black.

PC Bailey moves closer and looks. 'Yes, I see. Are you hurt anywhere else?'

She shakes her head. Apart from the bruises, there's no sign of injury. No pain below or tenderness to her thighs that would indicate she's been assaulted in any way. Nothing's been taken from her bag either: not her money, not her cards, not her keys. In a small voice, she tells him this.

'That's good. Is there anything else you remember?'

Amy's arm is around her and Maya can feel the warmth of her body through the throw that's draped across her shoulders. She's comforted by it, especially as her dad, instead of sitting next to her, has taken the seat on the other side of the conservatory.

As she struggles to think, her eyes fill with tears and noticing this, Amy gives her shoulder a gentle rub.

'Take your time, Maya. There's no hurry,' she says.

Maya's eyes leave her reflection and fix on the policeman's black shoes instead. 'I don't know what else I can tell you.'

He flips back in his notes. 'I've got here that the last thing you remember was walking to Weymouth Station. You don't remember getting onto the train to come home or even if you got to the station?'

Maya shakes her head. 'I don't remember the train, but I do remember the test.'

Her teeth are chattering, and Amy hugs her closer.

'This is the one you were taking at the test centre at Phoenix House?'

Her dad answers for her. 'Yes, she already told you that.' He's sitting with his elbows between his knees, his hands covering the lower part of his face. 'She was sitting the UCAT test.'

The other officer, PC Southerland, turns to him, his voice a study of practised patience. 'We just need to be clear of the facts, Dr McKenzie. It's easy to miss something.'

'I'm sorry. Yes, of course.' He sits back, looking out at the dark garden beyond the glass, and Maya sees how his concern is masked by his discomfort at having police in the house.

'So you remember doing the test, Maya?'

'Yes. It wasn't as difficult as I'd thought, and I was relieved. They hand out the results when you leave, and I'd passed. But…'

PC Bailey looks up from his notes. 'Yes?'

'I was definitely nervous about the journey home. I knew it would be getting dark, and I'm not very good in new places.' She remembers how the exhilaration had started to leave her as she left the test centre and started to walk, how she'd crossed the road to avoid the people flooding out of the cinema, taking a short cut between some buildings.

He smiles sympathetically. 'I understand.'

Does he? Maya lifts her eyes from his shoes to his face. How much does he know of their history? About her mum and how her death affected her. Did her dad fill them in before taking them through to the conservatory?

'I was about halfway to the station when I stopped and thought about messaging Dad.' She stops and takes a sip of the tea Teresa made her before going home, not caring that it's grown cold.

'But you didn't do it.'

'No.' How she now wishes she had. Maybe if she'd just phoned him, everything would have been okay. 'I decided to wait until I got home to tell him I'd passed. I wanted it to be a surprise.'

Her arrival at the house had been a surprise all right, but not the one her dad had been expecting.

'And you've no idea how you got home?'

She searches her memory, but there's nothing. 'No, I'm sorry.'

'We'll check CCTV in and around the area and make some enquiries in the local shops and pubs. See if anyone noticed anything.' He looks at his colleague, then turns back to Maya. 'You don't remember anyone acting strangely or the feeling that you might have been followed?'

Maya shakes her head. 'No, I don't.'

PC Bailey closes his notebook. 'I think we have all we need at the moment. Leave this with us, Maya. It looks like you could do with a good night's sleep. Be assured that we'll do everything to find out what happened and if anything comes back to you, here's my card with the number you should call.'

Maya takes the card and closes her fingers around it, but she knows it's unlikely she'll be making that call. This isn't the first time she's had a blank in her memory. There's the day of her mum's death.

Her dad gets up. 'Thank you. I'll show you out.'

When the front door closes, Amy stands and holds out her hands. 'Come on, Maya. You're done in. PC Bailey is right, what you need now is some sleep.'

Maya nods and allows Amy to help her up. The shivering has stopped, but she's bone-tired from trying to remember what happened. She lets Amy help her up the stairs, and when she falls into bed, her eyes close immediately.

Later that night, she cries out, waking herself. Her dreams have been filled with dark shadows and fear. Sometimes, she was on the clifftop. Then the scene would change, and she'd be standing in the alleyway in Weymouth, her phone in her hand. Each time, she knew something bad was going to happen. As she lies still, her hair damp against her forehead and her heart still pounding, the door opens.

'Maya, are you all right? I heard you cry out.'

It's her dad, his hair awry. His worn plaid dressing gown belted over his pyjamas.

'I had a bad dream.' It was what she used to say to him when she was little.

'It's going to be okay.' Her bed creaks as he sits and pushes the damp hair from her face, just as he used to. 'You've had a horrible experience, but you're home now and safe.'

'What happened, Dad? Why don't I remember?'

'I don't know, darling. I wish I did.' He straightens the cover around her, his eyes full of pain. 'The not knowing is destroying me. What if it had been worse? What if I'd lost you too?'

'You haven't lost me.' She takes his hand and presses it to her cheek. 'I'm here.'

'I know and I thank God for that.'

'I had a dream, Dad. I don't know what it was about, but it scared me. There was nothing but darkness and shadows, but I couldn't get rid of the feeling that someone was trying to hurt me. It was so real.'

'It was just a dream.' Leaning forward, he kisses her forehead. 'You need to concentrate on getting better, and you can't do that if you're anxious. Remember what I taught you. Whenever you feel overwhelmed, you must find your happy place. Let's say the words together.'

'All right.'

Maya lets him guide her as he did all those years ago. Allows him to take her back to a place of safety. He used to do this with her whenever she was upset: remind her of the good things, calm her down. She hears the whisper of the wind. The warm sunshine. Sees each tiny green blade of grass beneath the strong metal legs of the pylon that protects her. There's a daisy near her hand, and she brushes the petals with her fingers, thinking she'll make a daisy chain for her mother. Each movement guided by her dad's gentle voice. Below her, where the white cliff touches the beach, the waves surge and retreat, the sound hypnotic. Above her, the sun shines through the fog, the edge of it hazy as though she's seeing it through a gauzy curtain. She smiles, knowing she's back in her happy place.

The image holds for a moment, and then it starts to distort. The sun shines brighter, and light deflects off the metal structure above her head, creating flashes of light that make her screw up her eyes and turn her face away. She's fighting the feeling of peace, pushing herself up from its embrace. It's hot. Too hot. Every flare of sunlight branding her skin. And when she tries to sit up, there's a weight on her chest that pushes her back down.

When she wakes again and pushes her hot duvet away, her room is empty. She closes her eyes and drifts back into sleep, but this time when she hears the murmur of the sea and the whisper of the wind, she feels nothing but fear.

CHAPTER THIRTY-ONE
Maya

Maya sits on a flat rock, a metre or so from the edge of the sea, watching the tide crawl in. Seeing how the stones change from dull brown and grey to shiny amber and seal black. She's taken off her trainers and socks and has sunk her toes into the band of pebbles, glad that the beach is empty.

She looks at her phone to check the time. The day is turning to evening, the sky stained a tangerine pink. Soon she'll be joined by the evening dog walkers, but for now, she has the beach almost to herself.

If she was at work, she'd be helping the residents in the dining room: cutting up their food, lifting plastic beakers of tea to the lips of those whose hands are too shaky to hold a china cup. All the while, listening to stories that lose their thread… or never had one to begin with. Despite what the doctor had said when she went to see him, she wants to go back. Being with the elderly people in her care is where she feels safe, the routine of bed-making and the giving of comfort guaranteed to numb the thoughts that invade her mind. Thoughts that she hasn't told anyone for fear it might make them real.

For she's started to remember things and she's scared. Unsure if the images that come to her unbidden are memories of what happened the night of the attack. Whether she's starting to remember what happened. It's not the whole thing she sees – just flashes.

Images. Someone is behind her, but when she turns her head, she can't see their face. There's nothing else. No glimpse of hair colour or echo of a voice. The picture she gets isn't as solid as that. It's just a presence… and the certainty she's not alone.

The images come to her unexpectedly when her brain is idle. Taunting her. Teasing her. But just as she thinks she might remember more, they slip away, no more substantial than a wisp of smoke on a breeze. What they leave behind, though, is fear and, however much she wants to remember, she's scared of what might be there if she looks too closely. So, instead of trying to grasp the edges of her memories to make them firm, she locks them back down, forcing herself to think of other things.

The sea has been calm today. Healing. As the sun lowers, Maya watches the glistening sheet of water foam and hiss up the stones, sees how it pools around the rock where she's sitting. She digs her toes deeper into the pebbles, feeling them shift and settle, then picks one up and throws it as far as she can, watching the water devour it. Should she tell the police? But if she did, what would she say?

The only thing she knows for sure is she doesn't want to tell her father. She no longer feels comfortable around him. The memory of his slap always in her head and the evidence of his temper not something she can ignore any longer. Was her mum concerned too?

Slowly she gets up and walks to the steps. Now that the sun has set, she's cold, the air raising goosebumps on her arms. There's an emptiness inside her that even the healing rhythm of the sea can't take away. She wishes her mum was here. Wishes she had something of hers to bring her closer to her memory. Closer to the truth of what happened the day she died.

When Maya gets home later, the day has slipped into evening and a wash of stars cover the sky. She slips her key in the lock and, out of habit, listens. Usually, when she comes home, there's the smell of dinner cooking, the clink of glasses on the kitchen worktop, her dad's and Amy's voices filtering through to the hall.

Today is different. The kitchen is in darkness, and the only light is coming from the conservatory. If this was any other time, she'd cross the living room and join them, but tonight, something makes her hold back. They're arguing, their tangled voices rising above the silence.

'You know that's nonsense.' Her dad's voice is weary. 'We're friends, that's all.' Amy says something in reply, but Maya doesn't catch it. 'For Christ's sake, don't make it into something it isn't, Amy.'

From the shadow of the doorway, Maya can see them. Her dad is in his usual chair, Amy at the window. The argument has a dull exhaustion to it as though they've been over this before. As she watches, Amy turns, and she can see, even from this distance, that she's been crying.

'I thought you were different, Steve, but you're just the same.' She wipes under her eyes with the heel of her hands in frustration. 'Why don't you just admit it?'

Maya sees her dad's face change from hurt to something less easy to recognise.

'Because there's nothing to admit.'

Amy turns wet eyes to him. 'I've seen the way she looks at you.'

Her dad's voice rises in frustration. 'Shut up, Amy. Just shut up. You don't know what you're talking about.' He pushes himself out of his seat, and Maya sees how red his face is. How dark his expression. She also sees the tumbler of whisky in his hand.

He puts the glass down.

'If I'd known you were a womaniser, I'd have steered clear.'

'For Christ's sake, I'm not a womaniser.' He clasps his hands behind his head, elbows wide. It's a gesture she recognises… one that signals his despair.

'Then how do you explain this?' She bends and reaches into the bag that's beside her, pulling out what looks like a wedding album. 'Were you ever going to tell me?'

He takes a step forward, a little unsteady on his feet, reaching out a hand to steady himself against the glass panes of the window.

'Where did you get that?'

'Does it matter? The fact is, I didn't know, Steve.'

Amy slings the album onto the settee, and Maya frowns. She's never seen her parents' wedding photographs. She'd presumed her dad hadn't kept them.

'So you've been snooping around…'

Maya doesn't want to hear any more. Doesn't want to see.

When Amy first came into their lives, Maya hadn't wanted her there, but what she's just witnessed has brought home to her how much she wants her to stay. More than that, she's scared of what her dad will be like if she doesn't.

She turns and crosses the hall as quietly as she can, taking the stairs to the sanctuary of her bedroom. Not bothering to turn on the light, she sits on the edge of her bed, her arms crossed, her fingers making contact with the soft bruised skin. Yesterday, the police had come round again. They'd asked if there was anyone who knew she was going to Weymouth that day or what time she'd be getting off the train – anyone she'd argued with or who might have a grudge against her. She'd told them she couldn't think of anyone, didn't socialise much outside of work and hardly at all when she was there. How sad her life had sounded when she'd recounted it, how simple the routine: get up, go to work, come home. Going to Weymouth had been the first exciting thing she'd done in a long while.

How long she sits there she doesn't know, but the room is dark when she eventually plucks up the courage to go back down and see what's happening. The kitchen light is on and she goes in, expecting someone to be in there, but the room is empty, and when she looks out of the window, she sees that her dad's car has gone. Amy's is still there though, and she goes to look for her.

The living room is in darkness, the conservatory too, except for a small table lamp in the corner of the room. Presuming Amy has gone to bed, Maya goes over to it to turn it off, but just as her fingers reach the switch, she hears the creak of wicker. Startled, she looks over to the settee.

'Amy?'

She's curled up in the corner, her legs tucked under her, her dark hair falling across her face. When she lifts her head, her cheeks are wet with tears.

Quickly, she wipes them on her sleeve. 'Oh, Maya. I didn't hear you come in. I wondered where you were.'

Maya's glad Amy doesn't know she witnessed the argument. Doesn't *want* her to know. 'I was on the beach and lost track of the time.'

Amy unfolds herself from the settee and manages a smile. 'I was getting worried and thought I might have to send out a search party.' She gives a laugh, but it doesn't reach her eyes.

Maya thinks of her bed upstairs. How lovely it would be to lie on it and shut out everything, but however much she wants to, she can't just ignore the black smudges of mascara under Amy's eyes.

'What's happened, Amy?'

'Nothing.' Amy pushes her hair back from her face. 'You go to bed. You've had enough worry this week.'

Maya looks over her shoulder. 'Where did my dad go?'

'Just out for a drive. He needed some time to himself. You know what he can be like.'

The lamp casts a yellow glow over Amy's face, making her appear much younger than she is. So much like the photo of her mum on the beach. The one where she's holding out the fossil. There's a guarded look to her face that's much the same.

'Amy, just tell me what's going on.' Maya turns pleading eyes to her. 'I have to know.'

Amy takes a tissue from her pocket and blows her nose. 'Please just leave it, Maya.'

The wedding album is still on the settee where Amy threw it, and Maya can't take her eyes off it. 'You found their wedding album.'

'Yes.'

Maya takes a step forward. 'I've never seen it before.' At the thought of seeing her mum in a wedding dress, Maya's worry about Amy retreats into the background. 'I need to see.'

Amy shakes her head sadly. 'He never told me about her.'

If Maya hadn't been so excited to see the photographs, she might have taken more notice of what Amy had said, but she doesn't. Instead, she picks up the album and opens the cover.

The bride is beautiful, the dress not long but a ballerina style that offsets her slim legs. Her hair hasn't been styled or drawn up into a bun, but hangs to her shoulders in soft waves, a single white bloom pinned into it.

Maya's dad, so much younger than he is now, looks up at the woman with adoring eyes. A woman with hair like her mum's and a figure like her mum's.

A bride with the face of a stranger.

CHAPTER THIRTY-TWO
Maya

Maya sinks heavily onto the settee and places a cushion on her lap, hugging it to her. Nothing makes sense. Nothing is as it should be. 'I don't understand. Who is that woman?'

Amy sits next to her. 'Are you saying you didn't know your dad was married before? Before your mother, I mean.'

'No.' Maya shakes her head in denial. 'He can't have been. He would have said. I would have known.'

Yet the photograph album is evidence, the date of their wedding printed in silver inside the front cover. Five years before her mother's. Maya doesn't know what to think or how to feel. It's like someone has taken her world and turned it upside down.

'And he didn't tell you either?' she asks.

Amy shakes her head. 'No, I've only just found out. She looks so much like me. It's so strange.'

Maya's eyes move from the photograph to Amy. Yes, of course she does. Her dad's first wife looks just like Amy. Just like her mother. The betrayal is a poison seeping into her veins. It's as though she doesn't know her dad any more. What has happened has made him as much a stranger as the woman in the photograph with the white flower in her hair.

Despite her rising anger, Maya manages to keep control of her voice. 'I heard you and dad arguing. Is this what it was about?'

Amy dips her head. 'Amongst other things.'

'You can tell me.'

A single tear runs down Amy's cheek, and she brushes it away. 'It's nothing and I don't want you to be worrying about it. You've had enough shocks this week.'

She looks vulnerable – no longer the confident woman Maya has been used to.

'What's wrong, Amy? Please tell me. Is it the argument you had with dad? Was it really bad?'

'It wasn't his fault. He's been worried about you and hasn't been himself for a while now.' Amy meets her look, then her eyes slip to the darkness outside the window. 'I should never have confronted him tonight. I should have waited until things settled.'

'But he shouldn't have kept something like that from you… or me.' Maya hesitates, wanting to know yet not wanting. 'Have you argued like this before?'

Amy's voice is slow and careful. 'We've just moved out of the honeymoon stage and into something more real, that's all.' She manages a smile. 'I think we should both go to bed. Things will look better in the morning.'

'All right.'

Amy reaches out and tucks a strand of hair behind Maya's ear. 'Try not to worry. It will sort itself out. I'll see you in the morning.'

Maya's left alone in the conservatory. The room with its glass walls is the same as it's always been, but tonight it feels different. Colder. Emptier. The windows looking out not onto the sea that she loves but onto a dangerous world. The hateful wedding album is still open on the settee next to her, and Maya closes it. She thinks about putting it on the coffee table on top of the family photo album, so her dad will know she's seen it when he comes in, but she doesn't. What if he blames Amy for showing her and it makes things worse? Instead, she takes the album into the living room and puts it in the cupboard in the sideboard. Then she turns off the lights and climbs the stairs to bed.

When she reaches the landing, Maya sees the door to her dad's bedroom is ajar. Amy is sitting at the dressing table, her cardigan draped over the back of the chair and, as Maya watches, she raises her arms to twist her hair into a bun.

Maya's blood stills, and she lets out a soundless gasp.

For on the flesh of Amy's upper arms is a pattern of dark bruises.

Without saying anything, Maya runs to her room, the sound of her feet muffled by the carpet. In the safety of her bedroom, she stands in front of the window, her dad's words in her head. Words spoken as they'd looked at the photographs of her mum in the family album. *Our love was perfect. We never had a cross word. I adored her.*

Maya stops, a prickle of unease barbing her. He may have told her this, but how does she know it was true? The card. Mrs Ellis. Shirley at the 7-Eleven. The evidence says something different.

She looks at her reflection in the window, sees how her arms cross over her chest, holding her in an embrace. Her mum had held her like this once. She'd wrapped her little daughter in her arms and told her she'd give her life for her. She remembers it. Remembers the words.

But whose words were they? She thinks of the stranger standing next to her dad, the white flower in her hair. Now she can't be certain. Because now she knows that her dad is a liar.

CHAPTER THIRTY-THREE
Teresa

Teresa moves one of the white chairs with its smooth chrome legs closer to the low table in the middle of the room, then plumps the cushions on the settee. She wants the space in her consulting room to be as comfortable and homelike as it's possible to be in a room with a metal plaque on the outside of the door.

This morning, she'd been surprised to receive a phone call from Maya asking if she could make an appointment with her. Since the incident in Weymouth, she hasn't seen her and hasn't liked to ask Stephen too much, not wanting to pry. Under normal circumstances, she wouldn't consider taking on a client that she knows, but she can't forget it had been her idea originally to have her make an appointment and besides, these are no longer normal circumstances. The fact that she was there when Maya turned up at the house traumatised makes her feel strangely responsible for her.

But that's not the only reason she's seeing Maya. She's doing it for Stephen as a thank you for everything he's done for her. She thinks of him in his room above hers. Does he even know his daughter is coming to see her? And, if he doesn't, should she tell him?

There's another thing that's pushing at her mind today, craving attention… and that's Dale, who still hasn't come home. Although she tries to cover it at work, she's worried sick about him. The things she'd said to him the day he left had been terrible. Unforgiveable.

And the look of hurt on his face was one she'd never seen before. His face closed in. His eyes darkening as she'd thrown Maya's achievement in his face. Praised her as if *she* was her child not him. Shining a spotlight on her courage and initiative in order to highlight his failings.

But, most terrible of all, she'd likened him to Gary. The worst thing she could possibly have done. What if she never sees him again? What if she's driven him out of her life? Teresa takes a notebook and places it on the low table along with a pen. Where has he been staying since he left? Her son might have been difficult at times, but she misses him dreadfully. She looks up at the ceiling. Dale had said she was obsessed with Stephen. What would he say now if he knew that soon she'll be counselling his daughter? Would he say she was getting too close?

The phone rings, and Teresa picks it up, knowing she needs to keep her worries in check and be professional. 'Oh, thank you, Louise. Send her in.'

There's a small knock on the door, and when she opens it, Maya is standing there, her fair hair tied back in a ponytail. In jeans and T-shirt, she looks younger than she does when she's wearing her blue work tunic.

'Come in, Maya. I'm glad you came. I wasn't sure if you'd change your mind.'

Teresa leads Maya to the settee and invites her to sit. She takes the chair opposite and is about to ask how she's feeling when Maya speaks first.

'You and dad were friends years ago. What was he like?'

'What was he like?' She smiles. 'Much like he is now, I suppose. Kind… funny… clever.'

'Did you know he was married before? Before my mum, I mean.'

The question takes Teresa by surprise. Yes, she knew, but clearly Maya didn't, or she wouldn't have asked the question.

'I did. Yes. He was going through the divorce when I first met him.'

She'd only met Anne once and had found her rather ordinary but pleasant enough. If Stephen hadn't been her soon-to-be-ex husband, she was the sort of woman she could imagine being friends with. But as it was, she knew where her loyalties lay.

'I like to think our friendship helped him get through that time. I'm not saying your dad's right keeping it from you, but he must have had his reasons. Have you asked him?'

Maya shakes her head. 'Not yet. I'm too angry. I'm afraid of what I might say.'

'Anger's not always a bad thing, you know. It's a tool that helps us to read and respond to upsetting situations. The trick is to express it properly. That's much healthier than bottling it up. As I said, you really should talk to him about it.'

'Maybe.'

Teresa sits back. 'You've been through a lot, Maya, and it seems to me that your father is always trying to protect you. Few girls lose their mother so young, and I would imagine getting through that was your father's priority...' She can see Maya softening. She must know her father isn't a bad man. She just needs reminding. 'And even now you have enough on your plate to worry about... It's been, what, a week, since the incident in Weymouth?'

'Yes.'

'And how are you feeling about it?'

Maya studies her hands. 'Tired. Useless.' She pauses. 'Scared.'

'Of what might have happened?'

'Yes. I suppose I'm afraid that if I've been attacked, it could happen again.' She shakes her head in frustration. 'If only I could remember more, the police would have something to go on. None of the CCTV in the area has caught anything and, apart from the woman at the test centre, no one even saw me, let alone witnessed anything unusual. If it wasn't for the bruises on my arms, I'd almost think I was making it up.'

'Nothing's come back to you, then? Nothing at all?' Teresa presses on.

'Nothing useful… just images. Dark ones that make me feel anxious. All I remember for sure is leaving the test centre for the station and stopping to look at my phone. That's about all. That's the main reason I wanted to talk to you, Teresa, so you can help me get my memory back and find out if I was attacked. That and to find out what you know about my dad's first marriage.'

Teresa looks at her with sympathy. 'I don't know anything really. Just that he was married to her for five years and that they divorced soon after your dad met your mum.'

'You mean he had an affair?' She sounds shocked.

'Yes, though I wasn't aware of it at the time.'

Back then the two of them had talked about a lot of things: new investigations and the research that had shaped their shared profession. They'd even talked about Stephen's dream of opening a clinic of his own. But the conversations had always been on his terms, and he'd never offered up much about his private life. Maybe if he had, she might not have done what she did.

She thinks of the kiss. It seems that nothing has changed… except this time it's not Cheryl who's put an end to her fantasy… it's Amy.

'They didn't have any children so, as far as I know, it was a clean break. There would be no reason for her to continue to be a part of his life. I guess they must both have been happy to keep it that way.' Teresa stops, scared she's said too much. She shouldn't be telling Maya all this. 'I really think if you have any more questions it should be your dad you ask.'

'Well, at least there won't be any half-brothers or sisters crawling out of the woodwork.'

Teresa smiles. 'No, nothing like that.'

'Thank God.'

Maya's relief is written across her face, but Teresa knows she needs to get back to the real reason she's here.

'Now I think we should talk about Weymouth. Although retrieving the pieces of your lost memories of the attack won't be easy, I'm willing to help if I can. And if I can't, then I'll at least be able to give you ways to deal with all that's been happening.' 'I think what we're dealing with here is a form of post-traumatic stress disorder. I'm sure you've heard of it.'

Maya nods. 'We have a resident at Three Elms who suffers from it.'

'At the moment, we don't know whether we're dealing with physical or emotional trauma, but either one can directly affect your memory. It's nature's way of helping you cope with what happened. Suppressing memories until you're ready to handle them.'

Maya runs her hands down her jeans. 'And you think that's what's happened to me… Why I can't remember how I got these bruises on my arms? How I got home that day?' She looks at her arm and her face pinches.

Teresa thinks Maya's going to say something else, but she doesn't. Instead, she bites her lip as if stopping herself. What was she going to say? No matter. These things have a habit of coming out in time, and, whatever it is, she's in the unique position to hear it first.

'Suppression would certainly explain why a big chunk of your evening is missing,' she says, looking at her notes. 'Extreme emotional arousal interferes with memory, and I think that would explain things.' She writes something else on the pad on her lap. 'If we work together, I'm confident we'll make good progress before you go to university.'

Maya looks up at her, and Teresa sees how pale her face is. She taps her pen against the palm of her hand, seeing that Maya is unsure. 'When something traumatic happens, even when we aren't sure what it is, it's important to recognise that our old way of looking at the world might not make sense any more. We might need time to reflect on what is important to us and rethink the way we live our lives. I can help you with that by cognitive restructuring.'

Maya frowns. 'What's that?'

'It's a way of identifying your shattered beliefs and rebuilding them in a more positive way. Even if I can't help you regain your memory of what happened, I can help you have more control over the way you act and feel because of it. We can start today, or if you prefer, we could wait a few days until you're more up to it.'

'No, I'm happy to start now.' She stares at her, eyes wide. 'This isn't the first time it's happened... my loss of memory.'

Teresa puts her pen down. Hoping that what she's about to suggest is right. Not wanting to upset her if she's not. 'Are you talking about when your mother died?'

'Yes. I hardly have any memory of it,' Maya replies.

'When you were found, were you conscious?' She tries to imagine Maya at the age of six... what she would have looked like. She hadn't known her when she was a young child. 'Do you know if you'd suffered any form of head injury?'

Maya shakes her head. 'No, nothing like that. I know I was only young, Teresa, but don't you think I should have *some* memory of it?'

'Not necessarily. Like in Weymouth, your brain might have been trying to protect you without knowing it. It's smarter than we are at concealment.' She stops, remembering something. 'But you *do* have a memory of something, Maya. When we were at your mother's bench, you told me you remember vividly the part when your dad found you.'

Maya looks to the window as though what she is seeing in her head is out there. 'I remember the grass, every blade of it. The tickle of the wind on my face. The sun glinting off the metal legs of the pylon. It's as clear as if I was there now.' She turns back to Teresa. 'But I don't even know if what I see is real. They're images

I use to calm my panic when I think about that day. When what happened to Mum threatens to overwhelm me.' She pauses and lowers her eyes. 'They're the pictures Dad painted for me.'

'Your dad?'

'Yes, in the days and weeks after it happened, when I thought about my mum, I would get so upset that the only way he could calm me down was to get me to close my eyes and then tell me a different story—'

Teresa can't hide her shock. 'Did he put you in a trance, Maya?'

'Sort of. He found me lying under the legs of one of the pylons on the cliff and the mere sight of them after would send me into hysterics. He managed to help me turn the place from something scary to something...' she searches for the word '... safe. That's what he called it *my safe place*. He taught me to visualise using all my senses and, even though I'm an adult now, whenever I feel overwhelmed or sad about Mum, I use it.'

Teresa forces the muscles of her face not to betray what she's thinking. 'And it works?'

'It always has... except when I tried it the morning after I was attacked, it didn't.'

'I see.' She's trying to digest what she's just been told. The enormity of it.

Maya's face brightens. 'Maybe Dad could use hypnosis again to help me remember?'

Alarm bells are ringing for Teresa, and she wonders how Stephen could be so irresponsible. Even though paediatric hypnotherapy is not an uncommon treatment option for certain behavioural problems, it should be carried out by someone who has undergone extensive training. As far as she knows, Stephen hasn't had that, but what is worse is that he used the technique on his daughter.

'No, Maya. I don't think that would be a good thing. Look, I think it might be better after all if we leave things for today. I'll work on some exercises we can use, and if you'd like to make another appointment, we can continue where we left off.' She consults the calendar on her computer. 'I'm presuming you've been signed off from work?'

'Yes, for two weeks, but I think I'll go mad if I stay at home that long.'

Teresa smiles sympathetically. 'Take it one day at a time. The job you do is both physically and mentally challenging. You need to allow yourself time to heal. How about we make an appointment for tomorrow at ten?'

'Yes, that would be good.'

Teresa stands and shows Maya to the door. She smiles reassuringly. 'You'll be fine, Maya… just give it time. Is your dad giving you a lift home?'

'No, I'm getting the bus.'

'Okay. And try not to worry. We'll work this out together. Oh, and there's just one other thing… Was working with me your dad's idea?'

She likes the idea that Stephen might have suggested her. Trusted her with his daughter.

'No. I didn't discuss it with him. If I'd told him I'd been thinking about it, he'd only have tried to talk me out of it. It might come as a surprise to you, considering therapy is his job, but in our family, we don't talk about stuff. I suppose that's why I'm here.'

'I wonder if it might be better if we don't mention your appointment. That way you'll feel freer to talk about things. What do you think?'

Maya nods. 'Yes, I'd prefer that. I don't know what he'd think if he knew.'

'Very well then. I'll see you tomorrow.'

Teresa waits at the window and parts the metal blinds, watching until Maya's disappeared from view. Then she goes back to her desk and closes her eyes. Wondering what other secrets might come out in their next session and how she can protect Stephen.

CHAPTER THIRTY-FOUR
Teresa

When Teresa drives into work the next day, the sun is shining, and the roads are mercifully clear. She's had a restless night and has the beginnings of a headache. Reaching into her glove compartment, she searches for some sunglasses. Finding none, she tilts the sun visor down instead.

What Maya told her yesterday has been going round and around in her head. How could Stephen have been so stupid? Doesn't he know that using hypnosis to soothe his daughter could have got him into serious trouble if it had come out? She can only hope that Maya doesn't tell anyone else. The fewer people who know, the better.

When she gets to the clinic, she finds a couple of paracetamol in her bag and swallows them down with water from the cooler in reception. Her first two appointments go well, but she can't concentrate. It's Maya she's interested in.

Just after ten, Maya arrives. She takes a seat at the far end of the settee, her back ramrod-straight, her hands between her knees. She has the pale face and dull eyes of someone who hasn't slept, and Teresa knows how that feels.

'How have you been feeling since our talk yesterday?'

Maya raises her head. 'I don't really know.'

Her eyes flick to the ceiling and Teresa sees.

'This is a safe place, Maya. I know I work with your father, but whatever you say between these four walls will be in strictest confidence, as it is for any of my clients. You do believe that, don't you?'

She gives the smallest of nods. 'Yes.'

Upstairs, in the consulting room above them, Stephen will be sitting in the swivel chair he likes to use when he has a client. He'll be asking the person who sits in front of him questions in his kind, encouraging voice. Drawing them out of themselves. Helping them to find a way through whatever problem they've presented to him.

Teresa's eyes settle on Maya's drawn face. Why is it that she and Stephen can be so good at what they do yet, when it comes to their own families, the people they love, they find it so hard to do the right thing? Last night, when she wasn't thinking about what Stephen had done, she'd lain awake worrying about Dale, wondering where he was, and when she'd eventually fallen asleep, his face had followed her into her dreams. Accusing. Distorted with hurt. *Christ, you're obsessed with him!*

Maybe he was right. Maybe that's always been the problem.

She can't fix things for her son, yet Stephen's daughter is sitting in her consulting room, picking the loose skin from one of her nails. Her features pinched. Her eyes haunted. She has to do for her what she couldn't for her own child.

'Maya?' she says gently. 'I'd like to follow up on what we were talking about yesterday. In particular, any emotions you've had in response to the things you told me.'

'I've been so angry. I hate that my dad lied to me.'

It's said with such force that Teresa's taken aback.

'Not telling you he'd been married to someone before your mother was an omission not a lie, Maya.'

'I'm not talking about that.' A faint pink flush has crept up Maya's neck and she rubs at it. 'I've been thinking about it all night. Worrying about it. Everything he told me about their marriage was a lie.'

'Your parents' marriage?'

'Yes. All my life he's said what an amazing wife she was. How she was his soulmate. The love of his life.' She bites her lip, tears brimming in her eyes. 'I believed him.'

'And what makes you think he's been lying, Maya?'

'I didn't tell you before, but the day I found out about his other marriage, he and Amy had been arguing. They didn't know I'd heard.'

Teresa tries to keep her face neutral. Tries to ignore the tiny part of her, buried deep inside, that's pleased. The feeling grows that this is it. This is the thing Maya was keeping from her yesterday. Her secret.

'Are you able to tell me what the argument was about? If you'd rather not say, I quite understand.'

'It was about the other wife but also…' Maya stops and looks at her. Her lip caught between her teeth. Then she looks away. 'It doesn't matter. It wasn't anything important. I think Amy had got the wrong end of the stick about something, that's all.'

Teresa tries to push away her disappointment. This is not about her. It's about Maya. 'And how did their arguing make you feel?'

She thinks for a moment. 'Helpless. My dad has times when he's down and finds it hard to pick himself up, but I've never heard him shout. Her rarely loses his temper.' Maya's hand rises to her cheek and she stops, uncertainty written across her face.

Teresa has to admit, she's finding it hard to believe; Stephen is the gentlest man she knows. 'Arguments happen in most relationships. It doesn't mean they're about to end. Is that what you're worried about?'

'I suppose so. Things have been better since he and Amy got together. I haven't had to worry about him so much.'

'That's good, but your father is a grown man, Maya. It's his life, and it's not your job to worry about him.'

'I know, but I do.'

'And just because they were arguing, doesn't mean it was the same with your mother. All relationships are different. Some personalities clash, others don't. What's given you this idea?'

'It was something Amy said… like she knew.'

'Do you think your dad might have told her something about his relationship with your mum?'

'Maybe.' She covers her face with her hands. 'People in the town who knew them both said it had been a volatile relationship, but I didn't want to believe it. Yet now Amy's said it too—'

'I'm sure it was nothing, and you should put it out of your mind.' Teresa leans forward in her chair, hating what she's hearing about Stephen. Desperate to protect him from this new woman's words. 'No marriage is perfect, believe me.' She thinks of Gary. His threats. His control. She knows that better than anyone.

But it's like Maya isn't listening. She leans forward in her chair. 'There's another thing. Mrs Ellis, my old teacher, said her husband who worked at my primary school had to break up an argument between my parents one day when they'd come to pick me up.' Her eyes fill with tears, her words tumbling out. 'And I found a card Dad had written to my mum apologising for hurting her and begging her not to leave.'

Maya rubs the tops of her arms, her distress obvious. 'But the worst thing is… I think he might have hurt Amy too.'

Maya's words hit Teresa with such force she can't hide her shock. She glances up at the ceiling. It isn't true. It can't be. She'd wanted to know what Maya had been holding back from her yesterday, but now she wishes it had never been said.

'No, I can't believe that. Is there any way Amy might have made it up?'

'No.' Maya's fingers continue their rubbing. 'I saw what he did. I saw how devastated she was.'

Teresa looks down at the notes she's made, trying to match the Stephen she knows with the one who's been painted here and fails.

He's the friend she's always gone to for advice, the colleague who's been so supportive as her family life's fallen apart. Is she to believe the words of a woman he's known for barely five minutes? Can she trust those of a girl whose happy childhood ended abruptly at the age of six and who's recently been through a trauma she can't explain?

A car horn blares outside, forcing Teresa to refocus. She turns back to Maya. 'I want to tell you a story. Yesterday, a ginger cat wandered by my back window with something in its mouth. When I went out to see what it was, I realised it was a baby bird and of course I was afraid the cat had hurt it, or that it was dead, but it wasn't.' She smiles, remembering how delighted her mum had been when she'd told her the same story on her visit to her yesterday. 'Imagine my surprise when instead of running off, the cat just dropped the bird at my feet. Except for its feathers being a bit wet, it was totally unharmed, and I could hardly believe it when it flew away into the bush.'

Maya shifts in her seat. 'I'm glad.'

'I was too but the reason I'm telling you this, Maya, is that sometimes things aren't what they seem… or as bad as they seem. Just like me, you will only have been seeing part of the picture.'

She doesn't look convinced. 'Maybe.'

Teresa locks eyes with her. 'And I don't think you should repeat what you've said to anyone else.'

'I won't.' She looks out of the window. 'I'm actually thinking of going back to work. Being at home is making me anxious.'

'I think that might be a good idea.' The question Teresa asks next is one she shouldn't be asking. It's unprofessional, and also none of her business, but she can't help herself. 'Do you know what Amy's going to do? Is she going to stay with him?'

Maya nods. 'This morning when I came down, they were having breakfast together. They seemed to be okay. Do you think she might be in denial?'

Teresa thinks of the number of times she's sat at the breakfast table with Gary, pretending everything's okay for Dale's sake. Thinking that the next day things will be different and that it will never happen again. But Dale's her son. Why would Amy do the same when Maya isn't her daughter?

But when Maya speaks again, she has her answer.

'I think she's in love with him,' she says.

Green fingers of jealousy twist at Teresa's insides. Maya hasn't said it, but sometimes what's left unsaid is as powerful as what's verbalised. Stephen loves her too. It's obvious. And with that thought, any hope she might still have been harbouring dies.

She looks at Maya and remembers Stephen's hypnosis when she was six. The situation is worse than she thought and any other secrets he's keeping are bound to come out if he continues to see Amy. It's inevitable.

He's been such a good friend to her... it's her duty to make sure they don't.

CHAPTER THIRTY-FIVE

Maya

As Maya cuts a sandwich into four and places it in front of one of the residents, she thinks how good it is to be back at Three Elms. It's the only place she feels safe. Once her place of safety would have been Crewl House, the only home she's known, but not any more. Despite her dad and Amy trying to persuade her not to, she'd phoned up her manager and told her she felt well enough to come in. Being at home was making her anxious when what she really needed was to get back into some sort of routine – a rhythm to her days that would stop her thinking.

Too many things have happened recently that she doesn't understand… that have unnerved her. The attack in Weymouth. The bruises Amy had tried to hide from her. Evidence of her dad's temper. For the first time ever, shutting the door behind her and walking down the hill to the bus stop had been a relief. And now she's here, she knows what a good decision she's made as her energy is taken up with the residents' needs and requests, and there's been no time to think about things. No time to dwell.

As she helps someone out of a chair or arranges flowers, she wonders how she could have been so stupid as to think she'd be able to go to university, to leave what she knows: her job, her home, her dad. If it hadn't been for Mrs Ellis putting the idea into her head in the first place, she'd never have even thought about applying again. Nothing's changed since the first time she wrote out her application. She knows that now. Her dad won't want her to leave this time either.

Teresa's mum, Jean, is sitting with two other residents playing cards, though the game is unrecognisable, and she suspects they don't know the rules either. She stops beside her and smiles, pleased to see that she's settled in. 'I'd put the ace on top of that one, Jean.'

Jean smiles. 'Thank you, dear.' She puts the card face up on the pile on the table. 'Is my grandson coming today?'

'Your grandson? I don't think so, but your daughter will be coming later.'

'Not Gary then.'

Maya frowns. 'I thought your grandson's name was Dale?'

'Gary. Dale. They're just names.'

She pats her on the arm. 'Of course they are, and when Teresa gets here, you'll be able to ask her yourself. Let me know if there's anything you want.'

Her face, so phlegmatic a few moments ago, falls. 'I want to go home.'

There are so many things Maya could say, but none of them seem appropriate so, instead, she bends and hugs her. It's at times like this that her job is the hardest.

'Not that Teresa wants me there,' Jean says, her voice muffled by Maya's cardigan. 'Any more than she wants her husband even though he was a good man. Would do anything for me. But despite what she says, I think she still loves him. Stephen. Stephen. Stephen. It's all I hear.' She moves out of Maya's embrace and puts her hands over her ears as if to accentuate her point and Maya shakes her head. Jean's confused again, and there's no point in correcting her.

'I'll see you later, Jean,' she says. 'Enjoy your game.'

The house is quiet when Maya lets herself in, which isn't surprising as she's been on an early shift and her dad will still be at work. The space where Amy's car had been parked this morning is empty too, and she's relieved to have some time to herself without having to skirt around the two of them, wondering what's really going on in their relationship. She listens to the silence and realises that without knowing it, she's been waiting for this moment. The chance to look around while no one's here. A chance to find out more.

As she walks into the kitchen, she notices that the blue cardigan, the one that had once belonged to her mum, is draped over the back of one of the kitchen chairs. Maya picks it up, and brings it to her face, smelling it as though there might be some residue of her mother's scent. Of course, there isn't – the soft fabric smells of nothing in particular and it makes her sad. Just like at the beach, she has the urge to find something, anything that will give her that closeness again.

Putting the cardigan back where she found it, Maya wanders into the hall and looks up the stairs. Would it harm to look? To see if her dad has stored anything else away?

Walking as quietly as she can, even though there's no one in the house to hear, she goes up to the first floor and stands outside her dad's bedroom. Once, she wouldn't have thought twice about walking in, but now that Amy's here too, it feels wrong. She stands a moment, her fingers on the doorknob, before mustering up the courage to go in. As the door swings open, she's expecting the room to look different in some way, but it doesn't. It's exactly as it's always been: her dad's clothes strewn across the chair in the corner, his hairbrush and other paraphernalia on the chest of drawers. Books and folders are piled up on the floor beside his bed and three empty mugs stand on the windowsill, their insides stained brown. Picking one up, she smells it, surprised when it's the aroma of whisky that comes to her not coffee. Wrinkling her nose, she puts the mug down again.

For as long as she can remember, her dad has liked to sleep on the side of the bed nearest the window and so Maya had been expecting to see Amy's things on the bedside table on the other side, but there's nothing. Neither is there a make-up bag or toiletries. No books or magazines on the floor beside the bed. In fact, there's no evidence that Amy has been staying here at all. Crossing over to the wardrobe, she looks inside, but it's only her dad's clothes that hang there: the cords that he favours and a selection of soft shirts and casual jumpers. Many of which she's chosen for him.

Maya frowns, trying to remember if she's seen Amy go in or out of the room. She comes to the conclusion that she hasn't. Until she was signed off, she'd been on a run of early shifts, which meant she was up before either of them. And the last couple of days, Amy has already been in the kitchen when she's come down. Yet, the night of the argument, she'd been sitting in front of the dressing table mirror, her cardigan draped over the back of the chair.

Leaving the room, she crosses to the spare bedroom and looks in. The bed is neatly made but beside it is a small weekend case, zipped closed. Nothing has been put out on the dressing table beneath the window or on the big oak chest of drawers and when Maya goes over to it and slides out one of the drawers, it's empty. Her breath catches. Maybe Amy is thinking of leaving.

Returning to her dad's bedroom, Maya opens the wardrobe doors again, guilt making her check first to make sure no car has arrived back on the drive. Above the hanging space is a shelf full of bags and boxes. Dragging over a chair, she climbs up and pulls down the nearest bag. It's filled with nothing more exciting than old scarves and gloves. Another offers up a spare duvet and when she lifts the lid on one of the boxes all that's in there are some old psychology journals.

She climbs back down and looks around the room, her hands on her hips. Where could he have kept her mum's things? There's no point in looking in the drawers as, despite him telling her she doesn't have to, she's the one who puts her dad's clothes away after they've been washed. She knows everything that's in there. Every sock. Every handkerchief. Bending down, she looks under the bed, seeing nothing but dust balls, an old slipper and a balled-up tissue.

The drive outside the house is still empty of cars, and Maya's not ready to give up yet. She goes onto the landing and thinks where else she can look. There's nothing in the garage and, if there had been anything stored away in the rest of the rooms, she'd have come across them when she was cleaning. It's then she looks up. Above her head is a loft hatch, but it's too high to reach even with a chair. She stands with her head tipped back, looking at it. She's never been up there. Has had no reason to.

Looking around, she can't see anything to reach up with, but then she remembers the pole they use to open the fanlights in the conservatory. Getting it, she stretches up and slips the metal hook into the ring and opens the hatch before drawing down the ladder.

She climbs and when she reaches the open loft hatch, the opening is dark. With one hand on the ladder to steady herself, Maya reaches into her back pocket and pulls out her phone, turning on the torch. At first, as she sweeps it across the dingy space, all she can see are dust motes, but then the beam picks up some larger shapes in the far corner. Two wooden kitchen chairs, a roll of carpet and the whale hump of an overstuffed suitcase.

With a hand either side of the open hatch, Maya pushes herself up until she's sitting with her feet through the hole before manoeuvring herself into a standing position. Relieved to see the loft is partly boarded, she steps across the wobbly squares of wood until she reaches the case and trains her torch on it.

Everything else in the loft is covered in a layer of dust but the case is clean. Maya kneels and places a hand on it, her heart racing. Her mum's things are in there, she just knows they are, but now she's found them, she's no longer sure she wants to see. But if she doesn't, the case will always be up here calling to her. She stares at it, wondering if she dare open it for this is where her dad's secrets are, the things he's been hiding from her... the truth of who or what he is.

Reaching out a hand, she grasps the metal tab and slowly unzips it.

CHAPTER THIRTY-SIX
Teresa

Teresa signs the visitors' book and walks through reception into the living area where she's been told her mum will be. As always, as she catches sight of her and makes her way between the chairs and the walking frames, her guilt accompanies her.

When she reaches her mother, she bends and kisses her cheek. 'Hello, Mum.'

Today, her mother is sitting in a chair near the window, her eyes glued to a television the volume of which is turned down so low it can barely be heard. To compensate, large subtitles in white lettering dominate the lower half of the screen and she's pleased to see it is *Pointless*, one of the programmes her mum likes.

'Mum,' she says again, but her mother shushes her, frowning and pointing a finger at the screen.

'It's nearly finished.'

While Teresa waits for the programme to end, she looks around the room. It's pleasantly decorated with large colourful pictures on the walls and comfortable seating, but the residents who occupy the chairs seem so much older than her mother. Probably because they are. Her guilt returns, threatening to take her down a familiar path. Refusing to go there, she turns her attention back to her mother, reminding herself that this is the best place for her. The safest place.

'There, that's all done and dusted.' Her mum turns from the TV, where the credits have started to roll, and smiles at her. 'Have you come to take me home?'

It takes all Teresa's strength not to say yes. Throw her arms around her and tell her that of course she'll be taking her home. But she doesn't because she knows it's not true. Her mum's house is already on the market, and there's simply no way she can look after her as well as holding down her job and trying to keep things together. There's too much going on. She's gone too far. She's hanging on to her sanity by a thread.

Teresa doesn't answer her mother's question. Instead, she asks one of her own. 'What have you been doing today, Mum? It's been lovely and sunny. Have you been outside?'

Her mum glances at the window. 'I don't think so. Have I?' She directs the question to one of the nursing assistants who's walking by with a trolley on which sits a large tea urn and some cups.

The girl stops. 'Yes, Jean. Don't you remember? Maya took you out after lunch.'

Teresa's mum looks confused, then shrugs. 'Did she? Oh, well that answers your question then, doesn't it?'

She's glad that it was Maya who took her mother out. Stephen's daughter has the same underlying kindness and empathy as him. Although all the staff seem lovely, when Maya's on duty, she knows that her mum's in an especially safe pair of hands.

She touches a hand to her mum's shoulder, the wool of her cardigan soft under her fingers. 'Would you like to go out now? It's still sunny.'

'I suppose we could.' Her mother doesn't look too sure. 'Maybe we should wait for your husband. He said he'd help me with the gardening the next time he visited.'

Teresa's heart stops. 'Gary's visited you here?'

'What? No, no. Don't be silly. When I was at home. He said it the last time he came.'

Teresa kneels down beside her and takes her hands in her own. 'When are you talking about, Mum? Was it the night you had the break-in?'

Except nobody *had* broken in. Her mum had opened the door to whoever it was, and they'd gone upstairs to rifle through her things. Searching the cupboards. Emptying the drawers – that's if her mum is to be believed. What if it *was* Gary, though? She thinks of the address she'd written carefully in capitals in the little rose-covered book her mum kept in her bedside table drawer. The new address where she's living now. What if that was what he'd come looking for? Her mum wouldn't have remembered the details of where she and Dale had gone, but it wouldn't have taken much searching for Gary to have found it.

Teresa feels sick. There's been no evidence that he's been any-where near the house, but he could be making her wait. Biding his time until she's alone so he can ruin things.

'Maya and I were having a chat about him,' her mum says. 'She's a good girl. She has time for me.'

'What did you say, Mum?' she says sharply. It hadn't occurred to her that the two of them might discuss her situation. What has she been telling her?

Her mother shakes her head as if to dislodge the memory. 'Oh, I don't know. What does it matter?'

But it does matter.

She stands and helps her mother to her feet. 'Come on, let's go out now while it's still nice.'

Together they walk to the large French doors that lead into the garden. It's been carefully tended, the lawn newly mown, the beds still full of late summer flowers. There are two benches facing the flower bed, and they sit on one of them, admiring the dahlias. A sparrow hops across the lawn in front of them, and her mum watches it.

'A funny thing happened when I was out here earlier… with Maya.' She looks pleased at having remembered this fact.

'What was that then, Mum?'

She smiles at the memory. 'A ginger cat walked across the grass right here in front of us.'

Teresa takes her hand and squeezes it. 'That's nice.'

'It wasn't actually.' Her mum shakes her head sorrowfully. 'The darned cat had a bird in its mouth. I thought the poor thing would be dead and got up to shoo the cat away but then, would you believe it, it walked right up to me and dropped the wee thing at my feet.' She points at the paving stone by her shoe. 'Just there.'

Teresa sighs wearily, knowing what she's going to say next. 'It wasn't dead, was it, Mum?'

Her mother looks at her as though she's just given away the punchline to a joke she's telling. 'No, for your information it wasn't. It was as alive as I am. Flapped its little wings and flew off into that bush over there.' She smiles and runs her foot over the paving slab. 'I can still see it now. Its little feathers all wet from the cat's mouth.'

Teresa stretches her legs out in front of her and closes her eyes for a second. 'I told you that story, Mum.'

Her brows draw together. 'What do you mean?'

'I told you that when I visited a couple of days ago. It was something that happened to me when I was getting ready for work. The cat belongs to a man at the end of the row and it often walks past the back of my cottage. A ginger cat with a bushy tail like a fox. You must remember me telling you.'

Her mother leans back on the bench and folds her arms. 'So, we both have ginger cats.'

Teresa looks at her. 'No, Mum. There's only one ginger cat. There's only one bird. It's not you who saw it, it was me.'

Exasperation is taking hold of her, but she knows she mustn't let her mum see it. It isn't her fault, and anyway, what does it matter whose memory it was? At the end of the day, the story is a charming one whoever experienced it. Letting the matter drop,

Teresa tips her head back and watches the tops of the silver birches sway in the breeze, enjoying the late afternoon sun on her face. When she turns her head to look back at her mother, she sees that her eyes are closed.

She shuts her own eyes and listens to the shiver of the birch leaves. Then she empties her mind and focuses on her breathing. Noticing how the air draws in through her nose to fill her lungs. Concentrating on the rise and fall of her chest.

But, try as she might, her mind won't still. Something's snagging at her. It's the story her mum told her about the cat. It's not that she took her story and made it her own that bothers her. Nothing as simple as that.

No, the false memory has made her think of Maya. Made her realise how easily they can be created.

CHAPTER THIRTY-SEVEN
Maya

The case is full of clothes that spring up when released from the pressure of the lid: trousers, blouses, jumpers... shoes even. Maya picks up the top item and shines her phone on it. It's a navy T-shirt with a Gap logo on the front in red.

Suddenly, her mum's face is vivid in her head. She's lying on her back on the wicker settee in the conservatory, one arm thrown across her forehead, the other resting on the red 'G' of her T-shirt. As Maya watches, her eyes open. They're looking straight at her. The pupils constricting, her expression tight with irritation.

The memory is overwhelming, and she sways back onto her haunches, reaching backwards with her hand to stop herself from overbalancing. The picture is so vivid it's as if her mum's really there. This is not something her dad's told her, this is a real memory.

Maya lifts out item after item, coming to a dove grey blouse. She touches it with her finger, then brings the material to her cheek, feeling the cool silk against her skin. She lets it slip through her fingers, leaving an image of her mum in the dark attic space. Maya's at the kitchen table, a crayon in her hand, the bowl in front of her empty. She's hungry. Crying. Her mum's grating cheese, the sleeve of her pretty grey blouse brushing the yellow curls. As her arm reaches towards her, Maya thinks she's going to put some of the cheese in her bowl, but she doesn't. Instead, she reaches for the bottle of wine that's beside her and fills her glass.

Confused, Maya places a hand either side of her head to squash what she's seeing. That's not what her father had told her.

'Maya?'

It's Amy's voice she can hear. It's coming from the hall. The last thing Maya wants is for anyone to know she's up here, but there's no time to get back down the ladder and close the hatch. Within moments, she hears footsteps through the house.

'Maya?' Amy's voice comes again, from somewhere below her. 'Are you upstairs?'

Maya shoves the clothes back into the case and zips it up, her heart racing – wanting to keep what she's found to herself. She's halfway down the ladder when she turns and sees Amy at the top of the stairs, her coat draped over her arm, her hand on the newel post.

'Look at you,' Amy says. 'What have you been doing?'

Maya brushes a cobweb from her top, the grey strands sticking to her fingers, but doesn't reply. Reaching up with the pole, she pushes the ladder back into place and secures the hatch, but her hands are trembling.

There's a frown of concern on Amy's face. 'Maya, are you all right, love?'

Maya hadn't realised she was crying, but now she feels the tears tracing the curves of her face. Sees the damp material where they've dripped onto her top. 'No, not really.'

Letting her coat drop to the floor, Amy steps forward and puts an arm around Maya's shoulders. 'I think we need to have a cup of tea, don't you?'

Maya nods, not trusting herself to say anything else. She lets Amy lead her downstairs, through the house and into the conservatory, too bound up in her own concerns to notice the holdall in the hallway. Slumping down onto one of the wicker settees, she waits, her eyes fixed on the grey sea, as Amy makes them both tea.

'There you are.' Amy places a mug into her hands, then sits beside her, taking a sip of her own tea. 'Do you want to tell me about it? You never know, it might help.'

Maya thinks for a moment, then realises she does. Amy's kindness and concern are welcome, and there are so many things she doesn't understand. 'When I was in the attic, I found some of my mum's clothes in an old suitcase. They brought back memories.'

Amy leans forward. 'What sort of memories?'

'They weren't happy ones. My mum she...' Maya stops, trying to make sense of it all. She raises eyes, wide with hurt, to Amy. 'It was like she didn't like me. And when I think about it, she's never smiling in any of the photographs where we're together.'

'I'm sure that's not true. Your dad's told me how much your mum loved you. How much time you spent together before she died. You remember it too... you told me.'

Maya's heart clenches. 'But what if it's not true? What if the memories I have aren't memories at all... just things my dad's told me? All my life my dad has reassured me, made remembering Mum a part of our lives. Before bed every night, he'd tell me all about her, remind me of these amazing things we did together. But what if it was just a bedtime story? What if he was lying?'

Amy frowns. 'Is that likely?'

'I don't know. I'm so muddled.'

Amy turns away, but Maya's seen her expression. Her brows are drawn together, her bottom lip caught between her teeth as if questioning her thoughts. 'What is it, Amy? Tell me.'

Ignoring her question, Amy gets up and walks to the conservatory window. 'I'm sure you're overthinking things,' she says.

'No, there's something you're not telling me. I have to know.' Amy's holding something back. Maya knows she is. She can see it in the stiff angle of her shoulders as she stares out at the sea.

'Amy?' Maya leans forward. 'Please?'

Eventually, as if making a decision, Amy turns and comes back to the settee. She sits beside Maya. 'I've been part of your life for a few weeks now and have seen how much he loves you. How much he cares about you.' She swallows. 'Have you ever thought that he might be trying to shield you?'

The question is odd. Unexpected.

'Shield me?' Maya frowns. 'From what?'

Amy looks away. 'From the truth.'

CHAPTER THIRTY-EIGHT
Maya

Maya feels the colour drain from her face. 'What are you trying to say, Amy?'

Amy folds her hands in her lap. 'There's something I need you to understand, Maya. When I first met your dad, I won't lie, I thought he was wonderful. So caring, thoughtful and, above all, committed to you. Despite the age difference, we got on straight away, and I thought we had a really good chance of making a go of things despite the fact you clearly didn't like me.'

Maya shifts in her seat. 'You sound as if there's a *but*.'

'There is. I was happy at first, but overtime, since being in the house, I've become worried. I've begun to suspect your dad isn't the man I thought him to be. His dark moods. His temper. That night, after our argument, I lay awake thinking I should leave before your dad came home, but I couldn't. Not until I'd spoken to you. The truth is I'm not happy leaving you here alone with him… not until I know what's going on. Because it's not just me I'm worried about.'

'You think I'm in danger?' Even saying the words is shocking.

'I don't know but something has always nagged at me about your mother's death. You were found by your dad, which means you were on that clifftop alone with your mother… is that right?'

A cloud covers the sun, and the conservatory, that until a few moments ago had been filled with light, darkens.

'Yes, it was just the two of us,' Maya replies, hating what she's hearing. Where it could be leading. 'When they found me, I was on my own in the field beside the path. Underneath the electricity pylon.'

Amy draws in a breath. 'Do you really not remember anything, Maya?'

Maya shakes her head. 'Nothing. Dad says it's because I was too young.'

'Or maybe he doesn't want you to remember.'

Maya frowns. 'But why?'

'Because of what really happened. Because you were the only one to witness it.' She's silent for a moment, and Maya feels the colour drain from her face. 'Could it be your mum and dad weren't getting on? Maybe your mum was trying to leave – trying to take you with her.'

The way Amy's talking is making Maya frightened. She thinks of the hypnosis her dad had used on her when she was little. The pictures he'd painted of the vivid blades of grass. The warmth of the sun on her cheek. The wind whispering its secrets. *You're safe here.*

Then she remembers the card she'd found in the cupboard in the living room. *Don't leave me. I didn't mean to hurt you.* Suddenly, the pictures in her head of the clifftop don't seem so real.

Seeing how Maya's face has paled, Amy says, 'I know it's hard to hear, Maya.'

'You're talking nonsense.' Maya stands. She wants to get away from Amy, from the terrible thing she's implying, but something stops her. Her life has been dedicated to looking after her dad, making sure he doesn't sink into the well of despair that saw him line the pills up on the dressing table in his room. She's given up on ambition. She's given up on herself... and for what? A lie?

'You really think Dad was there?'

'Yes, I do. I'm sorry, Maya, but I can't live here any more. It was stupid of me to think that I could. I'm worried about him, and it doesn't feel safe. I came home early to get my things.' Her hand strays to her upper arm where the bruises are – the bruises she's kept hidden from her. It's true then. Her dad did this to her.

Maya's blood runs cold. 'You don't mean that.'

'I do, and I'm not trying to worry you, but I think you should consider leaving too.'

But her father's been her life. This house has been her life.

'I can't,' she says quietly.

Amy looks at her sadly. 'Then *I* must.'

'I don't want you to go, Amy.' It's said from the heart, surprising herself as well as Amy. 'Please stay. I need you here.'

Amy shakes her head. 'I'm sorry.'

She stands and hugs Maya, glancing at the door as though Stephen might appear through it any moment. 'I appreciate it, I really do, but I can't be here after everything that's happened. I'll stay with a friend and come back for my things another time. I think it's best you don't tell your dad the real reason I've gone. I'll message him and say I've been called away, a family emergency or something, just until I can think what to do. Are you sure you don't want to come too?'

Maya shakes her head. 'I can't. I know my dad, and it would make things worse. I'm shattered, and I'm going to get some sleep before he comes home. I need to clear my head before I see him.'

'I can't make you. Look after yourself, Maya… and be careful.'

'I will.'

Maya waits in the conservatory while Amy collects some things, and when she knows she's finally left, she climbs wearily up to her room. Whatever's happened, she needs to stay with her dad. For if they both leave, who knows what he might do?

Maya cries out, unsure if she's asleep or awake. Whether what she's remembering is a dream or real. The sky is that strange colour you get between day and night… or night and day. The shadows lengthening or maybe shrinking, she can't tell which. She's not sure where she is, but someone is hurting her. She feels the press of their fingers on the soft flesh of her arms. Their breath on her cheek. There's strength in those arms and when she tries to pull away, she's too weak.

Maya's heart is racing, and she's bathed in sweat. Slowly, her bedroom comes into focus, and she realises her throat is parched. With an effort, she swings her legs off the bed and pulls on her cardigan before forcing her feet to take her out onto the landing. The door of the spare bedroom is open. It looks onto the drive and Maya hears the metallic slam of a car door. Her dad is home. Crossing the room, she looks out. Watches as he bends to the passenger seat to retrieve his battered briefcase. He's wearing an old donkey jacket that's seen better days and his trusty cords. The sight of him is comforting, pushing away her fears.

Amy is wrong. She has to be.

CHAPTER THIRTY-NINE
Teresa

When Maya arrives for her appointment at nine, Teresa can see immediately that something's wrong. The girl is wearing a navy cardigan over her work tunic as she'll be going straight from the clinic to Three Elms and her hair, which she's scraped back from her face into a ponytail, only serves to accentuate the dark shadows under her eyes.

'Please, sit down, Maya, and we can make a start.' Teresa takes the chair opposite and folds her hands in her lap. Since she went to visit her mother at the care home, she's been worried about Maya. She knows too well the fragility of memories and she'll need to tread carefully. She hears Stephen outside in the reception area. It's important that Maya continues to trust her so she can guide her through what is true and what isn't.

Maya doesn't wait for her to say more but leans forward, the fingers of her right hand crossing her body, caressing her other arm through the material of her cardigan. 'I've had some new memories… but they're all very confusing.'

'That's not a problem. We'll work on whatever you have. Are they from the night you think you were attacked?'

'No. Nothing from that time.' She says it too quickly, her eyes sliding to the left, and Teresa wonders if this is true.

'I think it would help if you told me about them,' Teresa says.

'They're flashbacks from when I was little. I think it might be from the day my mum died.'

Teresa draws in a breath. 'What makes you think that?'

'I don't know. It's just a feeling.'

From above their heads, there's the scrape of a chair, a bark of laughter, then a door slamming. Stephen's client must have just arrived. Teresa's unsure how to continue. Would Stephen be happy for her to delve into the past? From what she's seen, and from what Maya's told her, it's not something he wants talked about.

But it's not the first time this has come up, and it's clear Cheryl's accident is playing on Maya's mind. From what little Teresa knows about her, the uncertainty of that day has remained with her for years. A fast-moving current flowing close to the surface, unseen, yet waiting for an opportunity to sweep her away.

'What can you tell me about these…' she hesitates, not wanting to commit '… memories?'

'Not much. Just bits and pieces. I found a suitcase of Mum's clothes in the attic. There was a top that I recognised, and it brought back something.'

Teresa nods. 'Do you want to tell me about it?'

'I wanted Mum to play with me, I remember that now. I asked and asked, but she wouldn't.' Maya presses her fingers to her forehead. 'I also remember raised voices. Mum and Dad had been arguing, and I think Mum might have been drunk as there was a glass in her hand. When I shook her awake, she looked like she hated me.'

'Oh, Maya. I'm sure she didn't.'

'That's what Amy said when I told her, but I didn't believe her.'

Amy. By now Stephen must have told her about the kiss. How she made such a fool of herself. A wave of embarrassment washes over her.

'Have you been discussing this with her?'

'Yes, a bit. She thinks that—' She stops and looks down at her hands.

'Go on.'

'I've been talking with her about what I remember, and together we've been trying to piece things together. She thinks there's a possibility that Dad might have been changing the memories I had of the past to shield me from something.'

Teresa doesn't like what she's hearing. From outside in reception, she can hear Stephen talking to Louise.

'From what, Maya?'

'From what really happened the day Mum died. Up until now, the only memory I've had is lying under the pylon... before they found me. When I think about it, there's no fear, just perfect peace, but I know now that I wasn't happy that day. I can sense it in the bits that have started to come back.'

'What new memories do you have?' Teresa asks, leaning forward, knowing she needs the answer – to push Maya on.

Maya's eyes fill with tears. 'I wouldn't eat my breakfast. Threw my porridge on the floor. Everything feels wrong. Mum was angry. Dad too.' She looks up. 'I'm scared, Teresa. I'm scared of what these memories mean.'

A sixth sense tells Teresa there's something she's still not shared with her.

'Is there anything else, Maya? Anything at all.' Turning her head, she glances at the door. 'I can't help you if you're holding something back.'

Maya crosses her arms, her fingers curling around the tops of her arms. She rubs at the cardigan she's wearing over her tunic, plucking and pressing at the navy wool. 'I've had a flashback that I think was from the day I was attacked. I thought at first it was a dream, but now I think it was a memory. Someone was hurting me. I remember their fingers pressing into my arms.' She rubs at her skin through her cardigan. 'I told you last time I was worried about Dad. That he might have hurt Amy. What if he did? And what if he did this to me?'

Teresa's skin grows cold at what she's suggesting. Not her father. Not Stephen.

'I think you might be getting a little bit carried away, don't you? On the day of your test, your father was here at the clinic.'

Teresa stops, her fingers pressed to her lips, realising something. He wasn't with her that day. It was the day he'd left early with a migraine.

Maya looks as if she might cry. 'I don't know what any of this means, but I'm scared. Dad doesn't like people leaving him. He didn't want me to go to university before. What if nothing's changed?'

Teresa knows she needs to take control of the situation. This is Stephen they're talking about. 'Is it Amy who's put this idea into your head?' At the thought of her, the green-edged knife gives a sharp twist in her gut.

'No, she wouldn't do that. It's the one memory I haven't shared with her.'

'Are you sure? Maybe you've forgotten.'

Teresa stops, realising how unprofessional she's being. If she carries on, she's in danger of giving away her feelings. Inside, though, she's seething. How dare this woman play mind games with Stephen's child?

She looks at Maya. So small. So lost. She has to know more.

'And anyway,' Maya continues. 'It doesn't matter now. She's gone.'

'Gone?' Teresa hopes she means what she thinks.

'Yes. She left last night.' Tears brim in her eyes. 'She said that after the argument they had, she no longer feels safe in the house.'

Teresa can't believe what she's hearing. 'Let's take a step back here a moment. You say your dad might have hurt Amy, but what exactly is it he's supposed to have done?'

Maya looks at Teresa through unshed tears. 'There were bruises on her arms. Just like mine. She doesn't know I've seen.' Her hands rub at the sleeve of her cardigan.

'I think we need to be cautious about something as sensitive as this,' Teresa says, stunned. This is worse than she'd feared. 'Maybe if we make another appointment, perhaps in a couple of days' time, we can talk about it some more.'

Maya's arms are still wrapped around her body, her fingertips pressing into the wool of her cardigan. 'I don't think I can. I just want things to go back to how they were before Amy. When it was just the two of us and things were still okay.'

But it's said with uncertainty, and Teresa knows it's because more often than not when secrets are revealed, it's no longer possible to go back.

She stares at the girl's fingers, watches the press and release of them. She sees her fear and knows it's her job to alleviate it. So that Maya can be happy again. So she and her dad can continue to live in their big house on the cliff and maybe in time Teresa can be a regular visitor.

'Maya, would you do something for me? I'd like you to take off your cardigan and lift up the sleeve of your tunic.'

'Why?' Maya says, confused.

'Humour me… please.'

Maya does as Teresa asks. She places the cardigan over the back of the settee and slides her sleeve up. Teresa gets up and walks around the table to her, taking her arm and gently turning it to see better as Maya watches her with a furrowed brow. The bruises, though now fading to yellow, are still visible, and it's almost as if Maya can't bear to look at them.

'Now cross your arms as you did just then,' Teresa instructs her.

Maya crosses her arms and straight away her fingers seek out the soft flesh. Wincing as they press down on the place where her bruises are. Teresa lifts each finger in turn, seeing how the pad of each one perfectly matches the bruising. She then returns to her seat.

'Look at me, Maya.' She sits forward, waiting until Maya's eyes meet hers. 'I want to tell you what I think has happened here.'

Maya sits and looks at her, her eyes questioning.

'In times of extreme stress, our brains can respond in unexpected ways. Ways that help us to cope with what is happening to us. You're not used to being away from home. The test you did, and the day itself, always had the potential to induce extreme anxiety.'

Maya frowns. 'But I was happy with what I did. I'd prepared well and didn't find it difficult. That much I *do* remember.'

'Maybe that's the point. If you thought you'd done well, it would have made the possibility of going to university all the more real. You would have become increasingly anxious about how your dad would cope if you got accepted onto the course and had to leave him alone for weeks on end.' She keeps her eyes levelled at Maya's, pushing aside the inconvenient fact of Amy and her own injury. 'The act of rubbing your arms is a well-documented way to rid yourself of distressing thoughts. It's called Havening and basically what happens is the action boosts the level of the mood-stabilising chemicals in your brain, helping to disrupt the link between the memory and the distress.'

Maya lifts her arm and studies the faint yellowing bruises. 'But how would doing that cause these? And how would I even know about it?'

Teresa thinks about her question. 'It could have been instinctive, or it might even have been another thing your dad suggested to help you through your distress when you were young. I've noticed how you often rub your arms when you're remembering something that makes you uncomfortable. It could be that on the night of the test you simply took the action to the extreme.'

'You mean you don't think anything happened to me on the night of the test?' Maya seems unsure, but Teresa can see that the logic of what she's saying is sinking in. No one wants to believe that their parent could harm them. That the person who is supposed to love you the most in the world could do something like this.

'I can't be sure but, no, I don't think it did.'

Maya's eyes flick briefly up to hers. 'I get that you think I caused the bruising myself because my stress levels were high, but what I don't understand is why I can't remember anything after leaving the test centre.'

Teresa thinks a moment. 'It's possible that being in a stressful situation, and out of your comfort zone, brought back the feelings of abandonment you must have had when you were left alone on the clifftop as a child. I've been thinking about it since our last session, and even if your dad helped you to bury memories of that time, they will only have been lying dormant... waiting for a trigger. If they started to emerge sometime during that evening in Weymouth, your body's natural defence mechanism might have kicked in to shield you from further trauma. It's only a guess, but it's possible.'

Maya covers her face with her hands. 'I was so worried. So scared.'

'You don't need to be any more. I think we've worked out what happened. Now we need to concentrate on how you can deal with these intrusive thoughts if you get them again. Shall we make another appointment?'

Maya smiles, and Teresa sees the relief in her face. 'Yes. I can come over after my shift tomorrow.'

'Perfect.'

She stands and shows Maya to the door, feeling satisfied with herself. She has protected Stephen, and it makes her feel good.

Going to the computer, Teresa opens the file containing her consultation notes. Her hand hovers over the mouse before clicking on the file marked with the girl's name. *Maya McKenzie*. Swiftly, her practiced fingers move over the keys, noting Maya's state of mind and the date when she had the first of her flashbacks. But however hard she tries to stop it, her mind won't focus on what she's writing. Instead, it strays to the other thing Maya told her… the identical bruises Amy had on her arms.

CHAPTER FORTY
Maya

Maya sits on her mother's bench, her chin cupped in her hands. Below her, the sea stretches out as far as the eye can see, blending with the horizon. This used to be her favourite place, somewhere she could go when she was feeling anxious, but now she wonders why she ever thought that. It's morbid sitting just feet away from the spot where her mum plunged to her death. How could she have not seen that?

Before, she would think of the beach below with pleasure. Would close her eyes and imagine the glistening sand that the sea would expose at low tide; the fossils buried deep in the rocks waiting to be found. Then her thoughts would turn to her mum, beautiful and perfect, her dark hair blowing around her face, holding out an ammonite for her to look at.

Now, all she sees is what everyone else who knows their family and their tragedy sees when they walk the beach: her mother's dashed and broken body on the rocks below the cliff. Her blood seeping into the cracks between their barnacled surfaces before the tide takes her.

Although she's relieved that Teresa has given her an explanation for her bruises and lack of memory on the day of the test, she can't help feeling as though she's been manipulated. That her dad's cast some kind of spell over her, making her believe things that aren't true to maintain the status quo of their little family. What was her mum really like? Instead of helping her move on, allowing her to deal with her grief as an ordinary father would, he's done the opposite. Made her a prisoner of her own fear. Trapping her inside her own little bubble, so she's afraid to take any new steps to change her life. When she gets back, she's decided to confront him with the things she knows. What the people in town have said about his relationship with her mum. The violent argument outside the school. The note she found written in the card.

She's just thinking about leaving when she sees someone walking towards her along the cliff path. They're some distance away still, and she stiffens, remembering the stranger Teresa and Amy had seen. The one who did nothing but stand and stare. As they get closer though, she's surprised to see it's Amy.

A week ago, she would have been annoyed to have her visit her special place, but now she's relieved to see her. Can't wait to tell her what Teresa said. When she gets closer, crossing the scrubby grass towards the bench, Maya calls out to her. 'Amy, what are you doing here?'

'I thought I might find you here.' She sits on the bench next to Maya. 'I wanted to make sure you're all right. How's your dad?'

Today she's wearing the blue cardigan that had once belonged to her mum, but Maya doesn't mind. It's comforting.

'He believed that you were at your aunt's, so he's been okay. I've been at work, so I haven't seen that much of him. And after work, I had my counselling session—' She stops, remembering that Amy doesn't know about it.

Amy looks puzzled. 'Counselling?'

'Yes. I've been having strange flashbacks since the night of the attack, and Teresa has been helping me.'

Amy stares at her. 'Teresa? Does your dad know?'

'No, and I don't want him to. I have to work things out without him. Oh, but Amy!' Maya clutches at her arm, desperate to tell her. To make her see that they were wrong about him all the time. 'It's brilliant. Teresa's helped me realise that everything's fine. There's no need for us to worry about Dad any more as she thinks she knows what happened in Weymouth. It's not what we thought, and I'm so relieved.'

Amy's brows pull together slightly. 'That's good, but I don't see—'

Maya wraps her jacket closer around her, starting to feel the cold. 'She looked at the bruises on my arms, and I told her how I thought they'd got there.'

She cringes at the memory, feeling sick at how disloyal she'd been to him.

'That was a brave thing to do, Maya.' Amy's hand reaches up to touch the top of her own arm through her coat. 'Does Teresa think we should be concerned?'

Maya knows what Amy's trying to say, but she's wrong. Has been wrong all the time. 'That's not what she thinks at all. She says I made the bruises myself as a way of coping when intrusive thoughts and memories come into my head that I can't deal with.' Maya feels her face colour. 'I think she's right, don't you?'

Amy doesn't answer. Instead, she leans her head back against the hard, wooden bench and closes her eyes, her brow furrowed.

Above their heads, the clouds are shredded by the wind. Maya tips her head to look at them, waiting. When the silence is too much for her, she pulls tentatively at the sleeve of Amy's coat.

'Amy, you haven't answered my question.'

Amy opens her eyes. She gets up and walks to the cliff edge, her hands in her pockets. Her dark hair whipped by the breeze. She looks down at the layers of mud, clay and limestone that fall in bands to the sea, their colours changing from dark grey to yellow. Scoured by the wind and the sea.

'You've forgotten something, Maya… what your dad did to me. How he hurt me. Just like he did your mum and maybe his wife before that.'

Maya doesn't want to hear it. 'But Teresa said—'

Amy turns to face her. 'Oh, Maya. Of course she did.'

'But why?' She doesn't understand.

'Because Teresa's in love with your father. Has been since the early days, apparently. Didn't you know?'

'In love with him?'

'Yes. She's jealous of me. Jealous of you. She'll do anything to protect him.'

Maya covers her face with her hands. 'Oh, God.'

'Maya, there are things I need to tell you. Things in the past I think you deserve to know.' Slowly, she turns and walks back to the bench, stopping when she's in front of her. 'You see, a few days ago, I managed to get your dad to talk to me a bit more about your childhood. He didn't say much, just a few anecdotes about you and your mum. I didn't tell you before because I was worried they might upset you. I can't stay long as I'm going to go back to the house in a minute to get the rest of my things but, if you want, I'll tell you.'

The wind picks up, flapping the end of Amy's scarf. Maya watches as she catches it and secures it inside her coat.

She nods, her stomach churning. 'Yes, tell me.'

CHAPTER FORTY-ONE
Teresa

Teresa knows she should go home, but something is keeping her here. Something that snags and picks at her mind. Since Maya left her consulting room and she wrote up her notes, she hasn't been able to settle. What she wants to do is tell Stephen he's making a mistake. That having a relationship with someone who looks so much like his wife isn't going to bring Cheryl back – that this person is putting ideas in his daughter's head and can't be trusted. But what if that puts their friendship at risk? She pours herself some water from the jug on the coffee table and takes a sip, glad the last of her clients has left, knowing she's been distracted and hasn't given them the full attention they deserve.

She's worried about the things Maya told her – ashamed at how easily she'd dismissed what she's been experiencing and how quickly she'd come to her conclusion. She takes another sip of water. Maya's bruising to her arms may well have been her way of banishing emotional pain, but she could be wrong. She's no detective, and it isn't for her to make these assumptions. But in her heart, Teresa knows why she did it. It was because she couldn't bear the thought that Stephen might in any way be connected to his daughter's injuries.

She turns off the computer and pushes her chair under her desk. Her unease about what might have happened fighting against her loyalty to him. For Stephen is the man who supported her when things in her life went wrong. Helped her to move on and leave her problems behind. He's been there for her when nobody else has.

It's getting late, the room darkening. With her thoughts in turmoil, Teresa gets up and switches on the overhead light, then goes to the window, twisting the rod to close the blinds. Stephen is still in the building; she can hear the slide and bang of the filing cabinet in the room upstairs.

She thinks she knows this man with his rumpled clothes and his unruly hair, but does she really?

There's a knock on her door, and she freezes, her hand resting on the windowsill. The knock comes again, and she comes back to life.

'Come in.'

The door opens, and Stephen grins at her. 'Not got a home to go to?'

She forces a smile. There's something uncomfortable about him standing there, blocking her exit. 'I won't be long. Don't worry about locking up. I'll do it when I've finished up here.'

'You look pensive.' Stephen leans his shoulder against the door frame. 'Anything happened that I should know about?'

'No.' Teresa moves away from the window. 'Nothing. I've just been trying to get up to date with my notes.'

'Well done. I'm impressed.' He straightens up. 'I'll see you tomorrow then.'

'Yes.' Her smile tightens. 'See you tomorrow.'

Teresa waits a couple of minutes, then hurries to the window and parts the blinds. Only when she's seen Stephen's car drive past the front of the clinic does she put on her jacket and turn off the lights. All the while, trying to ignore the disquiet that's lodged inside her. That in that house with Stephen and Amy, Maya is not safe…

CHAPTER FORTY-TWO
Maya

Maya sits alone on the bench. She needs time to herself to think about the things Amy has just told her. The first things had been innocuous enough – anecdotes, reminiscences of her dad's from when Maya was a child. Amy had told her about the time she'd refused to take off her new rabbit slippers even when she went to bed. Her imaginary elephant friend called Elvis. She'd smiled at the memories, delighted to find she could add more detail to them from the images that hovered at the edges of her mind, waiting to be captured. They were the good things.

But there were other memories too. Unsettling things. Like the time she'd hidden under the kitchen table when her mum and dad were arguing and the evening her dad had made her stay in her room and miss her supper because of something she'd done. How he'd called her an evil child and how bad he felt about it now. He'd told Amy these things when he was the worse for drink, the edges of the dark cloud still hovering. Had he thought that by confiding in her, he'd win back her trust?

Maya had forgotten about the time she'd been shut in her room, but now she can remember hammering at her bedroom door, her stomach rumbling with hunger, her face tear-stained. Beating and beating until her little hands were red.

Oh, how she wishes that memory had stayed buried.

Maya gets up from the bench. She doesn't want to go home, but she has to. What else can she do? As she walks back along the narrow track, feeling the cold wind against her cheek, she tells herself that it's all in the past and that she should forget it ever happened. But, as she sees Crewl House in the distance, she knows she can't fool herself any longer. It's not all in the past. When she'd come up here earlier, she'd been so sure about what had happened in Weymouth, so relieved at Teresa's explanation, but now she's no longer sure. Could Amy have been right all along? *Is* she in danger?

Lowering her head to the wind, she walks on. To her left, the gaps in the prickly hawthorn afford glimpses of sheep, huddled together for warmth. Rising above them, the solid structures of the pylons graze the sky, their metal arms joined by the power lines that run between them. Today, they give off a strange faint hum that she hasn't noticed before. She doesn't like it.

A gust of wind blows her hair, whipping it across her face, and she pushes it back. Dark clouds are gathering, and she's feeling the cold now, wishes she'd worn a warmer coat over her nylon tunic. To warm herself she walks quicker, each footfall cushioned by the close-cropped turf.

But now she stops abruptly. There's someone ahead of her on the path, pressed close against the hedge. Or is she imagining it? The scraggy hawthorns, bent almost double by the wind as though tired of arguing with it, might be making her believe she's seeing something that isn't there.

Above her, the power lines hum.

The wind stings.

Her shoes pinch… just as they did all those years ago.

Maya looks down, half expecting to see the black patent shoes her mum buckled too tightly in her haste to leave the house, her legs sheathed in regulation grey school tights. But it's just her trainers she sees, her tights the opaque black ones she wears to work.

She forces herself to focus on the here and now. On the surge of the sea below her and the moan of the wind in the power lines. She's not that six-year-old; she's an adult. Yet, the memory is very real. The fear too. However much she tries, she can't separate herself from the child she once was.

With panic taking hold of her, Maya starts to run back the way she's just come, towards the bluff. Brambles snagging at her tights. One of her laces has come undone, threatening to trip her, but she doesn't care. Someone is behind her. All she knows is she can't let him get to her. Mustn't let him stop her. Vainly, she clings to the present, but the past is crashing in again. She's six. Her legs won't move fast enough. Her mum is up ahead, and she calls to her, but she doesn't hear. She runs faster, her loose shoe slipping on her foot, and she turns in panic. He'll reach her mum before *she* can.

When she nears her mother's bench, Maya sinks to her knees, unaware of the sharp stones that press into her skin. The thistles that prick at her legs. 'Please, help me!'

But it's too late. Hands grasp her arms. Fingers dig into her skin, ready to drag her back. When she cries out, her words are snatched by the wind. Maya's breath comes in gulps, and she screws up her eyes, fighting to steady it, her fingers pressing into the flesh of her arms.

How many minutes she spends kneeling on that hard ground on the windswept cliff she has no idea. Maybe five. Maybe ten. But slowly, very slowly, she's drawn back to the present again, and when she opens her eyes, she's alone. It wasn't real, she knows that now. It was only a memory. One that had come to her with such clarity that she'd been swept away by it.

It's not the first time she's remembered those fingers digging into her arm. When the images had come to her before, she'd thought they were from the time she was in Weymouth, but now she knows for certain they weren't. That memory was from here at Crewl Point. From when she was six.

Pushing herself up from the ground, Maya waits for her heart rate to return to normal. For the first time since she can remember, she realises she hates it out here on this open clifftop. She wants to be home. The only place where she feels safe.

But even as she thinks the words, she wonders why she still believes it.

Those fingers. Those hands that dragged at her.

They were her dad's.

CHAPTER FORTY-THREE

Maya

Maya lets herself into the house through the back door, still shaky from what happened on the cliff. Straightaway, she goes into the kitchen and is relieved to see Amy's car still in the drive. She doesn't want her to go without saying a proper goodbye.

The house is silent as though waiting for something and she stands listening, wondering where Amy is. She goes upstairs and looks in her dad's bedroom, then in the spare room where Amy's been sleeping. Her clothes are gone, yet her car is still parked on the drive. Where is she?

'Amy?' she calls.

When there's no answer, she goes back downstairs.

'Amy?' She shouts it louder this time, a hint of desperation in her voice.

'I'm in here, Maya.'

Filled with relief, Maya goes through the living room and into the conservatory. Amy's sitting on one of the settees, her laptop in front of her. The rain that had been threatening for the last hour has started at last. She can see it slanting at the windows. Running down the glass like tears.

'I'm so pleased you're still here,' Maya says.

Amy looks up. 'Yes, I'm still here.'

'Something happened on the clifftop after you'd gone back.' Maya sinks down onto the settee next to her. 'It was another flashback, and I'm frightened. I think you're right about my dad. I'm sure now he did something terrible on the cliff the day Mum died and changed my memory of it... but how did he do it?'

Amy turns serious eyes to her. 'I think I know.'

'How?'

'Your dad has always been cagey about the time before he moved here and opened up the clinic. I know he was a professor at a university, but that was about it. I had no idea of his specialist subject or even what university he taught at. It seemed odd that he wouldn't want to say.' She rests her hand on her laptop. 'After everything that's happened, I thought I should find out more so after I packed up my things and put them in the car, I did some digging.'

Maya feels her heart skip a beat. 'Did you find anything?'

'Yes.' She looks at the laptop. 'I'm afraid I did.'

'Tell me, Amy. I need to know.' Her stomach twists in anticipation.

Amy's tone is grave. 'I started by googling his name. The first few results that come up were advertisements for the Wellbeing Clinic. I read your dad's bio, but it just brought up his qualifications and fees along with the title *Cognitive Behavioural Therapist*. There was no clue as to where he was practising or what he was doing before he opened the clinic. No hint of his area of specialism. When I scrolled on though, I found an entry from *The British Journal of Psychology*. It was an abstract of an article that had been published there, written by a Professor Stephen McKenzie.'

'My dad,' Maya whispers.

'Yes, your dad.' There's pity written in the downward turn of Amy's lips. The crease of her forehead. 'I think you need to read this yourself.'

She passes Maya the laptop and Maya balances it on her knees with shaky hands. The title of the study is *The Effect of Mood on False Memories* and, although she tries, it won't allow her access to the full article. But what's written there is enough.

Her heart thuds in her chest as she types his name into the search box on the journal's website. She needs to find more. Straight away, a list comes up, and she scrolls down the names of the studies her dad has published:

Is Changing a Person's Memory Just a Case of Changing their Minds?

The Persuadability of Memory.

Collaborative Remembering v False Memories.

She looks at Amy. 'The most recent study was twenty-five years ago.'

'Yes, I know.'

Maya clicks on the link and reads the title. *Can the Age of a Volunteer's Earliest Memory Affect How Easy It Is to Create False Childhood Memories in Adulthood?* Once again, the lead name on the paper is Stephen McKenzie.

Maya reads through all the abstracts, fingers of unease creeping up her spine as she does. Every single one of them is based around the idea that false memories can be implanted in a volunteer when someone, usually a family member, claims that the incident actually happened.

She sits and stares at the screen, goosebumps rising on her arms. There are no more doubts. No more uncertainties. 'My whole relationship with my dad has been a lie.'

Amy dips her head. 'Mine too.'

Maya reaches for Amy's arm and grips it. 'Recently, I've been getting memories of my childhood. Just flashes of things that start to fade when I grasp them. But they weren't of a happy childhood... they were the opposite. It doesn't make sense that Dad should put those memories there. Why would he want me to believe those things?'

Amy is quiet for a moment, her face pale, her lips colourless. 'Maybe he didn't. These new memories could be the real ones coming through at last. He'd papered over them with false good memories to make you believe you were a happy family.'

'He killed her, didn't he?' The rain is coming harder and faster now. Clattering on the conservatory roof. 'He said he was at home at the time of her accident, but he wasn't. He was there, I know he was. I can see him as clear as anything.' The shock is like a fist to her stomach as the realisation hits. 'He looked like he hated her.'

The words are out, hanging between them, never to be unsaid. She looks at Amy, willing her to say something that will give her hope, but she doesn't. Instead, Amy stands, her lips pinched.

'You have to tell the police.'

Maya's shocked. 'I can't. We're talking about my dad. What if I'm wrong and he's done nothing? It will damage our relationship forever.'

Amy crouches down in front of her, placing her hands on Maya's knees. 'And if you don't, knowing the lies he's told and the things he's kept from you, you will have to live forever with the uncertainty. Could you do that?'

Maya places the flats of her hand either side of her head. 'I'm so muddled I can't think straight. Maybe I should ring Teresa.'

Amy shakes her head. 'I'm not sure that's a good idea. She's obsessed with him, and I wouldn't put it past her to tell him what you've said. It's the police we need to tell.' She looks at her watch, and when she speaks again, there's a new urgency in her voice. 'Please, Maya, this is important. We've got to leave before he gets back.'

She looks out at the darkness. She's trying to cover it, but Maya sees Amy's fear in the pallor of her face. The hand that runs nervously over her dark scalp.

Amy's right. If they stay, they'll both be in danger.

CHAPTER FORTY-FOUR
Teresa

Teresa fumbles with the key, dropping it twice before she gets it in the lock. She glances behind her, thinking for a moment that someone is there, but it's only the empty wheelie bin, rocking on its wheels as it's buffeted by the wind. She'll need to take that round the back later.

She lets herself in and hangs her wet coat on the coat stand before shutting the front door and closing the curtain that covers the small pane of glass recessed into it. Not liking the darkness outside, she closes the living room curtains too, both the ones at the front of the house and the ones that look onto the narrow footpath behind the cottages.

How quiet the house is now neither Dale nor her mum is there. She'd imagined that Dale would have come back by now, his tail between his legs, but he hasn't. She ought to eat something, but she's not hungry so instead, she pours herself a glass of red wine and settles down in front of the TV. But as she flicks through the channels, she can't concentrate, and despite her best efforts, her thoughts keep returning to the things Maya's told her. Her fears and the bruises on Amy's arms.

She thinks of Cheryl and the wife before her. There were other women too when she'd first known him, though she'd conveniently pushed that knowledge aside. Stephen has never been short of women wanting to share his bed. And even though there's no one in the house but her, she feels her cheeks flush with shame as she remembers how flattered she'd been when he'd sought her out at the conference.

When she'd found out Stephen was in the process of getting a divorce during that first drink together, she'd been secretly pleased. Now she tries to remember the reason Stephen gave for them splitting up. Incompatibility, he'd said. Now she wonders whether it could have been something more.

She might be living in Stephen's house, but there's no way she can carry on living here without knowing what other things he might have revealed to either Maya or Amy. As she looks around the room, the haven Stephen found for her when her life was at its lowest ebb, she has the strangest feeling that it's no longer Stephen's secrets she needs to protect.

Her phone is on the table, and she picks it up. She needs to ring him. Get him to come over and talk about everything. And when he does, he'll help her see that her fears are unfounded. When there's no reply to her call, she leaves a message. *Can you come over, Stephen? There are things I need to talk to you about.*

As she puts the phone down, she sees her mum's eyes looking down at her from the photograph she keeps on the mantelpiece. Guilt floods her as she realises she's been so busy worrying about Maya and Stephen that she hasn't been to see her today. A sudden yowling outside the window startles her, and when she goes to the back door and opens it, she sees the ginger tom in the alleyway behind the houses. The story she told her mum about the time he had a bird in his mouth comes back to her. How frustrated she'd been when her mum had passed the memory off as her own. Teresa gives a shudder. And how easily a mind can be tricked into believing what it wants. She knows that only too well.

Teresa closes the back door and rests her head against it. There's a strange feeling in the pit of her stomach, and she knows what it is. It's the feeling she gets when she knows things are out of her control. What she needs is certainty.

Going to her laptop she puts Stephen's name into the search engine and scrolls through what comes up. It's mainly lists of the studies he carried out when he was a university professor. She skims through them, her heart sinking. How easy they had been to find. For *anyone* to find. Why had she not looked sooner? Stephen's secret is right there in front of her. Innocent enough unless the reader knows what *she* knows. What Maya's told her in her sessions.

She sinks down onto the settee. What should she do? It's no longer ethical to protect Stephen.

Teresa's just about to close the search window and shut down her laptop when she sees something that makes her stop. Her cursor hovers over the entry. It's a news article from twenty-five years ago, the headline demanding her attention.

She reads the article, then reads it again hoping she's been mistaken, fear coiling in her belly as realisation dawns. Her hand is at her throat, the pulse beating in the soft hollow. How could she have been so blind?

Jumping up, she grabs her coat from the back of the settee. She knows what's happened, and she needs to get to Crewl House as quickly as she can. For once acknowledged, the truth could hurt them all.

There's a thump on the door, and Teresa freezes, one arm in her coat. Who is it? Just as quickly, she slips her arm out of the sleeve again, chastising herself for being so jumpy. Is it Stephen at the door? Has he read her message and come straight over?

She drags back the curtain in front of the door and, without looking through the small pane of glass, pulls it open. She freezes, her hand on the door handle, her heart plummeting as she sees who's standing there.

'You!' she says.

CHAPTER FORTY-FIVE
Maya

Maya runs into the kitchen and looks through the window. The sky is dark, but the light from the kitchen is enough to see that the space where her dad parks his car is still empty. Thank God. Once she would have longed to hear the crunch of his tyres on the gravel, but now the thought of him returning fills her with dread.

The rich, pungent smell of tomato and garlic fills the room. Through the glass door of the oven, she can see the shape of the casserole dish she put in there before she went for her walk on the cliff. She'd forgotten about it. The plan had been to eat once her dad got home, but that's not going to happen now. Out of habit, she turns the oven to low... unable to cut the ties entirely. Knowing her dad will be hungry when he gets home.

'Maya, you need to hurry.' Amy has her coat on. The laptop under her arm.

'I'm sorry. I know.'

Maya runs upstairs and stuffs a few things into a bag. Hesitating a moment before placing her mum's photograph on top of her clothes and zipping it up. She's got no idea where she'll be going, what she'll be doing, when she leaves here.

Is her dad capable of murder? Could it really be true? Knowing she should call the police, she takes her phone out of her pocket and stares at the screen. Her finger hovers over the keypad, and she keeps her mum's face in her head. She owes it to her to do the right thing.

But… it's her dad.

Amy's calling up the stairs. 'Maya, will you be long? He'll be here soon.'

Quickly she puts her phone back into her pocket and picks up her holdall. She looks at her watch, and her anxiety increases. It's past the time when her dad would usually be home. 'I'm just coming.'

She runs down the stairs, her bag bumping against the wall, but just as she nears the bottom, there's the sound of a key in the lock and the door opens. Maya stops still, her hand gripping the banister.

'Hi, darling.' Her dad's voice is as warm and comforting as always. He shakes his umbrella outside the door, then leans it against the wall. 'Sorry I'm late. I've been out for a couple of drinks with Dan.' He shuts the door and chuckles. 'Ironic really, seeing as he's the addiction counsellor.'

He sounds so normal, so much like the dad she knows and loves, that for a minute Maya almost forgets what he's done. Forgets what he can be like when the dark cloud descends. She wants to step into his arms as she always does, but this time it's different. This time she knows the truth.

Her dad hangs his coat over the newel post, then looks at her, his head cocked to one side.

'Are you okay? You're as white as a sheet.'

'Dad.' The words burst from her. 'I know what you've done.'

'What?' He stands back, his brow creasing.

She stumbles on. Unable to stop. 'Those memory studies you carried out when you were teaching at the university, the ones you had published in the psychology journal, I've found them online. I've read the abstracts.'

'And what of it?' Her dad moves towards her and she backs up the stairs, feeling for the steps with her feet.

'You have to tell me the truth about what happened after Mum died. Did you feed me false memories about my childhood like you did the volunteers in the studies? Tell me it isn't true, Dad. Please.'

He clears his throat. 'You know about the hypnosis, Maya. I've never lied to you about that. Look, I'll put the kettle on, and we can have a cup of tea.'

Maya follows him into the kitchen. 'It's not just the memories from the time you found me underneath the pylon. It's everything since. You've used me as a guinea pig to cover up what really happened to Mum.' She stops, overwhelmed by tears.

'Your mum?'

'Yes. I'm not a child, Dad. You have to tell me the truth.'

'Listen, Maya.' Her dad's voice has lost its warmth. 'I don't like you talking this way.'

His eyes move away from her and by his look of surprise Maya knows that Amy has come into the kitchen. She turns her head and sees the look of warning in her eyes. Amy's trying to let her know that she should stop talking, that she's making things worse, but she can't stop. She won't. Not until she knows the truth.

'Tell me it's all nonsense, Dad. That I've got it wrong.'

There's a silence in the room and as she waits for him to answer, fear tightens her chest so she can barely breathe.

'Please. Tell me it's not true. That there's been some terrible mistake.'

But when her dad speaks again, his voice cracking, any hope she had that she's been mistaken is dashed.

'I'm sorry, Maya. I can't.'

CHAPTER FORTY-SIX
Teresa

'Gary,' Teresa says, her throat constricting as she says the name.

He's leaning against the brickwork, swaying slightly, his breath smelling of alcohol. It seems such a long time since she last saw or heard from him that she'd almost allowed herself to believe he'd forgotten about her. That her leaving him had been a blessing to him as well as to her. That he didn't care.

'Aren't you going to let me in?' he slurs. 'Show me around?'

She ignores his question. Not wanting to let him in with no Dale, no Stephen, to protect her. 'What are you doing here?'

'What do you think I'm here for? I've come to take you home.'

The door is only half-open, and Gary shoves his boot in the doorway. She stares at it, knowing that time is ticking away and she has to play this right.

'Why now?' she says. 'It's been weeks.'

'I knew you'd need time to come to your senses. Time to realise where you belong.'

Indignation makes her brave. Foolish. 'I don't belong in that house, and I don't belong to you.'

His face darkens. 'Shut up.'

He shoulders past her, slamming the door closed as he does, and the solid wood slips from her fingers as she's pushed to the side. 'I would have gone to your clinic only I didn't think you'd want a scene. It's better here. Quieter. Where is he?'

For a minute, she's not sure who he's talking about.

'Stephen's my colleague, that's all.' Her anxiety at seeing him is replaced with a sudden fear as she realises that in all the time she has been focusing on Maya and Stephen, she should have been protecting herself.

The blow to the side of her head is sudden and painful, hard enough to knock her to the ground. Teresa remains where she's fallen, shock making her pulse race. Gary is standing over her waiting for her to say something, but there's nothing she can say that will change what he's just done. Gingerly, she lifts a hand and touches the side of her face, and when she's sure there are no injuries apart from the raw and tender skin, she pushes herself up into a sitting position.

Years of counselling clients in abusive relationships has taught her that she mustn't let him see how scared she is.

'How did you find me?' she asks. 'How did you get my address?'

Gary frowns at the back of his hand as though it's acted with a will of its own. Then his eyes leave his hand, and he scans her face instead. 'You really don't know, do you?' Crouching next to her, he puts his face right close to hers. 'It's a good job your mother's always liked me. I can't do a thing wrong in her eyes.'

'My mum?'

'Yeh. She was delighted to see me. Couldn't wait to invite me in. While she was making the tea, it didn't take much looking to find what I was after.' Realisation dawns. The night of the burglary at her mum's house... it was him. Her poor mum. She wasn't to know what Gary was like. She'd always been careful to keep it from her. 'Stupid old bat started to come upstairs so I had to leave everything and come down.' He laughs and Teresa's sickened by his heartlessness. 'I guessed that by the time she went upstairs again later and saw the state of the room, she'd have forgotten I'd ever been there.'

Yet her mum hadn't forgotten. In her own way, she'd tried to tell her. It wasn't her fault her dementia had merged Gary and Dale into one and the same person. Why hadn't she realised?

'Your mum knows what a good husband I've been to you.' He stands and prods at her leg with the toe of his shoe as though she's something ugly that's been dropped in the gutter. 'The only bloody one who does. You're heartless shoving her into a home.'

His words hurt her more than the blow to her head. How could he ever know the sleepless nights her decision has caused her? How every day she questions whether she did the right thing even though she knows in her heart that she had no choice.

'I couldn't look after her. I haven't the expertise. Three Elms is a wonderful place and she's happy there.'

'Yeh, right.'

Struggling to her feet, Teresa squares up to him. 'Get out of my house, Gary. You're not good for me and you never have been. Dale knew it, it's just taken me longer to realise it.'

As soon as she's said it, she realises her mistake. Gary's face has changed to naked hatred. 'I should have sorted the little shit out properly when I had the chance. He clearly hasn't learnt his lesson.'

His words hit her like a slap. 'You struck my son?'

'He asked for it. Would you rather I'd hit you?'

Teresa's heart lurches as the truth sinks in. The reason why Dale would never go out if it meant she'd be left alone with Gary. How he'd wait until she was safely at work or late at night when they were both asleep before leaving the house. She thinks of the livid purple bruising around his eye socket… the way he was with her. All the time they'd been living with Gary, her son had been trying to protect her, and she hadn't known it. It should have been her protecting him. No wonder he was messed up.

Rage makes her fearless. With all her force, she shoves Gary in the chest. 'He's just a boy and you hurt him.'

Gary staggers back a couple of steps, then steadies himself, and Teresa realises what she's done. Before she can think, he's lurched forward, grabbing a handful of her hair. Yanking her head to the side.

'He deserved it,' he hisses in her ear. 'Always shoving his nose in where it wasn't wanted. Telling me to leave you alone.' He laughs. 'Or what? I'd ask myself. What did that little runt think he'd do?'

'He thought he'd do this, you bastard.'

Dale's voice comes from nowhere. His arm is around Gary's throat, dragging him backwards. 'Call the police, Mum. It's what you should have done years ago.'

Gary struggles, but Dale has youth on his side. Despite his lean appearance, he's strong and Gary is drunk. As he edges him to the door, Teresa runs and opens it, watching as Dale swings his stepfather round, the force of his shove sending him reeling into the road.

Quickly, Teresa slams the door closed, then pulls her son into a hug. He smells of stale sweat and the sea. 'Thank God you came. How did you know he was here?'

Dale shrugs. 'I saw him. I've been watching the place… watching *you*. Following you to make sure he didn't get you. I knew it was only a matter of time before he'd find where we lived, and I wanted to be there when he did.'

Everything suddenly becomes clear. The feeling she was being watched. The person she'd seen on the clifftop. Her son hadn't been able to share the same house as her, but he was still looking out for her. Making sure she came to no harm.

'I've been so worried. Where have you been staying?'

She feels him shrug. 'It doesn't matter.' Pulling himself out of her embrace, he stands stiffly. 'Call the police and tell them what he's done. It's over, Mum.'

Teresa should be relieved, but she isn't. Dale doesn't know anything, and she doesn't have the will or the time to explain. She knows what it's like to live under someone's control, and she owes Maya the truth.

Her son has got it wrong. It's far from over.

CHAPTER FORTY-SEVEN
Maya

Maya covers her face with her hands, letting her dad's words sink in. However hard she tries to make sense of them, she can't. The studies are proof of what he's done. And yet, if her dad had been such a monster, wouldn't she have known? Wouldn't she have felt it in her heart?

'Please, Dad. Tell me what's going on. You're scaring me.'

But her dad isn't looking at her any more, his hand is outstretched to Amy, his eyes imploring.

'Amy, love. You know I'd never hurt anyone. Please… talk to her. Tell her it's all a misunderstanding.'

Amy pushes up the sleeve of her T-shirt. 'Like this is a misunderstanding? Admit it, Steve. You're a liar. A violent, scheming liar. You didn't even tell her you'd been married before… What father would do that?'

He hangs his head. 'So you told her?'

'Of course I told her. Unlike you, I don't keep things from your daughter. Twist things.'

Stephen turns back to Maya. 'I'm sorry I didn't tell you. I never thought I needed to, as it was so long ago. Don't listen to her.' His tone is firm. 'This is about you and me. Trust me, Maya, you have nothing to worry about. Sometimes, it's necessary to do things that others wouldn't understand to protect your family from pain. I needed to protect *you*. Believe me… I had no other choice.'

There's a desperation to his voice that scares Maya, and she edges closer to Amy. 'There's always a choice,' she says.

Her dad holds out his hand to her, pleading. 'You have to understand what I did was for your own good.'

His words feel dangerous. His meaning uncertain. It takes all her courage to ask. 'What did you do?'

'Maya… sweetheart. Sit with me, and I'll explain.'

She looks at him, his hair mussed from the wind, his smile reassuring, and it's like an invisible thread is pulling her. She takes a step towards him, then stops as she feels the pull of Amy's hand.

'Stay away from her, Steve,' Amy says. 'Can't you see what he's doing, Maya?'

Ignoring her, Stephen moves closer. 'Please. Just let me talk to you.'

Amy takes a step back, drawing Maya with her. 'I said leave her alone.'

His eyes leave Maya now, locking with Amy's. 'What exactly is it you think I've done, Amy?' He beats a fist to his forehead. 'For Christ's sake. At least tell me what it is you're accusing me of?'

'Of deceiving your daughter.' She lets go of Maya's hand and taps her temple. 'Of filling her head with lies. What really happened to your wife, Steve? What did you do to Cheryl?'

'To Cheryl? I didn't do anything, I swear.'

Her voice is icy. 'You're a liar, Steve. A cold-hearted liar. You're so used to messing with people's heads, you don't know when you're doing it. Can you blame us for wondering what else you're capable of?'

'Don't listen to her, Maya.' He turns pleading eyes to her. 'I loved your mum. I would never have hurt her. I would never hurt *you*.'

'What about the card?'

'What card?'

'The one you wrote after she tried to leave you once. You said you were sorry for hurting her. I'm not stupid, Dad. I saw it with my own eyes.'

Maya sees how his fists bunch in frustration. 'It's not what you think,' he says. 'Yes, we'd had a stupid argument and she did try to leave, but I never touched her.'

He takes another step forward, and Maya flinches, remembering the slap. Remembering the feel of her dad's fingers on her arms. Memories flood into her head. Raised voices. Tears. Her fear. Her mum's scream.

She starts to shake, and Amy puts an arm around her. 'Admit it, Steve. You made it look like her mother's death was an accident, fed Maya memories to cover your tracks, but you didn't bank on her real memories coming back, did you? She knows you hurt her on that clifftop. She remembers how you grabbed her by the arms and dragged her away so she wouldn't see what you'd done.'

Maya sees how her dad's eyes darken. How his forearms tense. And for the first time in her life she's afraid of what he might do. Her heart's thumping so hard she's scared he can hear it, but she forces her voice to stay neutral, to diffuse the situation.

'Sit down, Dad. Let's talk about this… like you wanted.' Taking his arm, she leads him to the table, pulling out a chair so he can sit. 'Please, Dad.'

He does as she asks and, not bothering to take his coat off, sits heavily, his head in his hands. When eventually he lowers them, his eyes fix on something beyond Maya, as though the present has slipped away and only the past remains.

'I didn't hurt your mum, Maya,' he says again, quieter this time, the resignation in his voice showing he knows she won't believe him. 'There's nothing else I can say.'

Maya looks away, her throat aching with the tears she's holding back. 'You could tell me the truth.'

'I have.'

'No, you've only ever told me what you wanted me to hear. Abusing your profession, using techniques to make me think we were the perfect happy family.' She looks at the photograph of the three of them on the wall. 'Why would you do that unless it was to cover something up? I wasn't happy as a child… I was the opposite. I know that now. I hid under the table because I was scared of you. You locked me in my room.' Tears are streaming down Maya's face now. 'You said I was an evil child. You didn't think I would remember it, but I do. The arguments. How afraid Mum was.'

Amy pulls Maya back to her. 'How could you do it, Steve? How could you mess with a child's mind? Maya, come on. We have to leave.'

Maya can't speak, her mouth is too dry. She wishes she could wake up from this nightmare.

Her dad has his head in his hands. 'No, you've got it all wrong!'

CHAPTER FORTY-EIGHT

Teresa

The traffic lights are red and Teresa curses. She hasn't gone far and in the rear-view mirror can still see the lighted windows of her house, Dale standing in the doorway like a sentry in case Gary should return. She'd thought she'd needed Stephen to sort out her problems, but in the end, she and Dale had managed to do it themselves. Now it's Stephen's family who are in trouble. A tragedy unfolding up there in the house on the cliff that only she can avert.

Teresa taps her fingers on the steering wheel, thankful that the rain has stopped. Why on earth didn't she walk? If she had, she would probably be there by now. The lights are still red and with her impatience heightened, she wonders if they're stuck. A movement at the side of the road catches her eye, and instinctively she shrinks back into her seat. But it's only a bag that's got caught in the hedge, dragged there by the wind. Even so, just in case, she presses the central locking button. *Come on. Come on.*

Time is passing, and with every second, the danger is growing. She's got to try and ring Stephen again. His number is on speed dial, and she presses it and waits, hearing the dial tone ring out in the car. When he doesn't pick up, she feels her anxiety raise a notch.

There's nothing for it, she'll have to try Maya instead, but she'll need to tread carefully. She doesn't want to scare her.

It only takes two rings before the phone is answered.

'Maya? Is that you?'

Maya's voice comes back through the car speaker. It sounds as though she's been crying. 'Yes, it's me.'

'Is your dad there?' She wills the lights to change. 'Can I speak to him… it's important.'

There's a silence, and then the girl's voice comes again. 'Yes, he's here, but I don't think it would be a good idea for you to talk to him.'

Teresa frowns. Why ever not? She stares desperately out at the wet pavements, the illuminated shopfronts, wondering what she should do. Should she wait until she gets to the house to speak to him? Time is ticking on, and she can't be sure what she'll find when she gets there.

'Maya, you need to listen carefully to what I'm going tell you.' She takes a deep breath. Unsure where to start. What to say. Knowing she has to be believed. 'Your dad's in danger. Maybe you too.'

'What are you saying?' Maya's voice is louder now. 'I don't understand.'

There's a blast of a horn from the car behind Teresa. The lights have turned to green at last, but in her haste to move off, she lets the clutch out too quickly, making the car jerk forward before stalling. 'Damn.'

'Tell me what's wrong, Teresa.' Maya's voice drops a fraction. 'You're scaring me.'

Teresa starts the car again, but before she can move, the lights have turned back to red. She thumps her hand on the wheel. The driver of the car behind sounds his horn again, and for a mad moment, she's tempted to jump the lights. Only the oncoming cars stops her.

'Your dad did something bad in the past. He—'

Maya doesn't let her finish. 'I know about his university studies, Teresa. Amy told me.' Her voice wobbles. 'He did the same thing to me. Made me believe things that weren't true.'

Teresa's fingers grip the steering wheel tighter. '*Amy* told you?'

'Yes. And don't try and defend what he did. This time he doesn't deserve it.'

Panic floods her. 'I'm not defending him, Maya. You have to listen to me. Amy's dangerous.'

'What?' Maya stops and Teresa pictures her turning to the woman with questioning eyes.

'Is she with you?' Teresa asks, dreading her answer. 'Is she there?'

'Yes.'

Teresa speaks with urgency. She has to make Maya believe her. 'Amy's lied to everyone. She's not who you think she is.'

'What are you talking about?' There's suspicion in her voice. 'You don't even know her. You're only saying this because you're jealous of her.'

The words come as a shock, but they're not without truth, and Teresa knows she has to carry on. 'I'm going to tell you something, and I want you to promise you won't say anything in reply. Amy mustn't know what I'm saying… do you understand?'

'All right.'

'Amy's not her real name. It's Sarah… Sarah Fulkes. She was one of the volunteers in the last study your father supervised at university. It was a long time ago, back in the nineties.' The lights have turned green again, and Teresa pulls away, more carefully this time, turning right at the crossroads and then right again. 'The childhood memories the study supposedly uncovered were so disturbing that they caused her to have a serious breakdown. Over the years, she's attempted suicide and has been in and out of psychiatric units. It's only recently she's been considered well enough to live back in the community.'

Maya makes a small, strangled sound on the other end of the phone, and Teresa prays she won't say anything in reply.

She hurries on. 'The memories that were brought back were of her stepfather. She believed that when she was six, he sexually assaulted her. It was a shocking revelation. The study was stopped as soon as the university found out, and of course your father had no alternative but to report the findings to the police. The research carried on later without Sarah, and the results of the study were published in the journal.' She pauses and takes a breath. 'Her step-father was arrested and charged, but there wasn't enough evidence to convict him, and it was later found that the memories had never been real but implanted as part of the study. The damage had been done, though. Sarah was unstable before any of this happened and should never have been included in the study in the first place.'

There's a heartbeat's pause, then Maya speaks. 'How do you know all this?'

'One of the original newspaper articles reporting on the case came up when I was searching for information about your dad. There was also another more recent one containing an interview with Sarah's mother and a more up to date photograph of Sarah. Although she's a little younger, and her hair a different colour, it was definitely Amy. In the article, her mother said that over the years her daughter has become more and more obsessed with what happened and has read every article and paper your dad has ever published on the subject of memory. She'd agreed to be interviewed because despite at first believing that having more knowledge was a good thing for Sarah, as it might give her a better understanding of what happened, she had recently become concerned. Sarah's been off the radar for several months.'

Teresa hears Maya's sharp intake of breath, but mercifully she doesn't say anything. A wave of nausea passes through her. She can't let anything happen to the man she loves... or to Maya.

Ahead of her is the sea. To her right, the hill with Maya's house on its crest, bright lights shining from its windows. 'Listen carefully, Maya. I'm nearly at your road and when I get to you, I'll wait outside in the car. When I've ended the call, I want you to get out of the house as soon as you can.'

Maya says nothing, and Teresa doesn't know if that's good or bad. She has to make her understand the importance of what she's trying to tell her if her plan is to work.

'I mean it, Maya. Amy's seriously disturbed. I'm not sure what she's scheming, but I'm pretty certain the reason she's come into your lives is for revenge.'

CHAPTER FORTY-NINE

Maya

Maya stares at Amy. From the oven, the smell of burnt meat and garlic makes her stomach churn, and she wonders if she's going to be sick. Throughout the conversation she's had with Teresa, Amy's been watching her, her face dispassionate.

'What lies has she been telling this time?' she asks.

Maya hesitates. She no longer trusts Amy. No longer knows her. The story Teresa's just told her is too shocking to be made up. She knows she should be clever, be thinking up some plan to get out of the house, but she can't. She needs to know the truth.

'Who are you?' she asks, hearing the desperation in her voice. 'Why are you here?'

The ghost of something crosses Amy's face, then disappears again. 'What do you mean, darling? I'm Amy.'

Her dad pushes back his chair, looking from one to the other. Confusion slackens his face, making him look old. 'What is all this, Maya? What's Teresa been saying?'

But Maya doesn't reply. Her eyes don't leave Amy. 'You're Sarah, aren't you?' she says slowly. 'The girl from my dad's memory study.'

She hears her father's intake of breath, but still she hopes against hope that she's wrong. Waits for Amy to deny it. Prays for it. But she doesn't. The shrug of her shoulders tells Maya everything, and when she turns to Stephen and speaks, her worst fears are confirmed.

'Well, Professor McKenzie? I'd like to say the last few months have been a pleasure, but they haven't?'

Slowly, Stephen rises to his feet, taking in Amy as though seeing her for the first time.

'No. It can't be true. The girl in the study didn't look—'

'Like Cheryl?' The fingers of Amy's free hand trace a path through her hair. 'You've always liked dark hair, haven't you? Cheryl and the wife before her – you know, Stephen, the one you don't like to mention in case it puts you in a bad light – both were dark.' She runs her hand down her hip. 'Both slim.'

Stephen's jaw slackens as the hurt takes hold, and Maya's stomach twists at the cruelty. 'You made yourself look like them?' she says.

Amy smiles at Maya, then turns back to Stephen. 'It was the best chance I had of making you notice me… in the way I wanted. I read one of your earlier studies on attraction – one you carried out before you decided false memories were a lot more interesting to investigate. It proved what has always been pretty obvious to me. That people have a *type*.' She lifts a strand of her dark hair. 'It seems this is yours.'

'Sarah…' He stands there in shock, and Maya sees the effort it takes for him to control his emotions.

'I read everything.' Amy gives a small laugh. 'Even that final one, the one that carried on after I'd been removed from the study, even though you must have known how it had torn my world apart. Did seeing it in print make you feel powerful? Did it make you feel like God?'

Stephen puts a hand to his heart. 'It wasn't my study, Amy. You have to believe me. It was run by one of my PhD students.'

Amy shrugs dismissively. 'I know that.'

He carries on, desperation tightening his voice. '*She* was the one who used the information your family gave about your childhood to create new memories. And *she* was the one who steered your thoughts to the wrong conclusion. I had nothing to do with it.'

'Nothing? Are you sure?'

'Dad's telling you the truth.' The tension in the air is so thick that Maya feels she's drowning. 'He wouldn't do that.'

'Wouldn't he?' Amy spits out the words. 'I read the fucking article, Steve. Your name is at the top… right there for everyone to see. The lead name. It was *your* study.'

'You have to believe me, Amy, it wasn't.' Stephen drags a hand down his face. 'Look, I was a different person then. Younger. More arrogant. And, okay, I admit, I wanted the glory. The study was looking at whether it would be easier to plant false information in volunteers who had no memories before the age of seven, and it hadn't been done before. I wanted my name to come first when the study was published and made a convincing argument to my student to let that happen. I had no idea they were going to move away from the brief and introduce memories that were highly immoral.'

'Yet you still allowed the study to carry on, even after what happened to me.' Amy's face, framed by her dark hair, is pinched and white. Wracked with pain. 'Your study made me believe my stepfather had abused me. Can you know how that feels? Why would your student want to ruin all that? They didn't even know me.'

Stephen looks at her helplessly. 'It was never about you, it was about me.'

'You haven't answered my question.'

'All right. It was because they thought it would help me. They knew I needed something big to make my name known.'

She looks at him in disbelief. 'And they were happy to risk everything for that?'

His chin tilts defiantly and Maya's heart sinks. In that small gesture, she knows what he's going to say.

'The woman who did it was in love with me.'

The pain on Amy's face clears. It's replaced with naked anger. She jabs a finger at him. 'You should have known what was going on. It was your responsibility. The childhood anecdotes my family gave at the beginning of the study were innocent. When my brother said that our stepfather had dressed up as Father Christmas and come into my room on Christmas Eve, it was nothing more than what thousands of other fathers did on that special evening, but your student twisted it. Poisoned it. Played with my own sparse memories of that time until I started to believe what wasn't true.' She grabs Maya's arm, making her gasp. 'You know what that's like don't you, Maya?'

Stephen's face is ashen. 'As soon as I found out what had happened, I removed my student and finished the study myself. I left the university soon after it was published... I wanted to distance myself from it.'

He looks near to tears, turns pleading eyes to Amy. 'Please, Amy. We were good together.'

Amy doesn't respond, but Maya sees in her face what she's thinking. She never loved her father, she despised him. Sleeping in the spare room had never been out of respect for her. She just couldn't bring herself to sleep with the man who had ruined her life. The only emotion she'd ever felt for him was disdain.

Her dad has seen it too. He gives an almost imperceptible shudder, then holds out his hand to her. 'Maya, come here.'

Maya wants to, but she can't. Her body is frozen with fear, unable to move.

'Do it now, Maya!'

Knocking the chair to one side, he makes a grab for her, but Amy's quicker. Her arm is around Maya's neck, dragging her backwards. Despite her slight appearance, Amy's strong and Maya's struggles are futile. Amy's back is to the worktop now, her arm pulling Maya into her body, forcing her to twist as her free arm reaches behind her.

Before Maya can think what she's doing, she feels the cold press of steel against the tendons of her neck. Immediately, she stops struggling.

'Please, Amy. Don't hurt her,' Stephen says, taking a step forward, but Maya signals desperately with her eyes for him to stop.

Amy presses the blade closer. 'It was never my intention to hurt either of you. I just wanted your daughter to experience the same suffering as me. All these years I've been wondering if you've had any idea what a devastating effect implanting false memories can have on a family. After what happened, my mum's marriage was ruined, and she blamed me. Called me a liar. You may have distanced yourself from that study, but I haven't, and with every year that passes, the need to ruin your life as you ruined mine has grown until I think it might eat me alive.'

Stephen takes a step closer. 'Then you've done what you came to do. Just let Maya go.'

The blade presses, the tip pricking Maya's chin, and she forces herself not to move, terrified that the simple act of breathing might cause the knife to slip.

'No, I haven't achieved what I wanted... not now Maya knows the truth.' Amy's hand is shaking, and Maya closes her eyes, terrified of what could happen. 'You should have lived out the rest of your days under the weight of everyone's suspicion. Your own daughter never knowing for sure what you did – not just to her, but to her mother. You see, it's that uncertainty that kills you, Steve. Even after my stepfather was cleared of assaulting me, and everyone was telling me he was innocent, I still had flashbacks. I could never be one hundred per cent sure it hadn't happened. When he was released, I couldn't stand to be near him as I was always questioning myself and our relationship.'

Maya's dad shakes his head. 'But nothing happened. You know that now.'

But even without seeing her face, Maya can tell Amy isn't listening. 'What surprised me was how easy it was to do to Maya what your student did to me all those years ago. Take those self-inflicted bruises on her arms the day she came back from Weymouth. It didn't take much to use that to my benefit. By doing the same to my own arms after our argument, it was just one more small step along the road to making Maya believe you might have caused them. Teresa nearly ruined everything when she came up with her explanation for the bruises, but the seed of uncertainty had already been planted. Your daughter was beginning to doubt you and what you were capable of. All I had to do was use what little she remembered of the time when her mum was alive to create new memories. Just as *you* did.'

Stephen puts his hand out. 'Put the knife down, Amy. We can talk about this.'

Amy looks at him in disgust. 'Why would I trust anything you say?'

The knife's blade is cold against Maya's windpipe, and she tries not to swallow.

'Please, Amy.' Maya's voice is strained. 'It's the student you should be going after, not Dad. He told you he distanced himself from the study… and from them. Why don't you believe him?'

Amy's reaction is not what Maya is expecting. Her mirthless laugh echoes around the kitchen. Nothing's making sense, but before Maya can process things, there's the sound of a car's wheels on the gravel outside the window.

They all look towards the driveway, and Maya thinks she'll faint with relief. Teresa's here.

But then Amy speaks again and with her words, that same relief shrinks back into the very core of her.

'Only you didn't distance yourself from them, did you, Stephen?' she says, her eyes flicking to the window. 'You made sure they stayed close to you.'

CHAPTER FIFTY
Maya

From where they're standing, the car isn't visible, but Maya knows it's Teresa. Everything makes sense now. *She* was the one who had been her dad's PhD student. The one who'd run the memory study. It's why the two of them had always been vague about how they met. Why Teresa had shown such an interest in her.

She'll be sitting in the car. Waiting for them to come out. Does Amy know that too? She must realise Teresa would come here. That her love for her dad would be stronger than her fear of meeting Amy after all these years.

Amy has set a trap to kill two birds with one stone and in just a few moments, the three of them will be face to face once more.

Maya looks at her dad, willing him to help. But what *can* he do with the knife's sharp blade at her throat? And outside, Teresa is waiting. Not realising they know her secret.

Teresa, the woman she trusted.

Teresa, who helped her sort out her head.

Teresa who destroyed Amy's life for the love of her father.

Maya doesn't trust her either, but she has to do something to take control of the situation. What she needs is to keep her dad talking, so she can think what to do. Work out how they can get out of the house. If only she can get Amy on her side.

'Did you have an affair with Teresa?' It's all she can think of to say.

'Why are you asking? Why would you think that?'

'Because she's obsessed with you, Dad. Why do you think?' She feels Amy's arm loosen a fraction and continues. 'Amy always thought it. I should have believed her.'

Her dad stands helplessly in the middle of the room. 'When I first met Teresa, we hit it off straight away. One night we'd had rather a lot to drink, and she made it clear she'd like our new friendship to be something more. I was flattered, I'd be lying if I wasn't, but I was in love with your mum. I told Teresa we could be friends, but nothing more. It was terrible. She was so shocked. So embarrassed.'

Maya turns her head, so she can see Amy's face. 'You see, Amy. Teresa was young and infatuated. People do terrible things when they're scared that the object of their affection will be taken from them. She thought that by carrying out the study, she'd have a better chance with him.' Maya's clutching at straws here, but she's nothing to lose. 'Maybe if you talk to her, let her explain why she did it, we could sort this mess out. I'm sure she feels terrible about what she did…'

Amy turns her head to her. 'Teresa? What's she got to do with anything?'

'But I thought you said…'

Outside the window, the headlights of Teresa's car are picking out the lower branches of the trees.

'It wasn't Teresa who was your dad's student,' Amy says, and Maya hears the smile in her voice. 'Is that what you really thought?'

'Then who was it?' Maya asks, fear clutching at her.

It's her father's turn to speak. He looks at her with eyes full of anguish.

'It was your mother, Maya,' he says, his voice choked. 'It was Cheryl.'

CHAPTER FIFTY-ONE
Maya

Maya looks at her dad in shock. 'You're lying.'

'I'm sorry, Maya, but it's true. Your mother would have done anything for me in those days. Anything at all. She looked up to me. Thought that a shock revelation by one of the volunteers would elevate the study to new heights. She was young. Naive. Instead of giving me the academic recognition I longed for, what it did was destroy my career and cut hers off in its infancy.'

'Yet you still loved her. You must have done, or you wouldn't have married her.'

'Yes. You're right. I did love her.'

A picture comes to Maya. One she's never seen but has imagined oh so many times. Her mother's broken body at the base of the towering cliffs. The waves rushing in to drag away her body. Everything her dad is telling her is true. She knows it is. But if her dad didn't hurt her mum, it must have been someone else who did.

She struggles in Amy's arms as realisation dawns. 'It was you, Amy. My mum ruined your life, so you came after her. What did you do to her? Did you push her off that cliff? Did you kill her?'

Maya starts to cry, great sobs that swallow her words. Her dad's face is anguished. There's nothing he can do to comfort her. She wants the nightmare to end, but Amy's mouth is against her ear. The hair, so much like her mother's, tickling her cheek.

'I didn't do anything,' she whispers. 'I didn't need to. She did it to herself.'

'What do you mean? Tell me she's lying, Dad.'

'I can't.' Stephen's face crumples. 'How could you, Amy? What I told you was in confidence, and you promised you'd never tell her.' He knits his fingers together as though in prayer, then looks up at Maya. 'I've always tried to shield you from the truth, Maya, but you're grown now. Maybe it's time for you to hear it. I don't need to protect you from it any more.'

'What truth?'

Amy smiles. 'That your mother never wanted you. That she didn't love you enough to care what would happen to you if she threw herself off that cliff.'

Maya's heart aches. The memories she'd had when she found her mum's suitcase of clothes were the real ones. 'So I was right.'

Her dad looks wretched. 'She tried her best, Maya. But I'm not sure she was capable of loving anyone properly. Not even me. Cheryl was used to making the demands and now here was this little being making demands on *her*. She never had that maternal instinct most women have. I've always wondered if it was caused by some trauma in her past, but she never said, and it's something I'll never know now. We'd always had a volatile relationship, but, after a while, the fights she picked that had once been exciting, became more alarming. She accused me of all sorts. Neglecting her. Ignoring her. Cheating on her. But it wasn't true. The bizarre thing was that, even like this, I still loved her.'

'So what really happened the day Mum died?' Maya replies, the truth hurting her, but her fear loosening in her chest.

Amy lets go of her and shoves her onto one of the kitchen chairs, taking the seat beside her, the knife pricking Maya's ribs. She indicates with a nod of her head that Stephen should sit as well.

'Go on, Steve, this is something I'd like to hear too.'

Maya's heart is racing. For so long she's needed to know the truth. Her dad glances at her, and Maya can see the fear in his eyes, but he continues. 'It all started one morning when you were six, just before your mum took you to school. You hadn't wanted your breakfast and had thrown your bowl onto the floor so there was porridge everywhere. She lost her temper and slapped you.' He winces and Maya knows he's remembering the sting of his own hand on her cheek. 'I tried to calm her down, but she was out of control. She turned on me. Screaming that she hated me. That I'd been unfaithful. Hitting me over and over. She was wild, and I was scared by the strength of her emotion. It wasn't pretty, but at least you hadn't witnessed it… or that's what I thought. I presumed you'd run into the other room, but you'd hidden yourself under the table. Had heard everything. You crawled out and ran at her. Screaming. Pulling at her to get her off me.'

Maya presses her hand to her mouth. 'So those memories were real?' she says.

'Yes, Amy just used them and manipulated them. Made you think the argument was my fault, that your mum was trying to get away from me… not the other way round.'

'And the time I was locked in my room? Was that Mum too?'

He nods sadly. 'As soon as I realised what she'd done, I let you out, but it caused one hell of an argument.' He runs a hand down his face. 'I can't believe how weak I was. I should have just taken you then and left. But it's surprising what you'll do when you love someone.'

Like give up your life for them, Maya thinks. Your future.

Outside on the driveway, the headlights are still shining.

'Dad? What happened?'

'Your mum ran out of the back door and onto the cliff path, and I'm ashamed to say my only feeling at that moment was relief. She'd scratched my face, and I went to wash it at the kitchen sink.

When I came back, I couldn't find you.' He presses his fingers to his eyes, remembering. 'I searched the house, but then I realised you must have followed her.'

Maya's remembering too. 'My legs were tired from running and my school shoes were pinching. I had to stop to loosen one, then couldn't do it back up. It was foggy, and I couldn't see anything.'

'Yes. The fog had come from nowhere. I ran after you but could barely see a foot in front of me. And then I heard something.' He shudders. 'It was the most terrible sound I've ever heard, and there was no doubt in my mind what it was. I couldn't see the path or the edge of the cliff. I couldn't see *you*.'

A strange, strangled sound escapes him. Maya wants to go to him but can't as Amy is between them, the knife glinting dangerously.

'It's all right, Dad.' Maya wants to say more, but it's the best she can do just to mutter those words.

He looks across the table at her. 'I'd left my phone in the house and didn't know what to do for the best – whether to look for you or find out what had happened to your mother. In the end, I chose you. I blundered like a blind man through the mist and I thought I'd never find you. But then the sun broke through, and I saw you lying under the pylon, curled up in a ball. You were terrified, Maya. Terrified. Crying for your mother.' He's crying too, tears dripping from his beard. 'I scooped you up in my arms and ran back to the house. I phoned the police and the search and rescue, but your mother's body had already been swept out to sea. It wasn't found until several days later washed up further down the coast.'

Maya breathes in a juddering breath. How could she ever have thought him a monster? She's desperate to go and comfort him, but the only solace she can give is through her words. 'I'm glad you told me.'

'I'm glad too. You were so little. So traumatised.' He takes off his glasses and wipes his eyes with his handkerchief. 'In order to shield you, your brain had closed down your memories of what had happened. I just wanted to protect you. Help create a world in which you felt safe. One where you believed you were loved equally by both your parents.' His eyes move from Maya to Amy. 'I'm so very, very sorry, Maya. I know now I was protecting you from the wrong thing. Can this be the end of it now, Amy? You can see we've all suffered. There's nothing more to be gained by this.'

Amy sighs. 'Those are charming memories you both have, Maya. Are you certain you believe them? Are there doubts?'

Maya presses her hands to her ears. 'Stop it! I won't listen to you any more!'

She feels Amy's fingers dig into her arm, and she's forced to stand again.

'It's not over, Steve.' Amy holds the tip of the knife to Maya's throat and edges her to the door. 'Not by a long way.'

The chair's legs rasp against the floor as Stephen shoves it back. He moves forward, his hand outstretched. 'Don't make this worse. Let Maya go. I'll explain everything to the police, and they'll see there are mitigating circumstances. They'll be sympathetic to how the trauma you experienced during the study has affected your life and your mental well-being.'

He steps closer, his voice soothing. Coaxing. It's the voice he uses when he's taking Maya to her happy place. 'Look at me, Amy. Listen to my words and let me help you.'

Maya knows what he's trying to do, and when she moves her head a fraction, she sees Amy does too.

What happens next comes so quickly Maya's unable to react. She's pushed aside so hard she staggers back against the worktop, but not before she sees Amy lunge towards her dad. He doubles up, and Maya hears the sharp outtake of his breath. The moan of pain.

Then stares in horror as the knife Amy had been holding clatters onto the tiles, stained with blood.

CHAPTER FIFTY-TWO
Teresa

Teresa sits in her car waiting. What are Stephen and Maya doing? Why haven't they come out? Outside, the wind is tugging at the trees, rocking the car slightly, and she shivers. She has a bad feeling about this.

Instead of waiting here, maybe she should ring the bell and pretend she was just passing? But who *just passes* Crewl House? The track peters out to nothing after their driveway. But she can't just sit here. Shoving her mobile into her back pocket, Teresa opens the car door and gets out. The kitchen window is in front of her, and she takes a step towards it, keeping to the side so she won't be seen.

The lights are all on, illuminating the scene like a stage set, but the kitchen is empty. She can see an upturned chair but nothing else. With her heart racing, Teresa runs to the front door and rings the bell, but there's no answer.

Where is everyone?

It's dark up on the clifftop, windy too, the clouds scudding across the moon. Knowing she has to do something, Teresa walks over to an iron gate at the side of the house and unlatches it, hoping it will take her round to the back of the house. It does and as she follows the path, one hand on the wall to guide her, she picks out the white frame of the conservatory, its glass windows lit from inside by a standard lamp. It's empty, but the back door on the brick wall next to it is wide open.

Going to the door, Teresa listens but can't hear anything, just the wind in the trees and the pounding of the waves beneath the cliff. Something's happened, but she doesn't know what. Beyond the open door is a small lobby, and she feels along the wall until her fingers make contact with a light switch. Flicking it, the room lights up to reveal a tumble dryer, a clutter of wellington boots and walking shoes and a sink with a scrubbing brush on the drainer. Beyond the lobby is the hall and on the other side of it the kitchen light shines brightly. There's the acrid smell of burning food, but she doesn't want to go inside to investigate.

What makes her look down she's not sure, but when she does, her eyes are transfixed by the drops of blood on the grey tiles, the red smear on the tumble dryer.

Her hand rises to her chest. *Jesus.*

'Maya? Stephen?' Teresa's voice comes out louder than she'd intended, and she quickly steps back into the darkness of the garden.

Her breathing becomes shorter and she waits, the wind flapping at the ends of her coat. There's no answer. The house has a strange empty feel and now she knows why. The back door was open, the blood an indication that someone went out this way. Maybe all of them.

A sound from inside the house makes her turn back to it. A low moan, too deep for a woman. Realising it must be Stephen, Teresa kicks aside the wellington boots and runs through the small lobby to the hall. The groan comes again, the sound coming from the kitchen.

'Stephen!' This time she shouts it. 'It's all right. I'm here.'

The kitchen looks stark and bright after the darkness outside and as she sees the blood on the floor, her hand flies to her mouth. Something terrible has happened.

At first, she doesn't see him, but then she hears another groan. Stephen is lying behind the table, his arm clutching his stomach.

It's why she hadn't been able to see him from the window. Running to him, she kneels and puts her face close to his.

'What's happened, Stephen? Where are you hurt?'

There's blood on the tiles where he's lying. More by the door, smeared in places where she's run over it. *Oh God. What's happened?*

Dragging her phone from her pocket, she calls an ambulance and the police, then gently lifts Stephen's arm. Dreading what she'll see beneath it. His shirt is stained dark red down one side, and when she lowers his arm again and looks at her fingers, they're wet with blood. She tries to think what vital organs might have been damaged. His lung? No, he's breathing okay.

Teresa pushes herself from her squatting position and runs to the drawers in the kitchen units, pulling them open until she finds one containing clean tea towels. Grabbing one, she goes back to Stephen and holds the cloth against his side, pressing his arm down over it to keep it in place.

'It won't be long. The ambulance will be here soon.'

'Teresa.' Stephen tries to push himself up. 'You've got to—'

'Shh. Don't talk. You'll be okay, I promise.'

Putting an arm around him, Teresa helps Stephen into a sitting position, his back against the cupboard.

His eyes are dark with pain. 'No, you don't understand. It's Maya.'

For a moment, Teresa had forgotten everyone but him. She looks around her as if they might suddenly appear. 'Where are they? Is Maya hurt?'

'No.' He tries to move, wincing at the pain. 'But she's taken her.'

'Who has? Amy?' Teresa kneels again and pushes Stephen's grey hair from his face. Her mind is whirling, trying to take it all in. 'Yes.'

'Where have they gone?' But she knows. It's obvious. Amy's ultimate revenge. 'It's the bluff, isn't it?'

'I can't let anything happen to her.'

He tries to stand, but Teresa stops him. 'There's nothing you can do in that state.'

She looks up at the dark panes of the window. How long will it take for the police to get here?

Finally, she makes a decision. 'I'll find her.'

'No!' Stephen's face is white under the stark strip light. 'You mustn't. Leave it to the police.'

Her heart is racing. Adrenaline coursing through her. 'By the time the police arrive, anything could have happened.'

Stephen gives a moan that turns into a ragged cough. He screws up his eyes, and she wonders if it's possible to leave him alone in the state he's in. But what choice does she have?

'I'll leave the front door unlocked so the paramedics will be able to get in.'

Stephen opens his eyes again and clutches her hand. 'Don't…'

'I have to.' Teresa stands. 'The ambulance will be here any minute.' There's a fleece hanging on the back of the door. She unhooks it and lays it over him. 'Try not to move.'

With a last look at Stephen, she hurries back through the house and into the lobby, grabbing the torch from the top of the tumble dryer as she passes. Stepping outside, she listens, her senses heightened. There's a metallic squeak and clunk. A movement at the bottom of the garden. But it's only the garden gate swinging back and forth on its hinges. Nothing more.

Pulling herself together, Teresa shines the torch in front of her to light the way across the grass, straining her ears for the first sound of a siren. Hearing nothing but the complaining gate and the sea.

It's cold. The wind biting. Teresa runs across the grass and through the gate, the ends of her coat slapping against her legs, her hair flying around her face as the wind catches it. Then she's out on the coastal path, and the smell of the sea hits her.

The path stretches away to the bluff, but the darkness swallows everything. Without the help of the torch, she wouldn't be able to see more than a few feet in front of her. Is this the way they've gone? All her instincts tell her it is.

Her torch lighting the path in front of her, Teresa picks her way along the stony ground, feeling the brambles snagging at her trousers. She knows where she's heading, but not what she'll find when she gets there. Below her, the wind has whipped the waves into a frenzy. She can hear the crash of them on the rocks as the tide rolls in. It's difficult to see where the edge is.

Above her head, the clouds part to reveal a flat white moon and, for a moment, she can see further in front of her. The bent forms of the hawthorns loom at her on either side of the path, catching at her coat with their thorny fingers.

As she picks her way along the path, the cold light of the moon brings the metal legs of the pylons into relief, picking out the wires that run between. Then the clouds close in and darkness descends again. Ducking her head against the wind, Teresa pushes on, her breath coming in gasps. It's windier up here where the hawthorns break their shelter and the clifftop opens out. She must be near.

In the torchlight, Teresa sees where the path divides into two, the smaller of them bearing left. If she follows it, it will take her onto the bluff where Cheryl's memorial bench sits. A gust of wind batters against her, and she nearly loses her balance. If she continues, there will be nothing but sea on three sides of her. Below her, the place where Cheryl met her death.

She stands and listens, hoping to hear voices, anything that will tell her she's guessed right. All she can hear though is the howl of the wind. The thunder of the waves.

Teresa forces herself to carry on, wind tears streaming down her cheeks, not sure what she'll do if she finds them. Not sure what she'll do if she doesn't. Her hair is stiff with salt and her lips are numb with cold, and it's only now she realises how foolish she's been. She should have waited at the house…

Then, suddenly, she's there, the path to the bluff shorter than she'd remembered. She sees the bench, her torch picking out the wooden back, the armrests, the metal plaque with its memorial. And then, that same white beam picks out something else.

Maya.

She's between the bench and the cliff edge, so still it's like she's not made of flesh and bone but of something harder. She's staring in front of her and even when the beam of Teresa's torch passes over her, she doesn't look away. Beyond Maya is nothing but darkness.

The bleak wind lashes, rocking Teresa back onto her heels. She reaches a hand to the bench to steady herself.

'Maya!' she calls, but her words are snatched from her mouth and carried away.

Leaning into the wind, Teresa fights towards her, and it's only then she sees what Maya is looking at. It's Amy. She's standing at the edge of the cliff, her back to them, her long dark hair whipping around her head.

Maya is staring at her, her arm outstretched, her fingers reaching. It's like she's in a trance, and Teresa wonders whether it's really Amy the girl's seeing or if it's her mother... the past merging with the present once more. She watches as Maya takes one step forward and then another. She's going to try to stop her.

But the wind has blown the clouds away again and the moonlight catches the steel blade of the knife in Amy's hand.

Teresa's filled with horror. In another few steps Maya will have reached her.

'Maya, no!'

She trains her torch on her and is about to run forward when out of the darkness another shape appears. One that's bent over, their arm clutching their side, battling the wind.

Stephen.

'No!' he shouts.

He runs into the torchlight and grabs Maya by the upper arms, pulling her back into the safety of his own. Burying his face in her hair.

But it's not over yet.

Teresa steps to the side and sweeps the beam of light across the clifftop to where Amy had been standing.

But Amy is no longer there.

CHAPTER FIFTY-THREE
Maya

The sea is calm today, the pewter grey water dotted here and there with white frills. Seagulls scream in the empty air above them before swooping out towards the horizon, making Maya wonder what it would be like to be so free. She feels her dad's cold fingers wrap around her own as he takes her hand.

Even now, several weeks later, the enormity of what happened still hasn't really sunk in. Stephen had been wrong when he'd told Teresa that Amy had forced her out onto the cliff path. He'd been too doubled up with pain to see how she'd run out after her. For she'd guessed what Amy might do. Knew she had to stop her.

'All right?' he asks.

Maya nods. 'Yes. I think so.'

'I know what you're thinking, Maya, and there was nothing we would have been able to do to stop her. It was brave of you to try, though.'

'I wasn't able to save Mum, so I thought—' she begins, but Stephen interrupts her.

'I know, love.'

Maya feels nothing, and it's probably why she's been able to keep coming here. To sit on the bench on the bluff. The place of two tragedies.

'I've been thinking of putting the house on the market.' Her dad's voice breaks into her thoughts. 'Would it bother you?'

Maya looks at him then back at the sea, wondering at his need to ask. 'No, I think it's a good idea. A fresh start would be good for both of us.'

'I'm glad… and I'm sorry.'

She tilts her head to one side. 'What for?'

'For not talking to you all those years ago… for thinking I knew best. But I did it with the best intentions and, despite everything that's happened, Amy was right about one thing. I *did* want to protect you from the truth. You were only little, and I wanted you to be able to live your life without the memory of what had happened to your mum hanging over you. Is that such a bad thing?'

'No, it's not. It's probably what I'd do if I had a child.' Maya turns her eyes back to the sea.

'I did love your mother, you know.'

Maya gives his hand a squeeze. 'Of course I know. You've told me often enough. You've always had a lot of love to give, Dad.'

Stephen gives an audible sigh. 'I suppose that's been my failing. When I first met your mum, I thought she was the most beautiful creature I'd ever seen. Such beautiful eyes. The way her hair shone in the sunlight, the rays picking out the different shades of brown. But it wasn't just the way she looked; it was how she was in herself – so self-assured, ready to spar off anyone. I liked that.'

Maya frowns. 'Even though you were married to someone else?'

Her dad bows his head. 'I know. I'm not proud of it, but Anne and I hadn't been happy for a while and, well, these things happen.'

Did they? She wouldn't know. She's never allowed anyone to get close to her, her energy and emotions reserved for looking after her dad.

'My relationship with your mother was complicated.' He pulls the collar of his jacket up and settles back onto the bench. 'That edge she had was part of what attracted me to her.' He smiles at the memory. 'She didn't let me get away with things, and after I met her, I was never tempted to stray again, despite what she thought.'

'What about Anne? Did she know?'

'Of course she did. In an environment such as a university, nothing stays secret for long.' He bows his head and studies his fingers. 'When she found out about our relationship, she threw me out, but I didn't care… I was besotted. But it wasn't long before things started to go wrong.'

A seagull flies by, taking Stephen's attention. He waits until the bird disappears over the headland before continuing. 'Although no one said it to my face, I heard through the grapevine that my fellow academicians thought that by allowing the study to continue, even without Sarah, I'd put the university into disrepute. My affair with Cheryl was common knowledge by then and, despite my years of professorship, the knives were out. I made it easy for them and left.'

Maya shifts on the bench. 'And that's why you moved to Dorset.'

'Yes, I knew it was the end of my academic career, so decided on a change of direction. I bought the practice and within a few months the Wellbeing Clinic was up and running.'

'And you married her even knowing what she'd done. The terrible way she'd manipulated Amy during the study.'

'I loved her,' he says simply. 'And I blamed myself.' He sighs. 'I suppose I thought we deserved each other.'

He clears his throat, and Maya sees the sadness, the loneliness, in his eyes.

'But it wasn't the same between Cheryl and me once we moved here,' he continues. 'In her eyes a cognitive behavioural therapist didn't have the same gravitas as a professor at a prestigious university. We'd swapped the vibrancy of the city for the sea and a windswept house on a cliff. She grew bored and hankered for the life she'd had before. Then she became pregnant with you.' A chill wind has blown up and he draws her closer, smiling when she rests her head on his shoulder. 'Your mother might have struggled, but you were the best thing that ever happened to me.'

Below them, Maya can hear the waves rushing up the beach to meet the cliff. She thinks of her mother's body lying broken. Waiting to be found.

'Was she so terribly unhappy?'

While they've been talking, a sea mist has crept in, turning the sun hazy, blurring the contours of the cliff. Maya shivers, pulling her scarf higher around her neck as she waits for him to answer.

'Enough to make me feel I had to continually watch her. The week before she died, I'd come home late from the clinic. You were already in bed.' His voice breaks as he remembers. 'And when I'd gone into the bedroom to change out of my work things, I'd found on the dressing table a line of pills which she'd pushed out of their silver blisters. I don't know when, or even if, she'd intended to take them, but I swept them up and flushed them down the lavatory. We should have talked about it, but we didn't. Just carried on as if it had never happened.'

'I remember.' She sees again his anguished face, the shake of his hand as he carried the pills to the bathroom. Maya breathes in a juddering breath, realising how she'd misunderstood the significance all those years ago. How she'd misjudged the need to protect him. 'I'm glad you told me.'

'Do you forgive me?' he asks, not for the first time.

She lets out a breath, focusing on the sea. 'Of course I do. You were doing it because you loved me. Trying to protect me.'

'Yes. That was all I was doing.'

'And I know what that's like as I've spent my life trying to protect you too. I always knew you had a secret and I'm ashamed to admit that I thought you'd hurt Mum in some way when you were feeling bad, even if you didn't intend to.'

'They were migraines, Maya. I always told you that… You just chose not to believe me.'

'I misunderstood the card too… what you were apologising to Mum for. I should know better than anybody that there are two meanings for the word *hurt*.' Maya blinks back her tears. 'It's me who should be saying sorry.'

'There's nothing to forgive, darling.' Stephen gets up from the bench. 'If you don't mind, I'm going to go back now and phone Teresa. I thought I might invite her for supper to thank her properly for what she did.'

'I think that's a great idea.' She thinks how brave Teresa was and how bad she feels that they believed she could have been lying about her husband. That they didn't help her as much as they could. 'Tell me, Dad. What happened about Gary? He won't come after her again, will he?'

He shakes his head. 'I don't think it's likely. She told me she's applied to the court for a non-molestation order, but the police have also had words with him. If he has any sense, he won't go near her again.'

'I'm glad,' she says. 'I like Teresa.'

Stephen smiles. 'I do too. Someday, I hope I can make it up to her. I could have been a better friend to her.' He looks wistful. 'But let's talk about you, Maya. I didn't want to ask you before as I was worried you might feel pressured, but the deadline is creeping up, and I was wondering if you'd thought any more about submitting your university application?'

Maya thinks of the form her teacher helped her fill in. It seems so long ago now.

'Do you think I should?'

'It's not my decision to make, Maya, but yes, I do. I'll leave you to have a think about it.'

Maya watches him walk away, then sits back down on the bench he bought in her mother's memory. As she listens to the sea moving below her, she wonders about the strength of love. The lengths a person will go to in order to preserve it. She lets the rhythm of the waves soothe her, then when she's ready, gets up and heads back along the path to the house.

The mist is not lifting, and as she walks, she makes sure she doesn't deviate from the path. To her left, the shoulders of the metal pylons appear then disappear as the mist envelops them, flashes of sunlight striking the metal each time it clears.

A strange tingling has crept along her spine. The wires are humming as they did before. Something makes her turn and look back at the place where she was standing only a few minutes earlier, but the bench is no longer visible, the edge of the cliff slipping in and out of focus.

The memory that comes to her is fleeting, changing constantly, rearranging itself into new shapes. The siren past calling to her with seaweed-scented breath. Creeping towards her like an incoming tide.

Maya's six again, and her mum is standing with her back to her, but as she watches, the edges of the memory blur as the damp, grey mist envelops her again. Maya presses her fingers to her eyeballs, willing herself to remember.

She's running. Her patent shoes pinching. She bends to loosen the strap but can't buckle it again, so it flaps as she runs. If her dad gets to her mum first, they'll make up as they always do, and she can't let that happen. Maya shouts her mum's name, but she doesn't turn. Maybe she hasn't heard. She's glad. She doesn't want to see how her face will fall at the sight of her.

Maya carries on running until she's with her at the edge of the cliff, feels the fabric of her mum's jumper, cold and damp in her fist as she yanks at it. Fingers of fog curl around them. *I hate you!*

Her mother turns, the shock on her face changing to irritation. Gulls shriek and cry above their heads. She shakes her arm away from Maya's grip and, as she does, Maya feels her stumble, the soft material pulling from her grasp.

Maya screws her eyes up tight, scared she'll be told off. She tells herself the cry she hears is only a seagull, but before she can think any more, hands are grabbing at her arms. They're strong hands, the fingers digging into her flesh, pulling her back. Pulling her away from what she's done.

Her dad's hands.

She feels herself being lifted, buries her head in the roughness of his jumper as he runs with her. The next thing she knows, he's laying her gently on the frosty grass and when she opens her eyes, she can't see his face, just the legs of the pylon rising to the sky. She can hear him, though. His words comforting. Reassuring.

It will be all right, Maya. I'll make it all right.

A cry of a seagull brings her back to the moment, the mist clearing until the bench is visible once more. The flat of Maya's hand is against her chest. Her heart thudding. It felt so real… but already the image is fading, and she's no longer certain what she saw. Maybe it was something, maybe nothing.

She turns and carries on walking. Whatever it was, she'll let it sink back into her subconscious, for she knows nothing good will come from trying to make sense of it.

The past is the past and the present is where she needs to be.

A LETTER FROM WENDY

I want to say a huge thank you for choosing to read *His Hidden Wife*. If you did enjoy it and want to keep up to date with all my latest releases, just sign up at the following link. Your email address will never be shared, and you can unsubscribe at any time.

www.bookouture.com/wendy-clarke

In all my novels, setting has played an important role. *His Hidden Wife* is set in a fictitious village in Dorset and the idea to use the dramatic Jurassic cliffs as a backdrop to the drama came during a long weekend in the area to celebrate the New Year. As we walked along the clifftop, wind whipping my hair around my face, I was drawn in by the towering white cliff above the turbulent sea, the beaches with their hidden secrets where later we fossil hunted… I needed nothing more to get the creative juices flowing.

But what about the theme of the novel – the importance and implication of memory? Why did I choose it? It's probably something to do with the psychology degree I studied for many years ago. I was particularly fascinated by the different factors that can affect the way our memories are stored and how they are retrieved. Of course, my interest in this area might also be because my own memory lets me down on occasion!

I hope you loved *His Hidden Wife* and if you did, I would be very grateful if you could write a review. I'd love to hear what you think, and it makes such a difference helping new readers to discover one of my books for the first time.

I love hearing from my readers – you can get in touch on my Facebook page, through Twitter, Goodreads, Instagram or my website.

Thanks,
Wendy x

 www.wendyclarke.uk

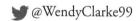 @WendyClarke99

 WendyClarkeAuthor

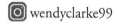 wendyclarke99

ACKNOWLEDGEMENTS

It's always hard to know where to start with acknowledgements as there are so many people who, directly and indirectly, help a novel come to fruition.

First, I would like to give a shout-out to my fabulous editor, Jennifer Hunt, without whose insightful direction there would be no book at all! Editing a book isn't easy. Thank you for having enough faith in my writing to give me the space I need to 'do my thing' before patiently guiding me until the magic happens! It's been an absolute pleasure to work on four books with you.

Thanks also to lovely Noelle Holten, Kim Nash and the rest of the Bookouture team who work tirelessly behind the scenes to get my novels in front of readers. An especially big thank you as well to the brilliant Lisa Horton for designing the most amazing covers for me. I love them all!

It's not just the people who produce your books who are important, it's the friends and family who support you. Thank you to my writing buddy, Tracy Fells, who has been with me throughout my writing journey and has sorted out my head over many a shared teacake! Thanks also to my lovely RNA writing chums… where would I be without our monthly meetup to sort out the writing world?

Not all the people I know are writers of course and I'd like to thank 'The Friday Girls', Carol, Barbara, Jill, Linda and Helen for their friendship. It's to you I gravitate when I need a break from writing, editing and general writerly stuff.

My family are the people who make it all worthwhile – my children, my stepchildren and their partners, my siblings and my mum. Thank you for all your encouragement and for reading my books… you don't have to!

And, no, I haven't forgotten my husband… I'm just leaving the best until last! We may have a dirty house, a settee covered in notebooks and an empty fridge when I'm in the throes of a new book, but you're always happy to go with the flow. I may be stuck on a plot, but you're always happy to talk it through until it makes sense. I may lack confidence sometimes, but you're always there to pull me back up. Thank you Ian.